DAWN UNEARTHED

A RAVENWOOD COVEN NOVEL

CARRIE ANN RYAN

DAWN UNEARTHED

A Ravenwood Coven Novel
By Carrie Ann Ryan

Dawn Unearthed
A Ravenwood Coven Novel
By: Carrie Ann Ryan
© 2021 Carrie Ann Ryan
eBook ISBN: 978-1-950443-51-2
Paperback ISBN: 978-1-950443-52-9

Cover Art by Sweet N Spicy Designs

For Lillie.
Witches, magic, covens, girl power, and bear shifters galore.

PRAISE FOR CARRIE ANN RYAN

"Count on Carrie Ann Ryan for emotional, sexy, character driven stories that capture your heart!" – Carly Phillips, NY Times bestselling author

"Carrie Ann Ryan's romances are my newest addiction! The emotion in her books captures me from the very beginning. The hope and healing hold me close until the end. These love stories will simply sweep you away." ~ NYT Bestselling Author Deveny Perry

"Carrie Ann Ryan writes the perfect balance of sweet and heat ensuring every story feeds the soul." - Audrey Carlan, #1 New York Times Bestselling Author

"Carrie Ann Ryan never fails to draw readers in with passion, raw sensuality, and characters that pop off the page. Any book by Carrie Ann is an absolute treat." – New York Times Bestselling Author J. Kenner

"Carrie Ann Ryan knows how to pull your heartstrings and make your pulse pound! Her wonderful Redwood Pack series will draw you in and keep you reading long into the night. I can't wait to see what comes next with the new generation, the Talons. Keep them coming, Carrie Ann!" – Lara Adrian, New York Times bestselling author of CRAVE THE NIGHT

"With snarky humor, sizzling love scenes, and brilliant, imaginative worldbuilding, The Dante's Circle series reads as if Carrie Ann Ryan peeked at my personal wish list!" – NYT Bestselling Author, Larissa Ione

"Carrie Ann Ryan writes sexy shifters in a world full of

passionate happily-ever-afters." – *New York Times* Bestselling Author Vivian Arend

"Carrie Ann's books are sexy with characters you can't help but love from page one. They are heat and heart blended to perfection." *New York Times* Bestselling Author Jayne Rylon

Carrie Ann Ryan's books are wickedly funny and deliciously hot, with plenty of twists to keep you guessing. They'll keep you up all night!" USA Today Bestselling Author Cari Quinn

"Once again, Carrie Ann Ryan knocks the Dante's Circle series out of the park. The queen of hot, sexy, enthralling paranormal romance, Carrie Ann is an author not to miss!" *New York Times* bestselling Author Marie Harte

DAWN UNEARTHED

NYT Bestselling Author Carrie Ann Ryan begins a new witchy paranormal series where a magical town keeps its secrets, but those in it must find a way to keep themselves safe.

The moment Sage Reed makes her way to Ravenwood, she knows the small town lives up to its mystical lore—even if she doesn't believe that she's a witch. After losing her husband, she's ready for change, and her aunt's bookstore affords the perfect opportunity.

Rome Baker has secrets of his own—even some that he's kept from the town he calls home. But when a striking and intriguing stranger saves his life the moment she steps into his path, his inner bear knows that she's the one for him. However, with the town under fire, he worries he might run out of time before he can show her what they can have together.

A new enemy is on the horizon, one who hides in the shadows, whose history is steeped in lies. And if Sage and

Rome aren't careful, Sage's new powers won't be the only thing that spirals into flame.

CHAPTER ONE

SAGE

I squinted as I looked at the GPS, trying to make sense of the directions. I had been across the Pennsylvania border for over an hour now, and I needed to find the right exit that would take me off the main highway and onto one of the many smaller roads that encompassed Pennsylvania. I needed to get to my new home, or at least what others would have me call my new home. I still wasn't quite sure what that would mean as of yet.

My hands clenched the steering wheel, and I told myself everything would be okay. I was making a dramatic move, with even more unknown changes to come, but it was for a purpose.

Because Ravenwood, Pennsylvania called to me.

I shook my head, frowning at myself as I checked the next exit.

The town wasn't calling to me. That was preposterous. Towns didn't reach out to people. And I did my best to ignore the odd whispers in my head, the pull to a place I'd never been to nor even thought of before. I pushed away the idea of a shadow person filling my vision. I wasn't being pulled toward anyone either. That was silly. The only people I knew in Ravenwood were my aunt and Rowen, who had sold me the building where I was setting up my business. Ravenwood was a place. Somewhere I would make my new home.

I couldn't go back to where I had been for so many years. I couldn't rebuild my life from the ashes in a place that still sparked with embers of sorrow and pain. I did my best to empty those thoughts from my mind because they wouldn't help anyone.

I was moving to a new place, in a new state, to a new home.

Ravenwood was a small town north of Philadelphia, and one I had only heard of because my aunt lived there. If asked to name cities in Pennsylvania, most people wouldn't even think of the town. She owned a small bookshop called Ravenwood Pages and frequently spoke of the warmth radiating through the town and how everybody was welcome.

Rupert and I had always meant to come north from Norfolk, Virginia, where we had lived for the entirety of our marriage, but things had never worked out. Between work, our conflicting plans, and life in general, we hadn't been able to visit my aunt Penelope at her bookshop. Looking back, I didn't know why. It wasn't as if it was too far of a drive—not when it meant seeing my aunt in her home. Now that I thought about it more, it felt as if something had been pushing us away. And, once again, that was an odd thought to have.

My aunt usually came down to visit us for holidays, or we went to Rupert's family's place. I last saw Penelope after the funeral when she came to make sure I was okay. Not that

I could *be* okay. Nothing about losing one's husband at twenty-four years old was okay.

Everyone kept saying that we had our entire lives before us, that they couldn't wait to see what would happen between Rupert and me. They wanted us to thrive, have babies, and create a whole family in our Virginia town. That hadn't happened. No, nothing had happened the way it should have. Rupert was gone. And so quickly, I could barely even pause to catch my breath.

A brain tumor had taken him before I'd even had a chance to come to terms with the idea that I might lose my husband. Now, he was gone, leaving nothing for me. Not his family, nor the rest of mine. Rupert's family hadn't wanted anything to do with me after Rupert died. They saw my pain *and* theirs etched onto my face every time they looked at me and had pushed me away because of it.

Now, I was on the long road to a new beginning, one where I needed to stop feeling the melancholy stretching over me, digging its claws into my flesh as I struggled to cope.

I shook away my thoughts, doing my best to breathe. That was all I needed to do. Breathe.

My dash lit up, and the sound of an incoming phone call filled the car. My lips turned up into a small smile as I saw the readout and answered.

"Aunt Penelope," I said softly, waiting for the next exit as I kept my attention on the road.

"Are you almost here?" she asked, her voice warm, soothing. She was always that way, as if every time I was near her, she infused me with warmth and magic. Not real magic, of course. Though my mother joked that my aunt was a witch, I knew that wasn't the case.

Magic didn't exist.

And, once again, here I was having odd thoughts.

"I'm almost there. I think it's the next exit."

My aunt was silent for a moment before she spoke again. "Take the exit and make sure you stay on the path. Don't take a detour or stop for anything that might come your way. Ravenwood is waiting for you."

I frowned, looking at the GPS again. "What do you mean?" Her words were weird. Then again, everything I'd been thinking for the past hour had been strange.

Another pause. "Nothing, darling. You'll be here soon. Finally. And Ravenwood will welcome you home. As will I."

"I hope so," I muttered as tension rolled over me again at the momentous changes I was barreling through. "Are we sure you need a bakery? It's a small town. There has to be one already."

"There was one a few years ago, but the tenants moved on. Lately, we've been dealing with the supermarket and their baked goods. Not that they aren't adequate, but there's nothing like bread and sweet treats from a true bakery. From *your* bakery. The town needs you, Sage. The building is ready and outfitted to your specifications. You'll be able to start soon."

My stomach clenched, but I still smiled. I hadn't made it up to Ravenwood yet because I had been dealing with estate issues and Rupert's family. Closing up my life and my house back in Norfolk while trying to open a bakery and a small business in a town I had never even been to, had been all-consuming. I still couldn't believe I was doing it, but things were falling into place.

Maybe they needed to after everything else had shattered around me. Grief wrapped its spindly fingers around my throat, squeezing, suffocating, the mere force of it over-whelming.

"It will be good to see you," I said, my voice choked.

"I can't wait to hold you again, my Sage. See you soon, darling. Remember, stay on the path and you'll find Ravenwood."

She hung up, and I frowned. "That was peculiar," I whispered. Though Aunt Penelope was pretty unusual. She was always giving advice, her voice filled with warmth and wisdom when she did.

She wanted me to come *home*. Such an incongruous word. Because I had thought I'd had a home for so long. Yet, now, it was gone. There was nothing for me back in the small house where I'd loved Rupert. Nothing for me in Virginia at all.

Rupert was gone, and all ties I had to that life had faded away with him, or perhaps they'd been snapped into pieces by the agony. The brain tumor had taken him quickly, even as he wasted away. I never wanted that image in my head again, even in the short years since I had lost him.

I loved him, and I would always love him, but I was ready to move on now. I'd spent these past couple of years finding out who I was. I needed to discover who I could be without him and outside of the place that held our memories.

I had gone through my grief differently than most. And I wasn't the same person I had been before. I was finding my way—a home to settle in.

Maybe that was healing. I didn't know, but I would find out. I needed to. And whatever pulled me toward Raven-wood urged me to do so.

My GPS signaled, and I took the next exit.

Ravenwood beckoned me.

I crossed over the exit and got onto the road, the same path my aunt had just mentioned. As soon as I did, dark clouds filled the sky. I frowned and looked up, wondering where the storm had come from. I hadn't known there was a storm on the horizon. I hadn't seen it, but maybe I hadn't been paying enough attention—which probably wasn't smart, considering I was still driving, and it had been a long day.

A long month. A long few years. A long agony.

I frowned and shook my head as the rain began splattering on the windshield. I quickly turned on the wipers, the sound almost...rusty. It hadn't rained in a while.

"This storm came out of nowhere," I muttered.

I hadn't remembered seeing it on my weather app that morning when I left, but storms did pop up here. Maybe this was the usual. I didn't know. I didn't know anything about Ravenwood. Other than the fact that my aunt had told me to come.

And since I had nothing else to do, I went. Now here I was, entering this small town as lightning streaked overhead, cracking in the sky. I swallowed hard, my knuckles going white as I kept on the road.

The rain began beating down harder, so loud that I could barely hear my thoughts. I had long since turned the radio down, and all I could hear was the sound of the storm raging outside. One I hadn't even seen until it surrounded me.

Dark clouds burst overhead, the rain becoming a deluge. The road was so slick that I was afraid I might need to pull off, but I didn't know where to do that. Would other cars be able to see me? My lights were on bright, even in the middle of the day, but I could barely see. It was as if night had come out of nowhere.

I swallowed hard, sensing the taste of metal on my tongue as fear encroached.

I needed to focus, to get through this. I had to find a place to pull off. There was nowhere, other than the embankment, and that didn't seem safe. I needed to find my way to a part of the road to pause, collect myself, and hopefully let the storm pass. And then I could get to my aunt and Ravenwood. The wind rattled my car, and I nearly skidded off the road.

"Crap," I whispered and slowed down. There weren't any other cars, no lights, and I had no idea where I was. I looked at the GPS, but all I saw was darkness. It couldn't seem to find me in the storm. None of this made any sense.

I looked up and screamed, slamming on the brakes even though I knew that was a stupid move in this rain.

A dark wolf stood in front of me, its eyes glowing gold in the headlights. I shouted, hoping to hell I didn't hit him.

I spun, fishtailing on the wet road, and did my best to steer into the skid, but I couldn't remember what direction that was. Was I supposed to go with my back wheels or my front wheels? All thoughts of driver's ed, and everything I had ever learned about driving through a storm escaped me. Tires screeched. I saw the eyes of the wolf again, and it lifted its lip, baring one fang.

I blinked as if lost in the moment. Everything froze around me, and warmth suffused me as I tried to focus. Attempted to see what was going on.

The wolf looked at me. When I blinked again, it was gone.

Everything moved quickly after that, and I was silent as I kept my hands on the wheel, trying not to roll over or skid off into the dirt and grass along the side of the highway, but there was no stopping my car.

The wet road, my overreaction, the storm, and that wolf had created this.

My car skidded horizontally through the grass, and the sound of my wheels popping as I slammed into the grass to the side echoed in my mind, nearly deafening me.

I blinked, my mouth dry as I tried to keep myself steady.

I was going to die. I wasn't even going to make it to my new home. I would die on this road with nobody around.

I would be alone. After so much time wondering who I could be as someone standing on their own two feet, I would die alone.

Finally, my car stopped, and I tried to breathe, my heart beating so fast I could practically hear it beating a staccato rhythm in my skull.

I quickly looked around and then looked down at myself.

There wasn't a scratch on me. I was fine. My car, on the other hand...I didn't know.

I couldn't see anything in front of me, not even the front of the car. Was I supposed to turn off my engine? I should call someone. I needed to do something. I looked down at my phone and cursed.

No signal.

Did Ravenwood have no cell service?

Someone had to come along soon. Though I needed to do something other than sit here. Someone would come and help me. Or maybe I could walk through the storm and find my way to help. No, I should stay in my warm car and then move towards the town once the storm let up.

That was the smart thing, right?

I looked through the window at the fallen tree in front of me and let out a relieved breath. If I had skidded a foot more, I would have hit it, and I could have died. The branches were sharp. It would have likely punctured the window and me.

Somehow, I hadn't hit that directly. I had to count that as a win.

I looked up the path once more and froze. A man lay under the tree. I couldn't be seeing this right. But *somebody* was there.

I pulled out my phone, even though it was a brick at this point, and scrambled for the door. It might be raining, and it could be a serial killer for all I knew, but I couldn't sit there and watch him practically drown in the mud. What if he was alive? What if he was hurt? I needed to find a way to help him.

My boots slid in the mud as I made my way towards the fallen man under the tree.

"Excuse me?" I asked over the rain, my voice shaking. "Hello?"

No answer. I knew that was stupid. It wasn't like he would answer if he was passed out or worse. I swallowed hard and moved forward before I knelt beside the man. His back rose and fell with his breaths, and I saw blood on his head from a small gash.

He was alive, though I knew I shouldn't move him. What if he had hurt his back? I didn't know *what* I was supposed to do.

I leaned forward and slowly brushed my fingertips across his forehead toward his temple.

He had a big beard, strong cheekbones, and a furrowed brow. His dark hair was slicked back, wet from the rain, and splattered with mud. He looked so strong, a little intimidating, but was passed out and clearly hurt.

I didn't know how to help. Yet something screamed

inside of me to at least try. To pull him back and attempt to save him. I'd never felt this way before, and I wasn't sure I liked it. I could barely breathe. I needed to help this man. I needed to do something.

"Excuse me?" I whispered again and brushed his skin with my fingertips once more.

Shock slid up my body and slammed into my arm. I fell back hard into the mud and scrambled away from him. He looked up at me suddenly, blinking, his eyes a dark brown ringed with a bright gold that seemed to shine in the low light the storm allowed.

He huffed out a breath and growled.

An actual growl.

Then I looked at his eyes again. They were no longer brown. They'd turned fully gold.

Just like the wolf I had seen.

That wasn't right. It couldn't be. I was seeing things. I had hit my head harder than I thought, and this was all a dream. A delusion. Because I didn't feel right. Not with something pulsating inside me: the sudden urge to reach out and touch this man, make sure he was real.

Lightning struck so close, it popped my ears. I let out a squeak. The man beneath the tree growled, cursed under his breath, and then slowly made his way out from under the large branches.

"You shouldn't...you shouldn't do that. You could be hurt." I wanted to reach out and touch him again, to help him. Something inside me pushed me forward, made me want to tell him that everything would be okay as I wrapped my arms around him.

I pushed away that strange urge.

"I'm fine," he growled. He tilted his head as he studied

me, his nostrils flaring. "It seems you're the one who saved me."

"What?" I asked, my entire body shaking with warmth and shock. I really couldn't breathe. What was going on?

He reached out as if to touch me, then let his hand fall. I wanted to move forward but I couldn't. We both sat there staring at each other as if we were the only two people in the world in a middle of a storm. It didn't make any sense. "It's okay, little witch. I think you shocked the hell out of me, but I'm awake now and fine. We should get out of this storm."

I scrambled away, my eyes wide. *Little witch?* Why had he called me that? I looked down at my hands and nearly shrieked again, but I had no breath left in me. It looked as if lightning scorched up my arm, white lines of power sliding up to my chest and down my sides.

My hips ached and burned. I scrambled for my shirt, lifting it. The man in front of me raised his brows and met my gaze.

"You okay?" He moved forward this time, his voice a deep growl of anger and... possession?

I shook my head, tried to catch my breath. As if waking from a dream, I realized that what I'd thought was real seemed to be wrong.

My memories were realigning, and I couldn't make sense of them. Part of me remembered waking up with inked abstract fish and waves across my hips in a belt when I was younger. I hadn't known why I'd gotten the tattoo. I didn't remember sitting for the artist, but I'd told myself that I had done it because tattoos didn't appear out of nowhere. Rupert had never liked it, but it had been *mine*. It had called to me, and I knew I needed it. It didn't make any sense. Only now, I remembered the truth. I'd woken up one day with my body inked in this anchor to...something as if I'd been meant to have it.

Why had I thought I'd gone into a shop and requested it? *Maybe because that was the rational answer.*

Only there was nothing sane about what I saw now.

The waves thrashed against my hips, moving around my body as if in a current. The fish swam in and out of the waves, breaking through the water and then diving back in.

Maybe I *had* hit my head.

My tattoo is moving.

The man looked at me and then over my shoulder. "I'm fine," he said, but he wasn't talking to me.

I turned to where he was looking, and my mouth dropped open, a scream ready. Then whatever had been pulsating within me, whatever hallucination arced through my brain, hit me again. I fell, my head splashing into the mud. I heard the man in front of me growl again, mumbling a curse as he reached for me.

All I could think about was the creature behind me. The large brown bear that I hadn't noticed before. I was sure it would finish me off if the burning that sliced through my body didn't do it first.

And then...there was nothing.

Nothing but questions.

And wrongness.

And darkness.

CHAPTER TWO

ROME

I looked down at the woman in my arms, taking in her long, flowing, honey-brown hair, and swallowed hard. My bear scratched at the surface, wanting to get a peek, wanting to know who exactly we had found. We knew everyone within Ravenwood's borders. We didn't know this girl. There was something else my bear wanted, but I couldn't figure it out yet.

I looked up at my brother as Trace began shifting back into human form.

"Good job scaring the crap out of her," I mumbled. The rain started to die down, and the wind slowly ebbed to a point where it wasn't all-encompassing.

Trace blinked at me, completely nude after his shift but not looking like he cared all that much. "You were bleeding and looked like you were hurting. I wasn't going to take the time to shift back until I knew you were healing. What if you needed me to be in my strongest form?" He growled, looking around. "Who is that? She smells strongly of magic, but I've never seen her before."

I shook my head and was grateful when I felt her pulse beneath my fingers. "I don't know," I said. "She saved my life."

Trace's brow winged up. "And how did she do that? With a spell?"

I knew Trace was hesitant around most witches, but that probably had more to do with his ex than it did the power running through the little witch's veins. He liked magic and respected it, but loving a witch who hurt because of their magic tended to scar a man, much like the magic had scarred his ex.

"I don't know what she did. I was having trouble getting out from under that tree that fell on me out of nowhere," I grumbled.

"You let a tree fall on you?" I didn't appreciate my brother's tone.

I scowled. "I didn't *let* a tree fall on me. Lightning hit it, and it slammed into me. It wasn't like I rubbed my back on it and was suddenly impaled."

"I don't know, I could make a bear necessities joke, but I'll refrain. The storm is letting up. I didn't realize we had weather like this in the forecast," Trace said as he looked up at the sky.

I followed his gaze and shook my head. "We didn't." Then I looked down at the woman in my arms. "Could have something to do with the new witch in town. Or something else that doesn't want her here." Stranger things had happened in Ravenwood.

"She shouldn't even be here," a third voice said as I looked up at my other brother, Alden, as he strode into the small clearing.

I met Trace's gaze, and he gave me a slight shake of his

head. He hadn't realized that Alden had been there either. Great. The three of us were triplets, and though we were nearly equal in strength, I was slightly stronger since I was the alpha of our pack. Alden hated it. Because Trace was beta, and that meant Alden didn't have a title.

It didn't matter that Alden was as revered in power as the rest of us. He still wanted more.

And he hated witches. Trace only growled at one witch for reasons of his own, but Alden *hated* them. I didn't know why.

"Alden, she's hurt." I pulled her closer, checking for any other injuries.

"She passed out looking at a little bear coming closer," Alden sneered. "She must not be that strong of a witch if she passes out at the idea of a shifter." His lip lifted into a snarl as he spoke, and I shook my head.

"I don't know if that's the case," I said. "There was magic ringing from her. And whatever she has in her, it shocked me out of the dizziness that hit me when I fell. I'd have drowned in that mud pit without her." Not the most honorable way to die. But she'd been there when I needed help.

"So weak that you can't even wake up from a little spell? Huh," Alden said, huffing and chuffing.

Trace opened his mouth to growl or say something he would probably regret later, and I shook my head. There were ways to deal with Alden. Though right now, I didn't want to worry about any of them.

"Do you think we should take her to Rowen?" I asked, looking down at the passed-out witch.

"We're not going anywhere near that sorceress." Alden snarled again.

I let my bear slide into my eyes, the gold glowing brightly

enough to illuminate the area, even in the semi-darkness from the storm.

"Watch your mouth. Rowen has done more for us than nearly anyone else in this town."

"Rowen is the reason our town is cursed," Alden snapped. "I don't have to be nice to the parasite who's killing Ravenwood."

Trace began to growl, his whole body shaking, claws extending from his fingertips.

I let out a curse and stood, the woman still in my arms. I ignored how she felt next to my chest—as if she were always meant to be there. I wanted to hide her from my brothers, keep her close, and make sure the world knew that she was *mine*. But that didn't make any sense.

"Stop it," I snapped. "We don't have time for this. Trace, go to Rowen and tell her what happened, about the storm, and that we found a witch. I'm taking her home."

"You're taking her to the den?" Alden asked, his eyes light gold as they shined from his bear being at the surface.

"I'm taking her to my home." My bear wouldn't let her be anywhere else—something I'd have to think about later. And, frankly, the man wasn't much better with his possessiveness at the moment.

"That's still part of the den, alpha," he said, snideness in the term, making my bear stand up and want to lash out. This was my triplet. I didn't get to fight and prove my dominance right now. Not if I didn't want to deal with an even bigger situation.

"My home is my home. And though it is part of the den, it's still mine. I'm going to make sure she's okay and wakes up feeling safe. Rowen can come to me if needed."

"I'll bring her." Trace looked between us. "Laurel, too?" he asked, his voice carefully bland.

I met my brother's gaze. My bear pulled from the woman in my arms to focus on the pain in Trace's eyes. "If needed. If she can. If *you* can."

There was so much left unsaid in those words, but I knew that Trace understood. He gave me a tight nod, glared at Alden, and then loped off towards the trees. He would probably shift back into his bear form. That way, he wouldn't run naked around town. He could find one of our caches of clothing around the area before he met with Rowen. Not that Rowen would care if a nude bear shifter showed up at her shop. She was used to it. This was Ravenwood.

I cleared my throat as I looked at Alden. "I'm going now. Please don't stand in my way. You could help by getting her car out of the ditch." I didn't put a command in my voice, not as an alpha. I wanted him to help me as my brother.

Alden snorted. "I'm not helping a witch," he said, glared at me one more time, then ran off, still in his human form. He hadn't shown up naked, so unless he had brought clothes with him, he had found us in his human form rather than his warrior or shifter form.

Warrior form, the halfway point between bear and human, was difficult to hold, and only Trace and I had a handle on it—and we only used it when we were in battle. And even then, not always. It took a lot of energy to maintain it and was hard on the system. Plus, it was more comfortable to be fully bear or man. Alden didn't have access to his warrior form without effort. I wasn't sure he even used it at all.

When Alden was out of sight, I brought the woman closer to me and inhaled. My bear chuffed, nudging at me, wanting out, wanting to see. I let my eyes glow, allowing the bear to rise to the surface. My nostrils flared, her sweet and intoxicating rose scent wrapping around me. It mingled with mine, forest and rose, acting as an anchor to something I didn't dare breathe. I shook.

I looked down at the unconscious woman in my arms— the witch, who I had a feeling knew nothing of our kind. I cursed.

Mate.

My bear couldn't speak, couldn't communicate with me, but I knew what word it wanted to use. What word it *needed* to.

Mate.

This woman could be my mate. The earth shattered beneath my feet as the gods looked down upon me. I'd found her. After all this time, I'd *found* her.

And now I needed to keep her. A woman who didn't seem to know about our world and who looked to be a witch from Ravenwood's lost coven.

I cursed again and brought her closer, running towards home. I had been out walking, surveying the storm that someone had seen on the horizon. I didn't have my car. I didn't even have my phone since the lightning hit had scorched it. I needed to call Jaxton, my friend and fellow fixer, to help clean up whatever had happened out here.

The town of Ravenwood was unique, and we needed to keep it that way.

I made it home without anybody noticing me. For a small town, that either meant that I hadn't caught their attention, or I had simply gotten lucky. Either way, it was a good thing. I didn't want to answer any questions yet as to who the woman in my arms was, and I had a feeling Rowen would feel the same way.

I went inside, closed the door behind me, and gently set the woman on the couch. I looked down at her as she breathed calmly. She didn't look hurt. I figured she could be drained from whatever magic had poured out of her and into me. I didn't know and only understood the most basic things about witch magic. I would be grateful when Rowen showed up.

I pulled out my spare phone—I had plenty since I tended to break them often with my strength—and dialed Jaxton.

The hawk shifter answered quickly. "Rome? You're out in that storm?"

"It seems to have dissipated, at least from what I can tell. Long story that I'll get into later. But, Jaxton? There's a new witch in town."

Jaxton was silent for a moment, and I knew his mind likely followed my thought process. "The three? The new coven?"

Not everybody knew of the Ravenwood curse and the need for a coven, but Jaxton did. As did I. Trace and Alden thought they knew, but they didn't have all the information. They weren't alpha or wing leader. They didn't realize that the true darkness was coming. We'd tell them soon. We had to with this woman's arrival. That storm had meant something, and the town needed to be prepared, not panicked.

I cleared my throat. "I don't know. Trace went off to get Rowen and maybe Laurel."

"Is that a good idea?" Jaxton asked dryly.

"About Laurel? Probably not. But we're seriously low on witches in this town."

"Maybe we gained one more. What do you need me to do?"

"I need you to get her car, her keys, and whatever else you can find out there and see if you can tow the vehicle to your place."

"Okay. What else?"

"Make sure I didn't miss anything in the cleanup. That storm came out of nowhere, and I don't think it was natural."

"Magic's sparking. Even the young ones are having a hard time right now keeping their human forms."

I cursed under my breath. "I'll need to go check the rest of the den soon if that's the case."

"We can do that. Let me know what else you need."

"Fine. Then we'll see what Rowen says."

Jaxton was silent for a minute before he cleared his throat. "I may have overheard something from Penelope," Jaxton began.

I held back a laugh. "May have overheard because you were in your hawk form, listening in? Or were you standing in her bookshop pretending to read?"

"I'm not going to dignify that with an answer," Jaxton said sagely. "Penelope said her niece was coming to town. The one who's opening that bakery shop?"

I cursed. "Shit, I forgot."

"I guess you'd better contact Penelope, too. It seems her niece is here." Jaxton hung up, presumably to get to work, and I looked down at the woman on my couch.

She was gorgeous, and from what I'd glimpsed, her eyes were piercing. Her hair was long and wavy, with nearly strawberry highlights that didn't make much sense in the honey-brown strands. But I liked anything with honey in it. Her eyes were hazel, and when she had lifted her shirt with fear in her gaze, I had seen the witch magic all over her skin. The ink running down her body had moved in waves. Her affinity must be for water. Still, she had looked so confused about it. I was terrified that she had come into her power in the middle of a forest, on the edge of Ravenwood, with no other witches to help her.

Rowen needed to get here soon.

"Not soon enough," I mumbled to myself as the woman's eyes fluttered open. She looked around, her eyes wide with fear. She sat up quickly, nearly falling off the couch. I reached out to steady her, but she shrank away from me. My bear growled at that.

We would never hurt our mate.

I pushed that thought away. Just because my bear liked her, didn't mean she was my mate. Though she scented of it, and I wanted to know what that meant. I ignored it. There wasn't time for that, not right now—and most likely not ever.

"Where...where am I? What happened?" she asked, her voice coming in pants.

I swallowed hard, wishing that Rowen was here. She'd be able to help. I'd probably screw this up. "You passed out in the forest. I brought you to my house." I swallowed hard, then remembered the blood on my shirt and all over my head. I hadn't had time to clean myself up after the tree fell on me. I'd been too busy making sure she was okay.

Fear coated the room, the smell masking her natural rose scent. I nearly gagged on it.

"Don't hurt me. Please. Let me go." She looked around as if trying to find a weapon or an exit.

I shook my head, my bear amused by her fierceness. "I'm not going to hurt you. You saved me from that tree. Remember?"

"Maybe?" She scrunched her brows. "How did I get here?"

"I carried you."

Her eyes widened. "Where are we?"

"You're in Ravenwood," I said softly. "Do you know what that means?" I asked, testing the waters.

"What do you mean? *I'm in Ravenwood...* Oh, God, I need to call my aunt. And get my car. What happened again? Why am I here?" She looked around my living room in a panic, and I heard her heart race. I wanted to reach out and steady her, crush her to my side and claim her as mine. Holding back the mating urge felt like trying to swallow nails, but somehow, I managed.

I wanted her.

I only knew her face, her fierceness, and her gentle touch.

And I wanted her.

Damn mating urge.

"I brought you here to make sure you were okay. Your aunt should be here soon." I hoped I wasn't lying. I hoped Jaxton and Rowen were taking care of things. Knowing them, everyone who needed to be here was probably already on their way.

"I'm sorry, I'm not usually like this. I'm so confused," she said, rubbing her hand over her face.

My lips quirked into a smile at that. She was adorable when confused. I didn't think me telling her that would help the situation, though. "I would assume so. Let me get you some water."

She looked up at me and smiled slightly. I counted that as progress. "Thank you. I think? It's been a bizarre day so far. I need...where's my phone?"

I went still and sighed. "Everything that you could have had was in or near your car. My friend's getting it all."

Her eyes widened again, the scent of her fear coating my tongue once more. "No, it's fine. I'm fine." She tried to stand up, her knees shaking. "What's wrong with me? Did you drug me? Wait. Sorry. That was rude. You saved me. Or I saved you? And my tattoos were moving, I think. They suddenly appeared when I was eighteen, but... I think I need to sit down."

I wanted to yell at her, my bear growling at the thought that we could ever hurt an innocent woman, but I didn't. I opened my mouth to say something, but the door opened behind us, interrupting me. The woman in front of me whirled and nearly fell again. I gripped her hips, keeping her steady. She tried to pull away from me.

I ignored how she felt against me, the way she felt *right*. Thankfully, she wasn't pressed too tightly to my body or she'd feel exactly *how* right she felt.

Damn it.

"That man there is named Rome. He's not trying to hurt you," Rowen said from the doorway. The storm was long gone, the sun bright behind her now, casting her in shadow. Her dark hair hung in waves, her blunt bangs highlighting her gray eyes that shone with magic as she stood in front of us, looking like a warrior with her height and strength in her sinful curves—as a friend of mine had once called them.

"What? What's going on?"

"Sage," Rowen said, and I stiffened.

I hadn't known her name. Sage. I liked it.

"How do you know me?"

"I'm Rowen, a friend of your aunt's. Penelope's on her way."

"Oh, you're the shop owner. I know you. You helped me with my store. I'm sorry," Sage said, shaking her head. She looked up at me then and smiled softly. "Did they say your name was Rome? I'm so confused. Uh...thank you." She looked down at my hands on her hips. I squeezed once, quickly, and her eyes darkened as I let her go.

My bear growled. I didn't want to release her but holding Sage like this would probably be considered out of the ordinary for anyone, let alone a witch who didn't seem to know that she was one.

"It's nice to meet you," I said, my eyes only on her.

Rowen cleared her throat, a curious yet knowing expression in her eyes. "Interesting," she whispered. "Penelope will want to have words, Rome."

"Nothing's settled yet," I growled, though I knew my bear had already decided.

"What are you guys talking about?" Sage asked, looking between us.

Rowen let out a breath. "This isn't exactly how I'd thought this talk would go, but I can feel the power in the air. You've already been triggered. That is interesting. The fact that I can even say that means that whatever spell was over all of us, keeping you away, seems to have lifted."

Rowen gave me an accusing glare, and I shook my head. "I didn't know anything. A tree fell on top of me," I said, a little petulantly.

Rowen's eyes widened, but she smiled a bit. "That's another Ravenwood story."

"What the hell are you guys talking about?" Sage asked.

I sighed. "Rowen?"

The witch smiled, and it was full of kindness and power.

"Sage Reed, formerly Sage Prince, welcome to Ravenwood. There's a lot you need to know."

Before I could say anything, before Sage could do anything, Penelope ran past Rowen into the house and threw her arms around her niece. I pulled away, reluctant to leave Sage's side, but I knew it was for the greater good.

"I was so worried. You're okay?"

"Aunt Penelope. I'm fine." Even I could hear the unease and worry in Sage's tone. *Fine* could mean so many things.

"You say that, but I want to get you checked out. Rowen will help."

"Rowen?" Sage pulled back, confusion etched on her face.

Penelope sighed and looked at me, then raised a brow before looking at the other witch. "It seems we have a lot to talk about, darling. Don't worry. We'll take care of you." She frowned and looked between Rowen and me. "Why didn't I tell her before? It doesn't make sense that I can speak so freely now."

Rowen scrunched her nose. "I have a feeling that damn spell was far greater than we thought."

Sage looked between all of us, confused, but no one said a word, no one explained anything. Not yet.

And I wasn't sure I could.

Because the more I stood there, the more my bear growled, I knew one thing for certain.

No matter who this witch was, no matter what it meant for Ravenwood, I had done something that would irrevocably alter my pack.

I had found my mate.

And she had no idea what she was in for.

CHAPTER THREE

SAGE

I stood looking at my aunt, my body aching, my tattoos burning into my flesh, and I couldn't help but turn to look at the large behemoth of a man behind me. His hair had fallen in front of his eyes, shaggy. It looked as if he had cut it himself. He had a big beard that hid most of his features until he smiled or looked right at you. He was broad, built, and I couldn't help but wonder why I had thought I'd ever be able to lift him when he was under that tree. And yet, here he was, looking as if a giant oak hadn't fallen on top of him. He had brought me here to his home, alone, and I had to wonder once again if he was a serial killer.

Still, I couldn't pull my gaze from him.

The more I looked at him, the more I thought of a bear. That reminded me of exactly *why* I had passed out.

"There was a bear...are there bears here?" I asked before I looked at my aunt and the gorgeous woman still standing in the doorway named Rowen. "What's going on?" My voice went slightly high-pitched.

My aunt sighed. "I didn't want to introduce you to Ravenwood this way, darling."

That wasn't helpful. My heart raced. I needed answers. Or a drink. Maybe a nap. I didn't know which, but I couldn't help but ramble in my unease. "What do you mean? Do random storms pop up out of nowhere, and bears frolic through the town all the time? Do people get knocked over by trees and then seem perfectly fine afterward? Why do you think this woman can help me? Come on, Aunt Penelope. Let's go. Maybe I hit my head or something. We need to go."

The gorgeous woman in the doorway sighed as she moved forward. "I hate when people tell me that I need to calm down, so I'm not going to use those words with you. However, I'm sure Rome here has some tea that we can make."

I looked up at the woman with her dark hair, fringe bangs, and cheekbones that I thought could cut glass. My head ached and I felt like I couldn't keep up. "Who are you again?"

"This is Rowen. The woman that I told you about. She owns one of the shops in town. The one next to your new bakery. She's renting you the cottage." Right. We'd gone over all of this already, and yet it didn't answer my question as to why the woman was here now. My aunt squeezed my hand so tightly, my pulse raced. I looked between the three of them and swallowed hard. Pain flared at my hip, and I let out a shout, pulling away from my aunt.

"What's wrong?" My aunt glared at Rome. I thought that was a little odd, considering no one knew what was happening.

"It's her anchor," Rowen said as if bored. "You should sit.

It will be easier to get through all of this if your knees don't go weak and you pass out again."

I narrowed my eyes at the other woman. "Pass out again? Don't make it sound like I swooned or something. There was a wolf... and a bear. And, I don't know...something happened. Maybe I got hurt in the storm, as well."

The large man beside me cleared his throat. "I should probably thank you for helping me. You sort of um, jolted me awake," he said quietly, his voice a low grumble. I looked up at him then. He winced, and I noticed Rowen glaring at him. *What is going on?*

"It would be easier if we did this all in the proper order," Rowen said before closing the door behind her and walking to the small kitchen in the corner.

"What do you mean? What order?" I winced again as my hip burned. I looked down, pulling up my shirt slightly. My eyes widened, and my mouth went dry. My knees did indeed go weak, and I dropped to the couch as I watched the waves crashing against my hip and the small fish swimming in and out of the crests, flipping their tails as if waving at me. Rome was at my side in an instant. I wanted to reach out to him but shoved that thought away. He let his hand drop as if he'd been thinking the same.

I licked my lips and looked at my aunt, my eyes wide. "I think I need to see a doctor. I've officially lost it. Just like Rupert's parents said."

"We're going to explain everything, Sage. I promise." Aunt Penelope looked at Rome. "Did she hit her head?"

Rome shook his. "No, I caught her in time. However, I think between whatever happened with her ink and then seeing Trace in bear form, it was all a little overwhelming. She passed out, so I brought her here."

"You should've brought her to my place," Rowen said. "I have things to show her that will make the transition easier. And I have better tea. You might as well have Lipton here."

I looked up as Rowen came striding back in, her hair billowing behind her. She was gorgeous, self-assured, and looked as if she could break someone with her fists.

"Should Laurel be here?" Penelope asked, and I looked between them, wondering when they were going to speak *to* me rather than at me or over me.

Rowen's gaze tightened. "Laurel can be wherever she wants to be. Though I don't think here is it."

"Once again, you're wrong on that, aren't you?" a redhead with plump lips and a slight scar above her right eye said as she walked into the room. "You must be the new little witch."

Rowen cursed under her breath. "We're not there yet."

Having enough, I stood up, ignoring the pain. "I don't know what's going on here, but we're leaving. Aunt Penelope? Is this a cult or something? No, I don't want to know."

"You haven't even begun if she thinks this is a cult. Or maybe you did," the woman named Laurel said as she leaned against the doorway.

A big man with shaggy brown hair, one who looked exactly like the man behind me, stood behind her, narrowing his gaze.

"Hell, Trace, you don't need to be here for this," Rome rumbled, and I looked between all of them.

My brain started to put things together, and the complete picture looked like something right out of a movie that usually gave me nightmares. Witches? Bears? Magic? Tattoos that moved? If I were awake and not losing my mind, then I'd surely fallen into something I wanted no part of.

"Trace. The man you said was in bear form. Who looks exactly like you..." I sucked in a breath, steadied myself. "I don't know what's going on. I'm sure you're all lovely people, but it seems I've made a mistake. If this isn't a dream, and if I can't click my heels and find myself at home, I'm going to head out now. Aunt Penelope, I'd like you to go with me. I need to figure this out. I don't know what I'm doing here, but coming to Ravenwood was clearly a mistake."

Rowen sighed, snapped her fingers, and the door slammed shut behind Trace and Laurel.

My eyes widened. She'd *snapped* her fingers and the door had shut. There were no pullies, no gust of wind. It'd just *happened*.

I pinched myself, the pain sharp.

Nope. I was awake.

I was either losing my sanity or my idea of what was real and far too surreal to make sense.

Rowen shook her head. "Everyone, stop. We're going to do this quickly, Sage. This isn't the way it was supposed to be. I didn't realize the effects of you coming to town would change everything so abruptly. I didn't expect the storm. Nor did I anticipate feeling as if we're all finally seeing things clearly. A spell gone to dust."

"I'm *shocked*. You not expecting something? Don't you always know the future?" Laurel asked, and I honestly didn't want to know the history between these two. The way they looked at each other with such...emotion. And yet, there was also something else there—so much misery. And since I knew all about grief, I wasn't about to ask.

"We should be at my shop, or even the bookshop for this. Not in your home," Rowen said as she looked at Rome. "I apologize."

I turned my gaze to the big man, unable to stop looking into his dark brown eyes. They seemed to pull at me, and I knew it must be the head injury. The one I didn't remember getting. Though I had told myself that I was ready to start looking at men again, and I'd found other men attractive since Rupert, this was *not* the time.

"You should listen to Rowen." Aunt Penelope reached out and cupped my cheek. "I promise it'll all make sense. While this isn't what we expected, it's Ravenwood. Nothing is as expected."

Rowen moved into my line of sight and met my gaze. Her eyes were a stunning gray, a color I had never seen before. I couldn't help but focus on them, wondering about her.

"You already know my name is Rowen. I'm the last of the Ravenwoods."

I tried to keep up. Since I didn't think they would let me leave anytime soon, I might as well follow along. I wanted answers, even if they didn't make sense. "Ravenwood. As in the name of the town?"

Laurel sighed. "If we're starting back that far, I'm going to need a drink, and tea isn't going to cut it."

"I've got it," Trace said as he walked into the kitchen.

Rowen handed me a coffee mug filled with tea, and I looked down at it. "We didn't drug you. Take a sip." Rowen paused. "I promise, nothing in that cup is anything special."

The large, bearded, very sexy man next to me snorted. "I would say I'm hurt, but you're right. That is the discount tea."

"You wound me, Rome," Rowen said, her eyes bright. It was the first hint of a sense of humor I had seen since she walked in here. The way Rome smiled, though? It lit up his entire face, and I nearly melted on the spot. The man should come with a warning.

What was wrong with me?

"As Laurel so eloquently put it, we are going all the way back," Rowen began. "Now, take a sip. The warmth will help you."

My Aunt Penelope gave me a soft smile and gestured for me to drink. I figured...why not? If this was the end, how I would be inducted into a cult and probably killed, why not drink the tea? I had to trust my aunt.

The brew was black, a little strong, but tasted decent enough. She'd also added copious honey, and that was delicious.

"It tastes great. Thank you." I looked at Rome. "Thank you."

"My tea is shit, but the honey is good."

A snort from the kitchen sounded. Rome's brother? "The honey's always good in our homes."

I looked at Rome, but he only shook his head. "I'll explain later. Or maybe it'll make sense in a few minutes once Rowen explains everything else."

"Nothing makes sense right now."

"Hopefully, it will soon." Rowen moved as the others came into the room. I was surrounded by strangers and my aunt, wondering when I would wake up from this very odd dream. "I'm the last of my family line. The last of my coven."

I blinked. "Coven. As in witch? I mean, that's wonderful for you, I believe everybody should practice whatever's in their hearts and beliefs, but I'm not quite sure what this has to do with me."

"It has to do with a lot more than you, honey," Laurel said, and I gave her an odd look. She shook her head.

"Maybe it'll make more sense if I show you," Rowen said and then held out her hand.

I took in her gray gaze, then looked down at her palm before dropping the mug.

Hot tea spilled over my boots and onto the hardwood floor. Rowen shook her head as the wind funnel in her hand poofed away, the tornado that had been there no longer present. Rome cursed behind me before catching the towel that Trace threw.

"I've got it," Rome said. "Maybe we shouldn't let people hold hot drinks when we're trying to change the world," Rome grumbled as he wiped my feet. "Are you hurt?"

I looked down and then gently, awkwardly, patted his shoulder as I tried to process what I had just seen. I was so embarrassed. However, as soon as my hand touched his body, he stiffened, and I felt a zing snap up my arm. I shook and immediately pulled away. "I'm so sorry. I'm fine. Really. I'm wearing shoes. Crap, is this going to stain?"

"It's why I don't have carpets or rugs anywhere. I tend to make messes. You're fine. Just breathe." He hovered over me and I let out a breath.

Rowen sighed. "It's been a while since I've done this. I'm sorry."

I shook myself out of my need to watch how Rome moved, and the concern I felt from my aunt, and instead looked at Rowen. "Done what?"

"Shown someone that the town of Ravenwood is special."

Special. That seemed to be a good word for it. If I were going to pretend that this was real, I might as well lean wholly into it. And, honestly, something tugged inside me, telling me to *listen*. I didn't understand, but it was as if I had remembered something I'd been forced to forget long ago. "How did you do that? What was that?"

"It's magic. I'm a witch with an affinity for air. Though I can work with all the elements, I mostly work with air. And I'm not the only witch in this room." She gave Laurel a pointed glance, and I looked at the other woman.

Laurel sighed and shook her head. "Yes, I'm a witch, but I don't have the type of power Rowen does. So, you're not going to see a little fireball in my hand."

"Fire? As in magic? Magic is real?" I asked, my voice choppy as my chest ached. The tattoos on my skin burned slightly as they continued moving around my body. I took a deep breath, trying to catch up. Rome knelt in front of me and gripped my hand. Somehow, he steadied me, and I didn't understand it. I looked into his eyes and let out a big breath. "What's going on?"

He stared at me then, and I inhaled his deep forest scent, feeling as if I were safe. As if no matter what happened, I wouldn't be alone. "Think about it. Think about every instance when you were younger and wished for something so hard that it sometimes came true. Or when you needed something, and someone was suddenly there to help. Think about the ink on your hips, of the water that flows around you. Think about the affinity that calls to you."

"Who are you?" I asked, staring at him. I wanted to move forward. I wanted to know this man.

And it scared me.

People didn't fall in love at first sight. It didn't happen. What was wrong with me?

"That's something for another time," he said and cleared his throat. He moved away, dropping my hand, and I stared at him, wondering about the curious looks everybody was giving me and each other. They knew something that I didn't, and I wasn't a fan of being kept in the dark.

"Shit," Trace cursed under his breath. When Rome shook his head, I wanted to say something, but I needed to get back to what Rowen had said first. I'd ask Rome and his brother what the hell they were talking about later.

"You're saying I'm a witch?" I asked. "You've got to be kidding me."

Rowen lifted her head, her eyes dark and full of lightning for a brief moment. "Yes, I'm saying you're a witch. And you've come to Ravenwood for a purpose. And not merely for baking, though the town can use you. This place is special, Sage. You know you're a witch. You can feel it. That's why you're not running away screaming right now. *You know*. Deep down, you know. And it might take you some time to understand it, to realize that you're not dreaming, and that you are a witch here for a purpose. The reason is to be part of our coven. Ravenwood is unusual. Our town knows that magic is real. It knows and protects that secret at all costs. There are many more than witches in town, but my family is the founders. We are the protectors. And we need you. For the town of Ravenwood knows that magic is might but not always right. And you were here at the time of the great becoming."

I stared at her, my heart racing, and yet...not in panic. I tried to comprehend her words as everybody nodded and stared at me. I looked down at the ink now sliding up my arms, moving from my hips. I had lost so much. I had lost my heart, my husband. Everything. If I were indeed losing my mind, what was one more thing?

"Oh, come on, show her more. Do something. When you get all high and mighty like that, it'll only make her think she's losing her marbles." I looked up at Laurel, and she shrugged. "I can't show you the fire, it hurts too much, especially when it's not a full moon. Walk around the town, and you'll see. I may hate it, but you're here for a reason. So, welcome to Ravenwood, witch. It seems we're a coven of three. Whatever we need to be."

"You're saying I'm a witch. And that this town is full of them. I know I can *see* you using your magic. I can see my tattoos moving. It's a lot. Do you get that?"

Rowen smiled. "You're not going to understand much of what we say right away, but maybe if we give you some peace, your aunt can explain it. After all, she's a witch, too."

My gaze shot to my aunt. "What?"

Aunt Penelope pulled at her shirt, her face blushing a pretty pink. "Not to the extent of others. I am more of an herbal witch. I don't have the powers that you have."

"That I have?" I repeated.

"Sage," she whispered, kneeling in front of me, "you consented to some of the ink on your body, but you didn't sit through sessions to get all of it, did you?"

I met her gaze, swallowed hard. "What do you mean?" I asked, fear in my voice. I knew what she meant. I had seen what I'd been missing as soon as the tattoos first moved.

"You told me you were called to the waves on your hips, that you did it out of impulse one night, but that isn't quite true, is it? They appeared one evening, right?"

"I don't know what you're talking about," I whispered.

"You do. And you need to see. You need to believe. Because Ravenwood needs you, Sage."

"Needs me for what?" I asked, looking at them, a sickening feeling settling in that maybe this wasn't a dream.

"We need you for the end," Rowen began. "And the

beginning. And everywhere in between. Ravenwood called you, and now you are home. You're here to protect it."

"Whatever the cost," Laurel added, and I looked at all of them.

I didn't scream, but I watched as the water rose in the fish tank in front of me. The others followed my gaze, and I had a feeling that my life had changed once again.

And this time, it was only the beginning.

CHAPTER FOUR

ROME

By the time Penelope spirited Sage out of my home, Rowen and Laurel on their heels, I felt as if I had been hit by a Mack truck. I was confused and left wanting. My bear shifted from side to side, angling for Sage's scent. For her touch. I'd never wanted a woman like I did her, and I'd only just learned her name.

My damn bear had lost his mind.

I wanted to run after her and keep her safe from anyone who dared to step in her path. My bear wanted to shift and roar and let the entire town—no, the whole *world*—know that she was *mine*. That I'd protect her at all costs. I knew that shifters could find their mates in an instant, but it usually took time for our inner beasts to fall for someone. To truly understand the soul within the other person—sometimes more than one person—until they knew who their mate could be.

And yet, that hadn't happened this time. Not at all.

Trace stood at the door, leaning against the frame as he stared at me, his arms folded across his chest. He was my mirror image, my closest brother, and right then, I felt as if I were seeing him for the first time. As if I saw *everything* for the first time now after holding Sage. "Do you want to tell me why you're acting so weird? How bad did that tree hurt you when it fell on top of you?"

I shook my head, trying to clear it, and then I rubbed my temples. Nothing helped, and I didn't think anything would until I had Sage. And that would be a problem since she was so new to the world of the paranormal. Not to mention, she didn't even know who I was, let alone about the idea of fated mates. "I got hit pretty hard, considering I passed out for a brief moment, but I'm fine now. I think." Better to talk about the tree rather than fate and bonds and the idea that my world had been rocked on its axis.

Trace gave me a look that spoke volumes. "You say that, and yet I don't believe you. What happened?"

I ran my hands through my hair and pushed my bear back so I could think. "I don't have time. We have to get to the pack circle. You know the others are waiting."

"You're the alpha. You can take a moment."

"Do you think Dad would make his pack wait while he tried to collect his thoughts?"

Trace shook his head. "That's the point. He is the Alpha of all shifters in the Americas. He can do whatever the fuck he wants."

I sighed and looked at my triplet. Our father was the Alpha of the Americas and ruled from our family's new stronghold outside of Montreal in Quebec. Trace and I had decided to stay in Ravenwood when the pack in Canada needed an alpha. Therefore, the *alpha* position and our other triplet had remained with us. No one had seen that coming since Alden wasn't a fan of Ravenwood, but the triplets had stayed together, nonetheless. Alden wasn't a bad person per se, but he wanted more power than he had and resented the fact that I was the alpha, with Trace as my beta. Alden was third in command, and barely hung onto the position.

If anyone challenged at the next pack circle, I had a feeling that Ariel would take Alden's position. The only reason she hadn't challenged him yet was that she had a family and enjoyed her position where she was in the pack. Although, if Alden didn't stop acting like an asshole, she might step in and take over the third spot, where I knew she should be anyway. However, right now, I couldn't step in and tell her to take over, nor could I insist that Alden step down. I could only monitor the situation, but I couldn't and wouldn't force a challenge. However, if they weren't careful, I'd have to make a decision and force the matter—not something I wanted to do. Some people liked that the three triplets held the top three positions. It seemed meant to be. I wasn't sure if I believed that, but I didn't want to push my triplet out of power. Or out of anything.

"Thinking about Alden and Ariel again?"

My gaze shot up to Trace's. "What?"

"You're getting that frown on your face. The line between your brows tells me you're thinking about Alden and Ariel. She's going to have to challenge him soon. For the peace of our pack."

I sighed and stomped to the kitchen, needing a drink. Alcohol didn't last long in our systems, at least not enough to do anything, but there were some bear-made honey beers that did a decent job of it. Our metabolism ran through alcohol far too quickly for my liking, but I needed a damn beer anyway.

"What happened out there before I found you? The others aren't here, you can tell me. You can trust me."

I opened two beers and handed a bottle to Trace. "Trust isn't the problem. Figuring out what the hell I'm doing is the issue."

"And what is that?" Trace asked, taking a sip of his beer.

"I don't know." I let out a breath. Trace stared at me in that unnerving way he had, and I knew if he was patient for long enough, I would eventually spill. So did he, and that was the problem. "I was out for a walk, checking the perimeter because of that unsettled feeling Rowen's been having, and someone said a storm was coming."

Trace nodded. "Do you think Rowen's weird feeling is because her new witch finally arrived?"

I shook my head, feeling certain of one thing, at least. "No, she's known Sage was on her way for a while now, though she never mentioned her by name. Rowen never had an uneasy feeling about it. But there seems to be something different in the air now. Maybe it has to do with why we need the coven to be stronger to begin with. As in what's coming to make all of us increase our patrols." I let out a breath and finally explained the darkness in detail, something I should have done long ago.

Trace's eyes narrowed, but he nodded. "I knew it was more than a feeling. There's an actual curse around the town, and something is coming to destroy us."

"We need to tell the pack," I said softly.

The witches had founded Ravenwood, but more than bears and witches lived within its wards. The town knew that magic and everything beyond it existed. It was an open secret, one the city, including the humans within it, protected fiercely. Shifters could walk around in either form and be welcomed here. Witches could openly practice magic, even if Rowen was the only true power left within the town's borders. Some witches, like Penelope, had minimal abilities, those who weren't part of the coven because it would be dangerous for them since their power was tied to their life-force. But they still had enough to help ward their homes or work essence and warmth into goods. And could help with a small healing spell or aid Rowen with some of her duties.

I knew Laurel had a complicated relationship with the coven for reasons of her own and couldn't give as much as she'd been able to when she was younger. I didn't blame her for not wanting to nearly kill herself every time she used magic.

The town of Ravenwood protected its people and its secrets, but Rowen had long known that *something* was coming. As our unofficial leader, our mayor being but a showpiece for the humans, Rowen knew when something was on the horizon that could threaten us all.

"And the storm came out of nowhere?" Trace asked. I nodded, pulling myself back to the conversation at hand.

"You saw it. We didn't know it was coming at all, let alone that it would hit as hard as it did. Lightning struck a tree, and I didn't move out of the way fast enough."

Trace's brows rose. "That must have been some tree, considering you're the fastest of us all."

That made me snort. "I don't think Frank would agree."

Trace's eyes filled with humor, his bear making the rim of his eyes glow gold. "Frank is nearing seventy. I don't think he's as fast as he used to be."

I laughed. "That old jaguar is still pretty damn quick.

Though not as fast as that cheetah that came through town that one time."

"It's too cold up here for either of them, but Frank likes it where he is—even if the cold makes his old bones ache," Trace said, mimicking Frank's voice.

I sighed, draining the last of my beer. "We need to get to the pack circle."

"We will, as soon as you tell me the rest of it. Lightning hit a tree, and it fell on you. I still don't get how that happened."

"I don't either. We both know that storm wasn't natural."

My brother sighed. "No, it wasn't. Since it happened when that new, pretty little witch showed up, it must have something to do with the coven."

I frowned. "You think she's pretty?"

"Hell, yeah. You saw those wide eyes and that plump little mouth." Trace raised a brow, and I realized my chest was rumbling.

I cleared my throat. "Sorry."

"Well, then. That answers that."

"That answers nothing," I growled, annoyed with myself and my bear.

"You're not going to tell your dear old triplet that you just found your mate?"

I froze and set down the empty bottle, even as my heart raced. My bear prowled deep within me. "It's not for certain." My bear pushed at me. I needed to run, stretch, do *anything* but talk about this. Because my bear wanted its mate, and I didn't know anything about her. Mating wasn't supposed to be this way. I wasn't supposed to fall for a stranger, one who had already saved my life—even accidentally.

"I saw how you reacted, and I can feel your bear pressing at your skin even now. You do realize that mating a witch right now is probably the worst thing your bear could be doing, right?" Trace asked drily. "What with this darkness, the witches' coven, and our pack?"

"And you would know all about witches, wouldn't you?" I lashed out, my bear pushing me. I cursed under my breath. "Sorry," I said quickly.

Trace held up his hand, his eyes filled with pity. "Oh, don't worry. Laurel and I are friends. You don't need to feel like you stepped in it about that at all," he whispered. "Not everyone in the pack will be okay with what could happen if you complete the mating bond with Sage."

"We don't even know if it's going to happen," I snapped. "Sage and I both have to agree to the bonding and the marking. It's not only what my bear wants. I can ignore it for now."

"That's only going to make you more agitated, and you have enough issues with control over your bear. Plus, with the factions rumbling about Alden's position and your handling of it, it's not going to be easy."

"It's fine. Come on. I don't know what I'm going to do, but I can't stand here wondering about the what-ifs. I don't even know her."

"No. And she's going to have a lot on her plate as it is, but she *is* pretty."

I narrowed my gaze. "Are you trying to get me to claim her, or do you want me to punch you in the face?" I asked, my voice clipped.

"You don't have to worry about me." He paused, his gaze filled with sympathy. "You know I'm not someone you ever have to worry about."

"I know," I said, letting out a breath. "Come on. We need to meet the others."

"Let's do it, then," Trace said, and I followed him out of my home, into the forest behind my house, on the outskirts of Ravenwood.

The den contained the pack circle and was carved into the mountainside, an intricate series of caves that protected us during the height of war back when the town was first formed. As time moved on, it was used less for its original purpose and more for training and as a place for our bears to stay when they needed to hibernate, even if our hibernation was slightly different than that of our natural counterparts. Many types of shifters called Ravenwood home, but bears were the most prevalent. Jaxton and the hawks were growing in number but weren't anywhere near the bears yet. There was a single jaguar and that cheetah who passed through. We had a couple of jackals, wolves, and a few mountain lions —even a badger or two who kept to themselves. Everyone was better off that way.

The bears were the most prominent, and our main den in the States was here. While my father was in charge of both continents in this hemisphere, my territory was nearly the size of Pennsylvania. However, there were alphas, wing leaders, and heads of every other type of shifter out there. My clan happened to be the bears in this territory. Therefore, I usually had the most say when it came to the shifters as a collective.

We made our way to the pack circle, seeing some of the others milling about. Today was an informal chat. If not, I would have been antsier than I already was. However, with the storm, my injury, and Alden running off as he had, I probably should have been more focused on this than I was. With the coven in flux and seeing Sage? I couldn't focus.

And that wasn't good for an alpha.

"I should have known," Trace grumbled from my side. I looked over to what he was glaring at.

Alden stood in the center of the circle, speaking as if he had a right to conduct the meeting. Thankfully, most of the pack ignored him, having side conversations of their own, but his small faction, ones who believed that Alden should be their alpha, listened raptly. Alden was the most political bear of our pack. He was the one who often traveled to the other alphas around the country and met with our father the most.

He wasn't the strongest, though, and that's what made an alpha. Still, the younger generation didn't always believe that. They had never been through a shifter war like the one my father had ended. They hadn't seen the gore, the bloodshed. Hadn't felt the terror. They wanted to follow the more elegant and sophisticated bear, not the one who could protect them against magic and the unknown.

"Thank you for waiting for my arrival," I growled, my bear in my voice. The others who hadn't been listening to Alden either growled at my brother or ignored him entirely before standing at attention. Alden's little crew glared at me, though they quickly averted their gazes. None of them was strong enough to face me in the circle nor meet my eyes directly. Good. They needed to remember who their alpha was. I didn't rule by brute force. I led by claw, fang, and the bear within. And that meant I wouldn't kill anybody who went against me, but they still needed to remember who their alpha was, even if they didn't always agree because they didn't understand what could be coming. None of us did. Not really.

"Ah, nice of you to show up." Alden tugged on his shirt sleeve. Most people wore jeans and T-shirts. Alden had on a button-down shirt, slacks, and nice leather shoes. I didn't understand why he dressed like that in the middle of a forest, but that was up to him. There was nothing wrong with having class. However, Alden used that class to look down on others. I didn't understand how he could be Trace's and my triplet, one-third of our souls, and yet not be anything like us.

"I was keeping the seat warm for you, brother." Alden winked, and I held back a sigh.

"The storm seems to be gone," I said, ignoring him. "Is everyone okay?" I asked.

"We're good," Ariel said as she walked forward, her arms crossed over her chest. "You were on the side of town that got hit the worst. Glad to see you're okay."

Her gaze moved to where the cut on my forehead had already healed, and I knew that Alden had likely told everybody I had gotten hurt. Great. Nothing like looking like a weak bear in front of others.

"It came out of nowhere and hit pretty hard, especially where I was. I'm glad everyone seems to have made it through unscathed."

I should have given all of them my attention to begin with. The fact that I had dealt with Sage and my issues first worried me. It wasn't easy to focus on everything all at once, but I needed to if I wanted to remain a good alpha. And while I might know who my mate could be now, it didn't change the fact that I was still these people's leader. They needed me. And I needed to focus on them.

Not on what could never be.

My bear growled at me, yearning to wrap itself around

my heart. I ignored the feeling. I didn't have time for anything of the sort.

I didn't think my bear cared.

"Come on, let's assess the damage and see what we can do."

The others began speaking in turn, going through everything that had happened since our last circle, while Alden slunk off to the side. I peripherally kept my attention on him and knew Trace was doing the same. We would have to deal with the triplet problem soon, but not now. Right now, I needed to ensure that everybody was safe.

I looked over to the other side of the circle, my lips twitching as three cubs came rolling in bear form towards me. I knelt and hugged them all close, watching their little paws waving in the air.

Others laughed, clucked their tongues, shook their heads. We continued our serious discussions of what we needed to do to clean up after the storm and going over any other pack business there was. All the while, three of our youngest members rolled around on the ground, their tiny little bear forms so small compared to the adults around them.

"You're interrupting," I warned after a moment. The littlest one, Honor, waved her little paw at me before scrambling up my leg. Jackson and Henry curled around my feet, so I sank to the ground and let the bear cubs climb all over me. An alpha on the ground in the middle of a pack circle might look odd to some, might not look like strength, but my father had always taught me that an alpha was only as strong as how they cared for their pack.

The bear triplets yawned widely at me before falling asleep in my arms, feeling completely safe and protected.

Their parents were off to the side, shaking their heads. They trusted me with their perfect babies. I figured that meant I was doing something right in this whole alpha business.

"We'll meet again in a couple of days," I said after a moment. I stood with all three bear cubs curled around me, Honor leaning into my neck, Jackson and Henry against my chest.

"Keep vigilant. Something's coming, and we all know it."

"We've got it," Ariel said.

Trace nodded tightly. "We'll keep on the lookout."

I moved to hand the cubs to their parents, a small smile playing on my face as Honor let out a chuffing noise. I shook my head and answered a few more questions before walking away with Trace.

"I'm glad the cubs came," I said after a moment.

"They seemed to know that you needed a hug," Trace said.

I laughed. "If you say something about a bear hug, I will have to hurt you."

"You're all bears, and they were hugging. But I'll refrain. The pack will feel your bear's unease soon. They'll know something changed. Alden might already."

I nodded tightly. "And if those who don't want a witch in the pack find out first, Sage might be in danger," I said after a moment, fisting my hands at my sides as my bear growled within me.

"We'll protect her, but you should probably let her know what's happening so she knows why she needs to be protected. She's a new witch and doesn't even seem to understand her power or the fact that magic is real. This probably isn't the best time for you to say, 'By the way, we're fated mates, and you're going to be mine forever.'"

"No, not even a little bit." I let out a curse and growled again. "Something's coming, I can feel it. And yet, all I want to do is go see where Sage is and make sure she's safe."

"I don't envy you, brother. Not even a little."

I opened my mouth to say something, but my phone rang. I looked down at the readout and answered.

"Jaxton, what's up? Everything okay?"

"I took care of your little witch's car, and Laurel is going to come and pick it up. Though I didn't call to talk about that or the storm."

I froze, uneasiness sliding through me. "What's wrong?"

"As I was checking out the damage, I flew over and saw something we need to talk about."

"What is it?" I asked again.

"Someone disturbed the graves. Disturbed them enough that I don't think everything buried over time is still there. We've got a problem."

I cursed. I knew that Jaxton was only stating the obvious.

Because if someone had disturbed the graves, we had more than a problem.

We had death itself.

And it was here. Waiting.

CHAPTER FIVE

SAGE

Even though I had slept the night before, I felt as though I were coming out of a fog. And not merely because of everything that happened the day before. It was as if a veil had been lifted from my gaze, and everything I had thought was real for so many years now had a different tint to it.

What Rome, a man I didn't want to think about just now, had said was right. Every little moment when I made a wish and forced change came back to me. Every time I needed help, every time I thought about my ink...each moment I saw something out of the corner of my eye that didn't look real.

Magic... magic was real?

Why did I keep thinking about Rome? Why did it feel as if I needed to see him? As if he were what I had been missing all this time. Nothing made sense anymore.

After the events at Rome's, Aunt Penelope had taken me to her house and set me up in the guest room. Somehow, I'd been able to fall asleep. I hadn't thought I would. Now I stood in her kitchen, wearing pajamas I didn't even remember putting on and staring at my aunt.

"All of this is real," I whispered, looking at her and then at the now no-longer-moving ink on my hips.

Aunt Penelope sighed and handed me a cup of coffee. "Yes. I had hoped to introduce you to Ravenwood and its quirks a little slower, but the storm and you meeting Rome as you did changed everything."

Her use of the word *quirks* nearly made me smile. Shifters, magic, and witches? That seemed far more than an oddity. My brain snagged on Rome's name, however, and I blinked, remembering the rest of the day. "I don't understand. I touched him, and it felt as if I had been shocked. As if he were a downed powerline. Yet, that doesn't make any sense."

My aunt smiled, her expression knowing. She was gorgeous and looked a decade younger than her fifties, her dark hair framing her face in a pretty bob. She had my eyes, *the Prince eyes* she called them. And unbeknownst to me before yesterday, there was also magic under there. "I think for that metaphor to work, *you* might be the downed powerline, darling."

I shook my head, trying to catch up to this abnormal conversation that seemed so normal to her. There was so much I was trying to understand. It was as if I'd been living two lives for my entire existence. I needed to bring them together. "He was hurt. And then, somehow, he carried me back to his place."

"Bears can do that," Aunt Penelope said, taking a sip of her coffee. I blinked.

"Bears, as in...?" They'd called themselves that before, but I had hoped maybe it was some slang I didn't know and not something else I'd have to figure out on my own.

"Rome is a bear shifter. Just like his entire pack. Or

perhaps they are a clan. I think it depends on the bear you speak to as to what they're called, but they're a pack—at least on this side of the equator."

I let out a breath, trying to remain calm. If I panicked, I'd only scare myself and probably my aunt. I could do this. I could be rational about the irrational. "The bear I saw...it wasn't just in my dreams?"

"No, but I don't know who you saw. It could have been Trace or Alden since the brothers are always around one another. They're triplets. Rome has two very handsome brothers who look exactly like him. As you well know since you already met Trace."

My ovaries nearly exploded at the thought, and I held back a frown. I needed to get control of my attraction to the very sexy, very large, very *bear-y* stranger. "I remember Trace. I don't know if I met Alden. So, they can shift into animals and don't eat people? And I'm a witch? Hence the water bubbling everywhere and me needing to pass out, right? Oh, and the tattoos that appeared out of nowhere and move. And this is all supposed to make sense."

"I think it's finally going to make sense for you. There were reasons I always kept up with you, Sage, and not only because I love you. You are like my own child, my favorite niece."

I snorted, even as my heart warmed. "I'm your only niece."

"Okay, you've got me there. But you must understand that you came to Ravenwood for many reasons, and not simply because you needed a fresh start. And not merely because I wanted you here. Because this is your home."

I swallowed hard, then looked down at my hands as I set my coffee mug down. "I don't want to believe you, and yet, unless I'm having a shared delusion with everybody or haven't woken from a coma, I saw things yesterday that I can't explain away. I saw the wind in Rowen's hands. I saw that bear come at me. And I felt the pain in my side as my tattoos moved. Tattoos aren't supposed to move."

"Yours do. It's your anchor."

"Anchor?" I repeated.

"All of those in our world, the supernatural and magical, have anchors. Mine is this." She pulled up the sleeve of her blouse to reveal a tiny dandelion planted in the earth but blowing in the wind. My lips quirked into a smile, awe filling me. "Yours are the waves on your hips and the abstract fish that swim around your body. They anchor you to the water you have an affinity for. The others will have air or earth or fire somewhere on their bodies, inked into their skin not by a needle but by the magic they were born with. It usually shows up around adulthood and is an important moment in a witch's or sorcerer's life. Shifters have anchors representing their animal form, as well, but I'm not sure when they show up on their bodies since they can shift at a young age. Of course, young witches and sorcerers can do magic, so maybe the anchors aren't tied directly to power and strength at all. It's a personal moment for those with an anchor."

I couldn't help but want to see what Rome's bear anchor and bear form looked like. After all, he was the first person I'd met in my new home, other than my aunt. He was an anchor himself.

At least, that's what I told myself.

"That means Rome has a bear on him somewhere. One that showed up one day." I was following along, going with it because I didn't know what else to do. I had seen it, the magic, and I couldn't let my eyes keep lying to me. My tattoos had appeared one day, and I'd told myself I must have drunkenly gotten the ink. And yet, they had never hurt. I hadn't even had to help them heal. They had simply appeared.

I had lied to myself and Rupert when I said it was something I had chosen to do. Only it hadn't seemed like a lie at the time.

Since I believed in many things, I had always known that magic could be real in the abstract. Though I had thought it was some faraway, out-there thing. Not something within me. I still didn't know if I quite believed that. Rowen seemed all-powerful, all-knowing, and I'd seen her wield her magic.

I had seen the ink on my flesh dance across my hips and up my sides, moving down my arms.

I hadn't imagined that.

If I wanted to remain sane, I needed to believe, at least about this shared delusion.

Because fighting it more would only hurt.

"There's so much for you to understand, Sage," Aunt Penelope said as she sighed, then took another sip of her coffee. "And I hope to tell you all of it. Although, Rowen and Laurel might be the best for that."

"Are they both witches, then?" I asked, trying to keep up.

"Yes, though there are some things I can't talk about as it's not my history to share. Nor my secrets."

"There seemed to be something there." I cleared my throat. Laurel seemed so angry. And yet, so had Rowen. I could practically feel the hurt radiating off them. I had always been good with emotions and feelings. I was empathic, at least in the sense that I could usually understand what broke others inside. When I lost Rupert, I had shattered within, trying to keep up with my emotions. Yet the grief surrounding me from everyone else had nearly drowned me.

I had left Virginia for many reasons, but now it felt as if I were coming home. I would say it didn't make any sense. And yet, it had to. All of this needed to be oddly logical.

My aunt sighed after taking her sip of coffee. "It hasn't been easy with those two. Honestly, it hasn't been easy with the town for a while."

"What do you mean?" I asked, tension gripping me.

"There's much that Rowen and the others will want to tell you, but the town used to have a lot more witches. Over time, the magic began to fade. Our town does its best to protect those around us, but that's not always something fate allows. There are so many types of supernatural creatures. Bears, wolves, dryads. So many. But witches founded this town, even though most of the witches left are latent like me."

"I don't know what that means," I said.

"Latent means that I have some power, I'm good with herbs, with finding the right book for the right person through intuition. But I don't have the same elemental power that strong witches like Rowen do. Like Laurel did."

"She *had* power?" I asked, worry for the woman I had met echoing in my veins.

"She did. But as I said, it's her story to tell. Rowen is the strongest of us all and protects us with everything she can. There's only so much she can do without a full coven of strength, though. She's lost so much, and I know she is at the end of her rope. She does her best, but now that you're here, well, I had thought *maybe* you were the one they talked about. The one they hoped for. But I hadn't known you would be this strong."

I blinked. "I'm not strong, Aunt Penelope. Not even a little. I broke when Rupert died."

"I know you hate the word *strong* because that's what everyone calls you when they see you trying to make a life for yourself, trying to rise from the ashes of what you had to become after losing your husband. And I'll try not to use that word when it comes to you. But the power within you? There is no other word for it. There is so much potential."

"I have tattoos that move, and I seemed to have messed with the water in Rome's home. I don't know what kind of strength you mean."

"You'll see."

"Yes, she will," Rowen said from the doorway.

I blinked, practically falling as I moved quickly to face her.

"Did you just pop out of thin air?" Visions of witches from TV shows who did that or showed up by wiggling their noses or blinking filled my brain.

I swore Rowen could see what I thought as a smile quirked her lips. "No, I used the door. Your aunt didn't lock it."

Aunt Penelope rolled her eyes. "You said you were on your way, and you can pick a lock in this house quicker than anyone I know. Maybe not Laurel. She always did have a knack for that."

Rowen sighed. "That is true. However, you should keep your doors locked, just in case. You never know what might be coming these days."

"Aunt Penelope mentioned the darkness," I said, wondering when I had fallen into this nightmare that I now believed to be real.

"Yes, there's that. And though this town may believe in

its magic and can protect itself, strangers drive through who don't understand what they see. My wards can keep them steady, can keep those under our power protected, but I need a full coven to keep it strong. As it is, Jaxton has to do a little bit of cleanup every once in a while."

"Jaxton? Isn't that the man Aunt Penelope said has my car?"

"Yes, he's a fixer. Much like Rome."

"Rome. The bear shifter."

Rowen smiled at me and shook her head. "You want to believe, yet don't. You're right on the cusp. You'll see more. Perhaps meet a dryad or two and understand the true meaning of our town. I know this isn't how any of us wanted you to be introduced to our people, brought into your town, but if you keep an open mind and try to believe, it'll be easier for all of us."

"I'm still waiting to wake up," I said.

"I'm sure. While you're waiting, follow along with the dream, and let's take a walk through town. I can show you your bakery, my store, and the bookshop, as well."

"I'd like to see Ravenwood Pages."

"My store is called Into the Wood," Rowen added. "I'm on one side of you, with Ravenwood Pages, your aunt's bookshop, sandwiched between us."

"Have you thought of a name for your shop?" Aunt Penelope said. "I know it was the last part you were waiting for, so you don't even have a sign or letterhead yet."

I sighed and winced. "I have. And I do have letterhead," I said. "I was waiting to show you in person." I didn't know why. Maybe I'd waited for a reason, much like everything else here.

"I think the name is quite nice," Rowen said, and my eyes widened.

"Did I send it to you by accident when we were emailing about the cottage?" I asked.

"No, she probably just knows," Aunt Penelope said, rolling her eyes. "So? What is it?"

"Ravenwood Sweets. Nothing too fancy, but I came here for a fresh start, in a new town to establish a new home. I thought I should include the name of that home in the place I'm building."

"I love it. And your baking is marvelous. It always puts me in a better mood."

Rowen's eyes sharpened. "I wonder what kind of spells you've been infusing into your recipes without even knowing."

I shook my head. "I'm not putting spells in my bread. That's not what I do." I panicked. "Right? Oh, God. What if I hurt someone?"

"You couldn't. Your soul is pure. You wouldn't ever hurt someone with your magic without your knowledge. It doesn't work that way. As for baking magic into your breads and sweets? Maybe not knowingly, but I have a feeling you've been doing magic all your life, even if you didn't realize it. For some reason, I think the curse or spell might have kept you from us but couldn't keep everything from you."

"I don't know if I like the sound of that. I'd want to know what I was doing."

"An untrained witch can be dangerous, yes. An untrained witch of your power? Immense. We'll figure it out. We always do."

"Now you're scaring the girl."

I looked at my aunt. "I think I need to lean into the skid,"

61

I said, reminding myself of the accident...and the big man I'd met and had seemingly saved. "Is Rome truly okay? A tree fell on him."

Rowen studied my face as if seeing something I didn't understand. "He's fine. They heal quickly. I'm sure you'll see him around."

"Because it's a small town?" I asked, not knowing why I pushed. And why I wanted to learn more about him.

"Perhaps."

I was already getting tired of Rowen's mysterious ways. I had seen the magic she wielded, saw it on my skin. Maybe I needed to believe. But I felt like I was two steps behind, no matter how far forward I moved, and this Rowen seemed to know all of the secrets but didn't want to tell me.

I left my aunt behind to work on a few pieces of admin, with instructions to learn the town and follow and trust Rowen.

I loved my aunt unconditionally. Maybe I needed to give in and figure out what was happening.

I had seen things, stuff I couldn't explain. Perhaps I needed to believe.

The town of Ravenwood was set up like any small town in Pennsylvania with a main street and a colonial street that ran perpendicular to the businesses. My aunt's home was one of the original, well-maintained houses on Ravenwood Drive. Rowen mentioned that her place was on the other end of the street, up a long, paved road that wound through the forest but was still technically located on Ravenwood Drive. Other homes seemed to have been there since the start of the town, well maintained yet kept to some code that meant they were all unique and painted in dark colors. Some had turrets. Many had circular windows that reminded me of a hobbit's or even a witch's home. That made me snort, considering the company I now kept.

"A penny for your thoughts?"

"I don't know if they're worth that much," I said, shaking my head.

"Never discount yourself. That's true for anyone, but especially for a witch."

"You keep calling me that, and yet all I've done is see my tattoos moving around my body and somehow raise water levels that nearly killed Rome's fish."

Rowen shook her head. "You'll understand soon. You're a Prince, after all."

My heart clenched ever so slightly. "No, I'm a Reed now."

Rowen reached out and squeezed my hand. "I'm sorry for your loss. Your aunt spoke highly of Rupert."

That made me smile. I didn't cry or scream when I thought of my late husband anymore. While I wasn't healed, not entirely—a widow never could be—I had moved on. I was on my path to finding happiness. Without his family, who always thought I was nothing. And without the town that hadn't known me at all.

"He was amazing. And though I *was* born a Prince, I'm a Reed now. My mother kept her maiden name, but I didn't. I don't want to think of myself as a Prince and forget Rupert, if that makes any sense."

The other woman nodded. "It does. And I understand. But you can honor both names to know where you came from. On both avenues, to see where you're going."

"It's hard to see where I'm going. And, sometimes, the past seems so tangled."

"The Princes were one of Ravenwood's three founding

families. The Ravenwoods themselves, my ancestors, built this town, but two other families came soon after—the Princes and the Christophers. Laurel comes from the Christophers."

My gaze shot to her. "All three of us are from founding families?"

"As it was written. The last coven should be of the three families, the ones who will bring us forward into the light."

"It sounds as if you're speaking from a prophecy or something." I tried to infuse laughter into my voice, but none came.

"Many things are written, but not all is seen."

"Now you sound like a fortune cookie," I said drily.

"You know, that's what I've always maintained," Laurel said as she walked towards us, her boots clicking on the cobblestones. "She likes to sound sage and wise, and yet, she sometimes sounds like a cracked, stale cookie."

"Let's not start today. I'm trying to introduce Sage to the town."

"You've told her about the founding families and some of the businesses on Main Street. Have you introduced the town?"

"I'd like to see my bakery if that's okay."

"We can do that. First up is Ravenwood Pages. Laurel works there."

I looked at the other woman. "You do?"

"Sometimes. I help my brother with a few things, but that's online, so I also help your aunt from time to time."

I noticed that Rowen had stiffened at the mention of Laurel's brother, but I didn't ask. It wasn't my place. And, honestly, I didn't have enough room in my mind to worry about anything else right now. It was enough that I was attempting to believe in magic and keep up with everything the residents of Ravenwood threw at me. I didn't need to add anyone else's emotions. Although, that was easier said than done. Rowen was so tightly wound that it felt as if she were suffocating next to me. Her feelings leaked through a tiny sliver in her control every once in a while. I could barely feel anything, but I did feel it. Laurel, on the other hand, burned brightly. Anger and pain wrapped around her as tight as a fist. Every once in a while, a flame of energy flicked off her as if the pain were screaming.

And even as I thought the words, I wondered if maybe I had known who I was my entire life. Yet, it had taken me taking my first step into this town to understand what exactly I had been feeling all these years.

I moved past the women and looked up at the building to our right. I grinned. "It looks like the photos," I said, smiling.

"Your aunt has been doing a wonderful job with the place. I always find the books I want. It's as if she knows what I need to read each morning."

"That's what latent witches do," Laurel said, rolling her eyes. "You can go in now, but your aunt isn't coming in until later today. You should probably go in with her then. She'll want to show you the place."

I nodded, my gaze still on the two-story building with its blue shades, cream wood exterior, and beautiful front porch. Each of the businesses looked as if they were older homes from the original town's founding and had been converted along the way. Everything was picturesque and set in an older time, with a few new-century editions like WiFi signs and streetlights.

I loved it. It called to me. Spoke to me as if I were finally home. However, I didn't quite understand how I could feel that way so quickly.

"Your building is next, and my shop is on the other side."

"Yes, the witch with a magic shop. I'm so surprised," Laurel said, and Rowen narrowed her eyes at her.

"Be kind or leave. We are introducing Sage to the town. I can't do that if you're acting like a witch."

I had a feeling that Rowen had wanted to use another word just then but had held herself back.

"Wait, you own a magic shop? I thought you owned a souvenir shop."

"We're in a town of magic. There are many souvenirs. However, it *is* my witch's shop. With magic for anyone, just not the kind they may think they need."

"Oh," I said, blinking.

"I sell jewelry, herbs, books, stones, and many other things that all walks of life can use. We're in a town filled with the supernatural, so I sell things that help shifters, our dryads, even the fae, who walk amongst us. And I sell things for the tourists who don't know what they're getting. Things that won't hurt them."

Shifters. Spells. Fae. Many words that didn't seem as if they should be in a conversation about reality. And yet, here we were. And there was no going back to the normal I'd thought I once had. There couldn't be.

"I feel like I have a lot to catch up on."

"Your aunt will have a book or two for you. At least things sent down through the Prince line. And between the bookshop and Rowen's, you'll find everything else you need. Don't worry if you feel behind. You didn't grow up here, but we'll catch you up. It's what we do."

I looked at Laurel and felt as if she wanted to say something else but didn't. She'd said that she couldn't do magic, but she seemed to know it quite well. I couldn't help but wonder what had happened.

"The town is full of people that you will meet, who will want to get to know you. Some will have secrets, but that's how it is with any small town. You are of the coven, or you will be. That means a lot will be asked of you."

"I'm trying to catch up. I don't know what any of that means."

"You will," Laurel said. "Sadly, you're not going to have a choice. None of us do."

"Laurel," Rowen warned but then froze and looked up. "Goddess."

"What?" I asked, and Laurel cursed before she pulled a sword out of nowhere. My eyes widened.

"Why...why do you have a sword?"

"Because I can't do the magic I want to use, and a girl has to improvise. Stand behind me. You're not going to like what happens next."

As I whirled, trying to understand what the hell was going on, darkness descended. Smoke enveloped the street, crawling through the grates, around eaves. And then, someone screamed.

CHAPTER SIX

ROME

I looked up at the sound of the scream, my bear pushing to the forefront. The tattoo on my chest warmed before the anchor ran down my arm, then back up to my neck, scraping at me. Claws extended from my fingertips, and I growled, huffing a bit. If I weren't careful, the hump on the back of my neck would rise, and I would scare any passersby, not that the mundanes would know what they were seeing.

The wards tied to Rowen's magic and soul worked hard to hide most of the magic from outsiders. It made some do a double take, to look over their shoulders one last time, but they wouldn't see shifters or magic.

All of the warding and spells to take-no-looks and no-sees, in addition to other magic, meant that the town was an incredible burden on Rowen.

That's why she needed her coven. That's why Sage had been summoned. A summoning that had been years in the making and had only now occurred—something we all needed to figure out.

And yet, I couldn't think about any of that right now.

I hurried out of Jaxton's mechanic shop after looking over Sage's car and growled. My bear pushed to the forefront harder, wanting to be in warrior form, but I refrained, at least for the time being, knowing I needed to assess the situation before I burned that much energy. Reserves that I might need later. Either way, my bear and I needed to see Sage.

Now.

"Is that smoke?" Jaxton asked, frowning. His eyes had gone bright gold, brighter than even mine, as he looked into the distance. As a hawk, his sight was better than any bear's or human's at long distances. And he could see things far clearer than anyone I knew. That was why he was wing leader of the hawks. "Damn it. It's the darkness."

I looked over at him, giving him a sharp look. "What? I thought that was an idea, not an actual entity."

My best friend winced. "That's what I'm calling what I'm seeing. It's fog-like, and I'm pretty sure something's about to walk out of it that none of us wants to see. And given the way my hawk is screeching inside my head, I have a feeling it has to do with those graves we saw earlier."

I cursed and started running towards the bridge over the stream on the other side of the main buildings where Sage was. The fog was close to her, that much I could see. And I knew I needed to get there as quickly as I could. My bear pushed at me even harder, and I had a sinking feeling that I knew who was at the forefront of the fight.

"Is that your girl?" Jaxton asked. I ignored the taunt, knowing that my friend was getting ready to fight. His talons would come out, and he could fight better in human form than he could in his hawk form. He was a larger bird of prey than any natural-born hawk, but he still fought better in near warrior form like I was currently in.

I ran towards the sound of the screams, the smoke dissipating slightly as forms began to appear in the gray haze. I made my way to Sage's side. She stood there, her eyes wide, Laurel and her sword in front of her. My bear relaxed marginally at seeing that Sage was unharmed, but part of me wanted to pick her up and run away with her to keep her safe. The other part wanted to tear at anyone who dared to come near her.

Mating urges weren't for the weak, and Sage had no idea who I was to her.

"Holy hell," Laurel said as Jaxton moved to her side. Trace came out of the Italian place across the street and ran towards me.

"Are those what I think they are?" he asked, and I cursed.

"It seems we have a necromancer on our hands," Rowen said as she walked forward, her eyes wide, and her hair blowing in the wind.

"*I am strong, and I will fight, I bring you forth into the light. Let our past not control our present, nor our future be as dark as night. I meet you with open arms and move you out of sight.*"

As she pushed out her hands and her words echoed off the small street, the haze went away. I swallowed hard, shoving Sage behind me as if to protect her.

"What?" she sputtered as she tried to look around me. My bear was having none of it and clawed at me. I pulled my shirt over my head, ignoring Sage's muttered curse, and let the ink on my body pulsate. I wasn't going to shift to full form, not when I might need to carry Sage out of here. She might have power deep within her, but she didn't have control of it. She didn't know how to use it. And even if she wasn't possibly my mate, I wouldn't let an innocent get hurt.

The anchor on my body slid around my chest, pacing from side to side as it focused on what was in front of us. Trace stripped off his shirt, too, showing off his anchor. They were nearly identical. His had a slight mark under one of its eyes, like Trace did in human form. Alden's had a different scar, as well. Alden wasn't here, and Trace was ready to shift if needed. Jaxton stood beside Laurel, his talons out, his whole body shaking. Mine rattled for a different reason: rage at whatever was coming at us with intent to harm.

"I don't think that protection spell worked," Laurel snapped, and Rowen glared at the other woman over her shoulder.

"It wasn't to protect us," she said, gesturing towards the bystanders as they ran.

Laurel gave her friend a tight nod. "Good, they'll need to protect themselves. We need to get rid of what's in front of us."

I shook my head. "My pack and the fae who aren't fighting with us will be on it. I've trained my pack well, and I know Ariel will have her team on this ASAP." As the mist faded away completely, I finally let myself catch up to what we now saw. "Fuck. Revenants."

"What?" Sage asked from my side.

I looked at her. Did my best not to growl and shield her from what was in front of us. "The shapes coming at us soon. They're revenants."

"Like...zombies?" She blinked as she looked between the revenants approaching and me, and I understood why she'd thought that word. Sadly, she wasn't that far off.

Rowen was the one who answered. "Yes, and no. Lower necromancers can pull the dead from the ground and use them as puppets. Those are lower revenants. Higher power necromancers can pull the dead from the spirit realm. Those are higher revenants, but still revenants. They play with the soul."

"My God."

"Precisely," Rowen whispered.

These revenants weren't like in the movies. They didn't move fast like spiders, nor did they stumble along without purpose or even searching for brains and flesh. They moved with care as if they were learning their new limbs but had a grace about them that spoke of their necromancer—their builder.

I didn't recognize the faces, and that told me that either the flesh in front of me was from older graves in town, those that had been built upon after they were dug up, or they were from cemeteries outside of town, and not those related to Ravenwood.

Revenants worked in different ways, depending on the necromancer. This one seemed to be strong enough to build new flesh on older bones. The revenants wouldn't remember who they had been while alive, though, for they weren't close to life now.

The necromancer had built flesh for their carriers of death. The revenants' eyes were vacant. They were unable to speak or think. With some of the strongest necromancers, I could sometimes see the pain and agony of those who had only partially come back but knew the horrors they had become.

The ones that lumbered towards us now didn't have that sense of recognition. I didn't think they had been in their flesh for long enough. No, these were newly built, and the necromancer who controlled them had to be close.

"You need to cut off their heads," Laurel said, her sword shining in the light. "It's the only way."

"You could also burn them," Rowen said.

Laurel flipped her off. "I could, but we know that's not happening."

I ignored the two of them and looked at Sage. "You need to go. Run."

"Where am I supposed to go? What the hell is happening?"

"We're about to be inundated with death," I said, still unable to quite believe the words coming out of my mouth. "A necromancer, a dark witch, is controlling them."

"Is this the darkness you spoke of?" She was sharp. That would help keep her alive. At least, I hoped so.

"I don't know. No one does. They're here, and they're not going to stop until they kill everyone in their path."

"So, where's the necromancer? The one controlling them?"

"That's a good question," Rowen said. "We need to do a seek spell."

"Do you have the power for that?" Laurel asked, and I knew it wasn't said unkindly, even if Rowen flinched. Rowen was already exhausted from using nearly all of her magic to protect the town. She needed her coven. She needed Laurel back to full steam, and she needed Sage to learn her powers.

"Yes, but it's not going to be strong. I'll need you to take them out while I do the spell."

She began to mutter under her breath, but I heard the words, nonetheless.

"*Ancestors, Watchtowers, sisters, and friends, lend me*

your strength to seek out the end. Find the darkness that now controls death, show me the hideout with next word and breath. Give me the power to find what we seek, this is my will, so mote it be."

She lowered her head and held her hands out to the sides, repeating the words silently as she chanted. "Stay behind me," I growled, knowing there could be more than the necromancers' pets behind us. I couldn't leave Sage on her own.

"I'm not leaving you alone." Her hands shook, but she stayed near.

"They're coming!" Laurel yelled and threw herself in front of Rowen. The two might seem to hate each other some days, but they were practically sisters. And Rowen would die for Laurel, and vice versa. That was why they tended to get along, even with the animosity.

Jaxton stood by Laurel's side as the first revenants came. The hawk shifter's talons slid through dead flesh, and then the fight was on.

The revenants made some sounds, but not many. They couldn't scream, though I swore I could see the pain and rage in their eyes. Sage was at my side and had picked up an aluminum bat from one of the alleyways I hadn't even noticed. Good. She could fight for herself, though I still wouldn't let her do too much. Trace was at my side, fighting as the first revenant came at us. I roared, rattling the windows, and looked over my shoulder to see if it had scared Sage. Her eyes widened only slightly, and her grip tightened on the bat.

"Okay, I don't know what I'm doing."

"That's fine, you'll learn," Laurel shouted over her shoulder.

I moved myself in front of Sage again and lashed out at the first revenant. It let out a silent screech before it fell, its head rolling off to the side. Sage blanched beside me, but she didn't stop moving. Instead, she looked as if she were ready to protect *me*. My bear growled proudly at the idea.

We stood near the bridge, the stream under us now roiling. I cursed because I knew who was doing it. Sage was a water witch, even though she didn't understand her powers. If we weren't careful, she might hurt herself. Or one of us.

"Breathe through it," I said, and she frowned at me.

"What?" she asked as she slammed the bat into a revenant as it came at us. I ripped off its head, and blood sprayed. She looked down at herself and shivered. "It's a dream. It's only a dream."

"No, it's not." I killed another revenant. "Don't let the power within you overwhelm you."

"What power?"

"Look down," I ordered as I killed another monster.

She did indeed look down and nearly tripped backward as she saw the raging stream below us. It had slowly started to rise, cresting into waves that weren't natural.

"That's your power. It's untapped, untrained, but you can figure it out."

"I'm not doing this. It has to be the others."

"It's you. Rowen is using wind in her spells to protect and to find. Laurel's using her sword. We're using the talons and claws we have. This is you. The water in you."

She shook her head, but as another monster came towards us, lumbering slowly, she held out her bat. Water slammed into the bridge, washing two of them away.

Trace cursed, sighed, and then leaped over the bridge's edge to deal with the revenants.

"Maybe keep them here so we can take care of them and not slowly move them downstream in the path of an unsuspecting innocent." I slashed at another revenant, and its head rolled to the side.

"I did that?" Her body shook, her fingers whitening around the bat.

"You did," I said and held back a smile. My bear was pleased. This woman was strong, far stronger than she knew. And she was mine—if she let me have her, and if I let myself pretend it could happen.

Because she was a witch, the one person my pack would never agree to have as its alpha's mate.

Interestingly, my bear didn't care.

And it wasn't time for me to think about how sexy she was with her power radiating in those hazel eyes. How her honey-brown hair floated around her as if caught in a hidden wind that only her powers showed.

She gripped the blood-covered bat for dear life, and yet, she kept fighting. She might not think she believed what she was seeing, but she still fought. Protected, even in this dream that she thought she waded through.

And she did all of it as if on instinct.

She was so strong, so powerful. I couldn't wait to see what she did next.

First, we had to survive.

Jaxton shifted quickly into his bird of prey, forcing a scream out of Sage's mouth. That was disappointing, but she had never seen Jaxton shift before. She had never seen *anyone* shift before. Maybe she would get used to everything and not cower when it came to the animals who lived within us.

Jaxton's talons pierced the air as he killed the final

revenant, the one that had come too close to Trace and Laurel. The three were friends—close friends—and they would fight and die for each other. Just like I would do for my siblings.

As the final monster fell, Rowen came towards us and cursed under her breath. "They had a spell blocking me. I can't find them. But did you get their scent?" she asked as she ignored Sage for a moment and stared at me.

I shook my head. "All I smelled was rotting flesh, but I'll check."

"Me, too," Trace said as he jumped over the bridge to get closer to us. Jaxton shifted back, and I ignored how Sage's eyes nearly fell out of her head as she looked at the naked man. He had shifted and burst through his jeans because we couldn't keep our clothes as we transitioned. I knew he hadn't wanted to do that but needs trumped wants. Trace sighed and pulled a pair of sweats out of the messenger bag I hadn't even realized he had been wearing this entire time.

"Put on some clothes. You're scaring the newbie."

Sage let out a breath, her eyes wide. "You're a bird. I mean, a *beautiful* bird, but wow."

Beautiful? My bear didn't like that. Hell, *I* didn't like the sound of that.

"I'm a hawk," the other man said as he put on the pants. I wanted to shield Sage's eyes and not let her watch the other man. I was already jealous, but my bear wanted more. Needed it. After a fight like this, one with just enough danger to push adrenaline through my body, I wanted it all. I wanted my mate.

Damn it.

"Hawks aren't that big," she said. "Are all shifters bigger than normal size?"

"Usually, birds of prey are a little different because of our mass issues, but Rome and his two brothers are bigger than normal grizzlies. I have a different conservation of mass issue than they do."

Sage looked around at the mess around us, at the gore on the bat in her hand, the water under the bridge, and let out a breath. "All of this is real."

"What was your first clue? The water that you were controlling? The revenants? Or the man who was naked just now after shifting from a bird?" Laurel asked dryly.

Sage narrowed her eyes, anger sparking. Good. She could stand up to Laurel. I loved Laurel like a sister, but the fire that burned within her made her harder than she used to be. "I'm going to go with all of it, and you're going to need to give me a moment to catch up. It's been what? A day? And, suddenly, my entire life is filled with witches and shifters and now fricking revenants. This isn't normal."

"It's our normal, Sage," I whispered.

She looked at me then and shook her head. "Maybe, but I still need to catch up. And all of you need to let me do that."

"We might not have time. Not in the way I wanted," Rowen said. "If a necromancer sent their progeny out like this, it means they're ready. Far more than we are."

"What does that mean?" Sage asked as I cursed. She gave me a weird look.

I sighed. "It means that we're not ready, and we need to be."

"Ready for what?" Sage asked.

Ignoring her, Rowen said, "And you need to begin training." My bear growled.

Training meant that Sage would become a witch. She

would find her powers. And danger would come at her quicker than ever.

And that wasn't something I was sure I would ever allow my mate to do.

Even if she didn't know who I was to her yet.

CHAPTER SEVEN

SAGE

I stood inside Into the Wood, my body still shaking as Rowen shoved a cup of warm tea into my hands.

"Drink up. There's nothing in there that will hurt you. Just some good strong tea with a little bit of sweet."

I looked down at the steaming cup and then up at her. "It's all real, isn't it?" I asked, my voice barely above a whisper. I didn't know why I was saying this. I'd already let myself believe, but watching the revenants come after my new friends and town had hammered everything home.

Rowen raised a single perfectly crafted brow but didn't smirk. Instead, she studied my face as if she expected me to say more. And perhaps I needed to.

"It's real," I said again. "I still can't believe it," I added. "I guess I have to, though. I saw them. I felt them as they came at me. As my bat connected with them."

"You're right. Those abominations were very real. I haven't seen them cross the Ravenwood borders since I was a child, and my mother was still teaching me how to control my powers. There were rumors of a necromancer coming closer to Ravenwood, and I believed them, of course, but it seems it was true. And they are no longer traveling. They're here. Though for what purpose? I don't know that as yet. What I do know is that we must get you trained. Soon."

"Will you tell me what's going on?" I asked after a moment, taking a sip of the tea. It was warm, sweet, and seemed to soothe me from the inside out, even though I was still energized from what had happened. The guys had left to go clean up or fix whatever had been broken by the oncoming horde.

Rome had given me a long once-over, had looked as if he wanted to say something, but had only left. Something inside me felt almost bereft at that. I didn't understand it. It didn't make any sense. I didn't even know the man.

Laurel had gone with them after glaring at Rowen and stowing her sword. It had disappeared as if it had never been there. Was that another kind of magic?

"It's time I explain as much as I can to you so you can begin training."

"Training," I repeated. Why did that sound ominous?

Rowen sighed and tapped her long fingernails on the workbench in front of her. "You're a witch, Sage. A strong water witch, from what I can tell. Which is good because I have air, Laurel used to have fire—and will have it again if I have anything to say about it—and you would be water. That's three of the elements there, three corners of the triangle."

I frowned, having so many questions. "Isn't there earth, as well?" I asked, trying to remember what I'd read in pagan books over the years.

Rowen's eyes tightened for a brief moment before she shook her head. "It's one of the four main elements, yes, but not one of the three for our triad. Earth is the base, but when the other three come together, we can create our own base, so we don't need earth."

For some reason, it sounded as if she was trying to convince herself of that rather than it being true. Or maybe I was thinking too hard about what she said.

"I was the one who moved the water from the stream."

"Yes. And you have so much untapped power, it's dangerous. We need to train you on at least the small spells. That way, you won't hurt anyone around you."

My heart raced. "Oh, God. I need to check on Penelope. I forgot," I blurted. "How could I forget?" I needed to get my head out of my ass and focus on what was important, not the idea that this was no longer a dream.

Rowen shook her head. "She already texted to check in. She's fine."

"She texted you?" I asked, a little hurt. Though I'd been the one so lost and trying to keep up that I'd forgotten to text my own aunt. I had no right to that pain. I was so caught up in current events and a certain man who could turn into a bear, I felt as if I were flailing about.

"Your aunt has been a surrogate aunt to Laurel and me for many years. I've known her my entire life. And she was checking on you. I'm sorry she didn't contact you right away. I'm sure she texted you, as well, but your phone is off," she said softly.

I frowned and pulled my phone out of my pocket. It was indeed powered off. I looked up at her, shaking my head. "How did you know?"

"Because you're a witch who was learning to use her powers. I was sure it shorted it out for a brief moment. It'll be fine," she said quickly as my eyes widened. "You can turn it back on, but we tend to hurt technology when we use our powers in bursts as you did."

"I don't understand," I said softly.

"There's a lot you don't understand."

Annoyance pricked at me. "Then why don't you tell me? I have to believe all of this. I can't ignore the facts in my face. But you're treating me as if you're an all-knowing vessel who's lording the fact that I don't understand over me, and it isn't helping things."

"I like that. You pushing back. That way, it's not me," Laurel said as she walked in. She put a small bag on the counter. "I brought biscotti. It's decent and from the Italian place. Your aunt says you can bake better. I can't wait to start getting some baked goods from your shop. And if you know what's good for you, honey buns will become your favorite thing. The bears here love honey. If you feed them, they will come."

"The bakery." I cursed. "I haven't even seen the building yet. And it's right next door. I've been so focused on everything else, I'm not paying attention to what I need to. To what I came here to do. I haven't even been to my cottage, other than to drop things off this morning after staying at my aunt's. I'm losing my way."

"Stop being so hard on yourself," Laurel said softly, surprising me. "You've been through a lot in the past day. Of course, you're not going to get everything right now. You're going to make mistakes, you're going to screw things up, but you'll pick yourself up because you're a Prince. And that's what you do."

"That's what my aunt does then, if you're saying that."

"That's what your family line does," Rowen added as Laurel nodded.

"Explain that to me," I said. "Please."

Rowen gave Laurel a look and nodded. "As I mentioned, our three families founded the town," she said softly. I nodded, knowing she was only getting started. "Over time, the families fought, got along, and then settled more. Some moved away, taking their magic with them, but others stayed, adding to the wards, protecting our people. The bears showed up around the time Ravenwood was founded and settled in their den here. Rome's ancestors. His father used to be the alpha here before moving to Canada to be the Alpha of the Americas."

My eyes widened. "What?"

"Your little honey bear has a lot of power," Laurel teased, and I frowned.

"He's not my anything," I said, wondering why something about that statement pricked at me.

Rowen glared at Laurel, but Laurel held up her hands and shook her head. "My mistake," she said, but I felt as if she didn't think it was a mistake at all.

I needed to clear the air. "I'm not ready for anything like what you might be suggesting." However, I wasn't sure that was accurate. I'd come here for a fresh start, and dating was a natural part of that. Though I wasn't sure why I was even thinking about that at the moment. Again.

"I'm sorry," Laurel said. "I was only teasing," she said, and though I felt like she was sincere about the apology and the teasing, there was some truth in her words that I didn't want to focus on. Not right now, anyway. Maybe not ever.

"As I was saying," Rowen chided, "the bears created their den here and are one of the largest packs in this part of the United States. Their kind is the main shifters here. Others have settled, knowing they can be themselves, and the wards will protect them from revealing their identities to any outsiders. Even if people come in as tourists or are driving through, they won't see the magic that lies within the town's walls."

I frowned. "Then why did I see?" I asked.

"Because you were meant to," Laurel said. "Because you're a witch. You're one of us."

"I'm a water witch," I clarified, a little worried how much I needed to believe all of this without reservation.

"Or you can call yourself a witch with an affinity for water," Laurel corrected. "You can use air and fire and earth and everything else with specific spells, but water comes naturally to you."

"Spells. Like the words you said on the bridge?" I asked.

Rowen nodded before flicking her wrist. Books rose from the bookshelves behind her. My eyes widened as they danced in the air before settling in a stack in front of me.

"These four are part of the Ravenwood line. They're beginner spells you should read and memorize, but do not practice independently. You should never do anything on your own until I deem you ready."

"She might sound like a know-it-all right now," Laurel added snidely, "but she's right. Some of these could be dangerous, even if they're simple."

"You want me to work on spells?" I sputtered as I looked at the leather-bound books. They smelled of age and warmth, and I wanted to reach out and touch them. But I didn't. I was afraid of what would happen if I did.

"Yes, you're a witch. And we need you here. Your aunt has some of the Prince volumes, but you need to promise me not to practice on your own. You could hurt yourself or others if you're not careful." Rowen gave me a soft look.

I bit my lip. "I don't want to hurt anyone. I don't even know if I want to do any of this."

"You don't have a choice." Laurel rubbed her hip and frowned. "Magic is within you. Like it's within all of us. Sometimes we don't have a choice in what happens. And you need to deal with that." She was practically growling now, still rubbing at her hip. Rowen gave her a sad look before schooling her features.

"Laurel, despite how she said it, is right. We need to be careful. You must focus on what you can and learn the basics. I will help you along the way."

"This is all so much." I pushed my hair from my face. "You expect me to do this, to learn magic, all while trying to settle here? I thought Ravenwood would be my home, a place for me to start a new life."

"That's what you're doing," Laurel said.

"No, I came here to be a baker. To open a shop and bake bread and brownies and honey buns," I said, my voice rising. "I didn't come here to learn about powers or magic or to change anything."

"As I said, you might not have a choice," Laurel reiterated. "None of us do."

"Because of what happened today?" I asked.

"We've always known that a darkness was coming," Rowen began. "I'm no seer, but sometimes we can scry and see what's headed our way. A necromancer's been on the horizon for a long time now, but it wasn't until today that I realized how close they were. It's either because of your arrival or we're where everything was meant to be at this point," she said.

"It's my fault?" I asked incredulously.

The other woman shook her head. "No. Not at all. Some

things are simply meant to be. You are a witch. You are a part of our coven. Part of the three—the power. We need you. But we don't have a lot of time. Not if the necromancer is so close already and able to bring their dead flesh to our borders and within it. That means they are farther along in their training than we are."

"It's going to have to be a coven of two," Laurel said, raising her chin. "You know that."

I frowned, looking between the two of them. "I don't understand." I held up my hand as both of them glared at me. "I know it's probably a painful subject, but if you're telling me that I'm going to need to fight a necromancer and not run away like I want to right now, then I need to know why you're saying it's only a coven of two."

Laurel growled before she pulled up her shirt so I could see her side. I gasped, I couldn't help it, and tears pricked at my eyes.

"What happened?" I whispered, my hand reaching out as if to soothe without me even realizing it. I let my hand fall, shaking.

"I'm cursed," Laurel snapped. "My entire family line is."

Rowen flinched at that, and I had to wonder what was left unsaid.

"Somebody trapped my powers within me. Oh, I'm still a powerful witch with a fire affinity, but I can't use it. Every time I do, it scalds me, etches its flames on my skin and burns me from the inside out. I am the phoenix flame with only ashes to bear. I don't get to use my powers to protect, only to harm, only to murder. That's my legacy. That's what whoever cursed me wanted. That's what plagues the Christophers."

"And there's nothing you can do, nothing *we* could do?" I added, my voice soft.

Laurel pulled her shirt down and shook her head. "No. We've tried."

"I'm still looking," Rowen said softly, her voice far gentler than I had ever heard it before.

"And it's not working, is it?" Laurel snapped.

"I've been trying for so long. And I'm going to continue."

"It's not enough," Laurel said before pausing. She let out a breath, her head lowered. "And I know you're trying."

"What do I need to do?" I asked after a moment, staring down at the books. It was all so much, and I felt like I couldn't keep up. But I had seen what came at us. I had felt them at my back, had watched Rome rip off their heads with his claws. He was a grizzly. An actual bear shifter. I had seen Jaxton shift into a hawk, the largest bird I had ever seen in my life, and then shift back into a human. The others had thrown him sweats as if his nudity weren't a problem for them but had wanted to keep his modesty. As if revenants and necromancers and witches and prophecies and towns that understood the supernatural were commonplace to them. My breath started to come in pants, and I gripped the edge of the table. Laurel gave me a sad look, and Rowen leaned forward and grabbed my wrist in a punishing grip. "You're okay. Breathe through it."

"You say that I'm okay, but I'm still so behind."

"You're allowed to be behind. But now you have to catch up. I know this isn't how we wanted this. It's not how anybody wanted it, but you don't have a choice. I hope you understand that. No matter what happens next, you need to learn. You need to practice. You need to remember these spells and try to protect those you love. And yourself. Because the town needs you. The coven needs you."

I looked at her then and saw the fear in her eyes she tried to mask.

"It's killing you, isn't it?" I asked as if knowing it had been there all along.

She pulled away as if scalded and shook her head. "I'm fine."

"She's not fine. It takes a full coven to keep this town safe. To keep it hidden. And she's doing it herself. Your aunt doesn't have enough magic to help, my magic is killing me, and you're too new. She's putting her life-force into the wards and the spells she does. So, she needs you. And maybe she needs me too, but I'm not someone who can help." Laurel looked at us and then down at the books. "I can never help. All I do is burn. All I do is make a mess—so, good luck with this. Be stronger than me. Be stronger than the Christophers." She gave Rowen a pointed look and then walked out, slamming the door behind her.

I didn't know what to say to make things better, but I did have questions. "My aunt and I are the last of my line." I looked at Rowen. "You're saying you're the same for the Ravenwoods. How many Christophers are there?" I asked, knowing the answer was important, even though I didn't know why.

Rowen met my gaze, her gray eyes pulsing. "Laurel has a brother. Ash. He doesn't live in town. He travels all over the world. He left us long ago. He's cursed like she is, only differently. It doesn't matter. He isn't part of the coven and never will be." She shook her head and pulled her hair back from her face, flipping it up quickly in a practiced move. "Read the first book and then come back so we can practice. You're not going to be good at it. You're going to have too much power, too much raw potential within you to tame. But we're going to protect this town. And I don't care what I have to do, but we will protect our people."

I nodded, letting out a breath. "Okay."

"Read, practice with me, bake your goods, become part of this town. Because the more you are settled, the more you become connected to the earth, to the people, to the new world around you, the better it will be for all of us. And the better for you."

As a customer walked into the building, the bell above the door ringing into the silence, she walked away, breaking whatever odd spell had connected us. It hadn't been magical but had held us together anyway.

I swallowed hard, looked at the books in front of me, and wondered once again how I had gotten here. In the time since I had lost my husband, I had been trying to find a new path, determine the way I needed to be. But I had been wrong.

If I had known who I needed to be, I didn't think I would've come here. Or maybe I was always meant to be here. I didn't know. I traced my fingers over the edge of one book, and my gaze caught on another on the shelf, one with a bear claw etched onto the spine.

There was so much history here. So much I didn't know. But I didn't think the witches would be the ones to tell me everything, not when I knew they were keeping secrets.

There was someone I could ask, though. Someone who might make sense.

Not that I knew why. Rome had been the first person I had seen, the first one to try and tell me the truth. I would speak to my aunt first, though she had been keeping secrets for my entire life. If she didn't talk to me, I would speak with Rome. Hopefully, he would help make sense of things.

At the moment, nothing did, and I knew if I wasn't quick about it, if I weren't careful, I wouldn't learn everything in time.

Even I could feel it. Something was coming. Something beyond what had crawled over the bridge today. Something beyond that which burned in my veins.

The water in the glass next to me started to spill out, and I cursed before I picked up the books, cleaning up the mess.

I was already three steps behind, and everybody else was running at full tilt. I needed to catch up. I needed to keep up. Or I was afraid all would be lost once again.

And I didn't even know what all of it was.

CHAPTER EIGHT

ROME

My paws pounded the soft ground, the stream having turned the dirt into mud on the banks after Sage had practiced with Rowen the night before. It squished between my claws, but I kept going, knowing my fur would likely end up covered in mats and muck. When I shifted back, the dirt would remain, but hopefully, the mats would go away. I could feel my bear laugh inside me, even though the human part of me was in charge as I ran. The magic of shifting wasn't like in the movies or any book. I was part of my bear, the spirit within me living as part of me.

I was born this way, and like the cubs who lived within our den, I could shift the moment I was born—though most waited at least a year or so. I had turned for the first time when I was two days old. Trace didn't change until a month later. Alden had waited until he was a year old. And while some might say it was because he had less control and power, for me, I always assumed it was because Alden wanted to do things his way and didn't want to be part of the three of us. It was odd to be a triplet and not be connected, not like most of the other bear shifters around us were anyway. There were many twins, quads, and triplets within the shifter culture, especially with bears. We tended to take a while to have children, but we usually did it in multiples when we did.

Multiples within dens were usually far more connected than any other siblings or interactions, except those of mated pairs or triads. It was as if they each had a soul yet were connected upon conception and split, though still with part of the others remaining as if forever bonded.

Trace and I had an enduring bond, but the one we shared with Alden seemed tattered, though not beyond repair. I couldn't believe that. Not when I needed my pack, my den, and my people. It was hard to understand why my brother was like this when no one else in our family was.

I grumbled, a low, deep sound that radiated through my chest as the call of a hawk floated on the air. I looked up to see Jaxton winging above me, his broad wingspan so immense, it nearly blocked out the sun. Jaxton's mother had once called him Icarus, afraid that her son would fly too high and lose his touch and freedoms—not to mention his wings. Jaxton was probably the safest of us all, at least those who had grown up in Ravenwood.

My brothers and I had been born in Ravenwood, not in Canada like some might have thought. Our father and mother had moved outside Montreal to run and rule the pack of both continents after my grandfather had passed. Most didn't know that our grandfather had been Alpha. We'd hidden that information to keep our pack and our grandfather safe. He had passed away in his sleep, making my father Alpha of us all. And I had taken the mantle of alpha of the Ravenwood pack. My bear had risen to the occasion, and the bonds within the den had understood what was needed.

Trace had quickly become beta, second in strength and command. And Alden had been relegated to third, his least favorite position, an opinion he made known to all.

I grumbled again, holding back a growl so as not to scare any innocent bystanders or bunnies that might be in my wake. I strode through the shallow part of the stream, contemplating fishing or maybe at least washing off the rest of the mud, relaxing, doing *something*. Running out my frustrations wasn't working.

My bear nudged at me, wanting to see Sage, but I knew I couldn't. I needed to hold myself back so she could become accustomed to her new life. If I went to her now, I'd be a growly bear who wanted to throw her over my shoulder like some Viking. I wasn't sure I could control myself around her, so I stayed away.

The longer I did, the harder it would be for her to get to know me and fall passionately and deeply in love, but I never said I was a smart bear.

I looked up to see Trace standing at the edge of the stream in his human form, his messenger bag hanging at his side—probably with clothes for me. He likely wanted to talk, though I didn't particularly feel like doing that at the moment. We had enough to deal with, and I honestly didn't want to focus on any of it right now. I wanted to growl, let my bear lead, and just be. But that wasn't an option currently, so I would have to be an adult, the alpha, and face my issues.

I sighed, shook out the water from my fur, and shifted. It was a painful mix of agony, bliss, and torment all rolled into one as I went from bear to human. Energy radiated off my body, and I shook off the pain, the pleasure, as I stood naked in the stream, glaring at my brother.

"Put on some clothes. I don't need to see that." Trace waved at my crotch.

I refrained from mentioning that he had the same as I did and saw himself daily in the mirror. "You're not supposed to notice that. Shifters don't."

"I don't want to notice my brother's dick at all, but I sure don't want to talk to it since I'm sitting here on the ground, and you're standing there all growly. Put on some clothes. Let's talk."

"What if I don't want to?" My bear was in a *mood*. It wanted Sage. So did I. And since we couldn't have her, I wanted to slap at someone with my claws. Trace was here. He wouldn't bruise...much.

"Don't you sound like a petulant alpha?" Trace smirked. Jaxton let out another call from above, and I swore I heard a laugh in the sound before he tilted one wing in a sign of goodbye and flew away.

We had work to do, cleanup to deal with after the necromancer's attack. And, honestly, we needed to find out who was coming at us. There was a reason Jaxton and I were the cleaners and fixers of Ravenwood. We had to clean up the magic and any unexplained things the wards couldn't protect. Rowen was only one person, and I was afraid that even with Sage's newly burgeoning powers, she wouldn't be enough to help with the coven wards. Not without Laurel breaking her curse, and I didn't know when that would happen. If ever.

It might have been easier if Ash were back, but then again, given everything that had happened when he left? Maybe not. Jaxton and I were needed more and more, and so were others around town, trying to help. I was afraid it wasn't going to be enough one of these days.

"You're growling again. What's wrong?"

"I'm thinking about everything we need to do, and all that we don't know. And, honestly, I was thinking about Ash," I said, shaking my head.

Trace's jaw tightened. "He's gone. He's not coming back."

"You say that, but maybe he needs to."

"To do what? Throw Rowen off her game again? Break his sister's heart? Ash is gone, Rome. There's no fixing it. He's not going to save Ravenwood. He never was."

"You're not going to tell me what happened with him?"

"There's nothing to tell. Seriously. Ash is gone. And good riddance."

I looked at my triplet and shook my head. I wasn't sure I quite believed that, but I couldn't break through his walls, not when it came to Ash Christopher and the broken shards he had left behind when he burned his way through Ravenwood.

"Why were you thinking of him?" Trace asked after a moment, his voice soft.

I sighed. "I was thinking about everything that Jax and I have had to clean up recently. And the necromancer. And the fact that we don't know who it was or why they came at us. There are all these unknowns, and it all happened right when Sage came to town."

"I bet Sage is another reason why you're so growly," Trace whispered.

I shook my head. "I can't. She doesn't even know who she is. How am I supposed to explain to her what the hell's going on inside me?"

"She's hurting, Rome. You know she lost her husband, right?"

I swallowed hard, giving him a tight nod. "I do. It's been, what? A couple of years now?"

"Yes, from what I heard from Rowen and Laurel."

"Do you know what happened?" I asked.

"No. And even if I did, I don't know if I'd tell you. If you want her to be your mate, you'll have to be the one who finds out more about her. From her. Though it's not like you've had a full conversation with her. This fated mate business is for the birds," Trace said, and another shriek came from above us.

I looked up at Jaxton as he flew down and landed. He shifted into his human form and dug another pair of sweats out of Trace's bag.

"A bird joke?"

Trace blushed. "I didn't know you were there. And it's a saying."

"Should I ask you if you shit in the woods? Would that be helpful?" Jaxton asked, his eyes filled with laughter.

I shook my head. "You waved goodbye."

"I saw another bear lumbering over here, so I thought I'd visit and see how things were going."

I turned as Alden walked through the trees. He lumbered, all right, though in human form. His bear was in his eyes, and he chuffed, the hump on the back of his neck rising.

I cursed under my breath.

"Alden."

"You're mated to that little witch?" Alden asked, his voice low.

"Stop," I said, this close to adding power to my words. I

could get my brother to stop. I could get him to bow to me and do what I ordered and commanded. Only I wouldn't do that. Not then, and only in dire emergencies. I was alpha, which meant I had to protect all of my people—even my asshole brother, who got under my skin like nobody else.

"You can't marry that *witch*," he spat as if *witch* were a dirty word. And to some of the old-fashioned bears, it was. A long-ago war had been waged between the witches and the shifters, the witches dying at the hands of those stronger than them far too quickly, and the shifters being forced to endure unimaginable pain by witches who needed to protect themselves. Wrongs and atrocities were committed on both sides, and yet, everyone had eventually come together through mated pairs and a treaty and truce that protected them all.

Still, some of the elders didn't understand that. They only remembered the pain, and Alden only believed what he didn't understand.

He didn't have immense power or magic, and he hated what he didn't have.

"Yes, she's my mate. The one I can truly bond with and have forever. I haven't told her yet." My bear growled at me in annoyance. "And if you go there and tell her, there will be consequences," I snarled, my bear in my throat. My anchor wrapped itself around my chest, the head of the bear near my throat. It seemed to want to growl at Alden and push me into doing something we would all regret.

My bear didn't like Alden very much, and right then, I wasn't sure I did either.

"You know the pack won't have this. You already think you're good enough to be alpha when others wonder, and then what do you do? You plan to mate with a witch?"

I didn't know this man in front of me. Not anymore.

Damn, I needed to breathe. If I didn't calm down, between my anger and the mating urge, I'd likely strangle my brother here and now. "Don't continue if you know what's good for you. You know it's forbidden to mess with mates."

"When mating bonds are real. You don't have one. And not with a witch. And a witch with no power? An abomination."

I growled and moved forward, but both Jaxton and Trace put their bodies between us.

"Don't," Jaxton whispered.

"Not now," Trace added.

"You're going to regret this," Alden said. "Having a witch for a mate? You can't. Not as alpha. Not if you want to *stay* alpha."

I tilted my head, my bear in my gaze as I studied him. Alden lowered his head a fraction, unable to meet my eyes. Good. "Don't threaten her or me. You and I may have problems we need to deal with, but that needs to come second to everything else."

"Always second. Or is that third? Always focused on everyone else instead of who you're supposed to care about: your people."

I shook my head, my bear still in my gaze. "That's all I'm doing, Alden, protecting my people. I need to keep our pack strong, and you know we can't control who our bears want as mates. Who we connect to. Despite all of that, Sage is here for a reason. You saw the darkness. You know it's here."

Alden snorted. "Isn't she the one who brought it? We were fine until she showed up."

I shook my head. "You know that's not true. You know it has been brewing for a long time."

"Because of witches. The bears have been fine. It's the

damn witches who keep doing things. And now you want to mate with one? No. The pack won't stand for it."

I pushed through Jaxton and Trace and threw myself in Alden's face. Alden lowered his gaze, and I growled, low and so deep the rest of the forest quieted as if there were a real predator in their midst.

"Leave before you say something you'll regret."

"We'll see," he muttered, but quietly enough that I knew he was blowing off some steam, trying to get the last word. So, I let him. *For now.* My bear was strong enough to allow it. Alden stomped off, growling under his breath, and I shook my head.

"You need to deal with that," Jaxton said.

"You're not a bear; don't get in the middle of our politics," Trace growled, but there was no heat in it. We were all friends here.

"I might not be a bear, but I am wing leader of the hawks, and I don't want my friends hurt. Go see Sage," he said after a moment, and I frowned.

"What?" I said.

"Your bear is on edge, and you need to decide what you're going to do about it. And, honestly? She needs to know who you are and what decisions you might be making for the both of you."

"I can't have a mating bond without her," I said. "There will be no decision-making without her."

"True, but can you reject the mating bond? Can you ignore the urge that's riding you right now?"

"Wouldn't it be better that way?" I asked, and my bear let out a painful growl inside me. I'd yet to voice that aloud, and I wasn't sure why I did now. I didn't want to walk away from her, but I also didn't want to scare her. Protecting her and needing her didn't seem to go hand in hand. I sighed. I had no idea what I was doing.

"You don't know what it means to walk away from a mate," Jaxton whispered. "The pain and agony you'll feel every day you even try to take a breath. They say there's a choice, and there can be in the direst of circumstances, but it changes everything. Sage is new to all of this, and you need to make sure she understands what else is out there. Because the pack is watching, and so is the rest of the town. The witches began this place. They're at the center of it all. We all watch them as we do you. You need to help Sage. Be there. There's a reason you're fated. And if you fight that, blood will be drawn. We all know that."

And then Jaxton flew away, leaving his sweats behind him. Trace let out a small laugh, though there was little humor in it. "He is good at that whole prophecy thing, isn't he?"

My stomach turned, even as my bear tugged at me. "Maybe. Or maybe he's saying what needs to be said."

"Go see her. Put on a shirt, though. And maybe some shoes. Don't act too much like an animal."

I snorted. "I *am* an animal. Maybe that's something she needs to get used to."

Trace shrugged. "You'd better go see if she can. Or else you'll be wondering *what if* for a very long time."

I nodded, then began running, my bear on edge as I made my way to my house. I changed clothes, washed my face, made sure I didn't have any mud in my hair, and let out a breath.

I already knew where she was, my bear could sense her, but I also knew because everybody seemed to keep me abreast of where she was at all times as if waiting for things to change. I didn't know what to think or what I was supposed to do.

I made my way to the town center and inhaled her scent as I walked toward the bakery she would open sometime in the next two weeks. The building had once held a small café that hadn't done well. The humans who hadn't sensed the magic tried to sell wares to the unsuspecting—only they were the ones caught unawares.

I cleared my throat and wondered what I should say. What *could* I say? Before I could even knock on the door, it opened. I stared at the woman in front of me, her honey-brown hair pulled away from her face and piled on the top of her head, her hazel eyes wide.

"Rome," she said, seeming startled. "I'm sorry, did I know you were coming here?"

I shook my head. "No, but I wanted to see you." I cleared my throat. "If you're on your way out..."

She shook her head. "No, no. I just felt like someone was at the door. Or maybe I heard something? I don't know."

My bear perked up at that. So, she'd felt me. She was a witch, and they had mates, as well. I didn't know exactly how it all worked, but the fact that she had sensed me had to mean something. "May I come in?" I let out a breath. "To see your shop," I added, knowing that that was the truth but not all of it.

Her gaze brightened for a minute, and she pulled back. "Of course. We're still setting it up—or at least I am. Aunt Penelope was here earlier, but she's next door working now. The contractors I hired from afar have done a great job."

"Jaxton helped organize them," I said casually, looking around at the space. It was a two-story building, much like many of the businesses on this street. This one had once been a house long ago and had a small apartment up top that I figured she might use as her office and storage for now. Still, there was a professional kitchen, as well as a whole front area for where she could show off her baked goods, and a section I figured would eventually be a seating area once the tables and chairs were out.

"It's looking great in here," I said.

"It had great bones to begin with. I did most of the work through video online because I couldn't leave my other job yet, not even to visit." She paused. "And I think because I wasn't supposed to be here yet. I don't know. It doesn't seem like something I would do, not seeing the town before everything changed. I hadn't even stepped foot in this building, yet there I was, making an entire business plan."

I nodded. "Ravenwood has that effect. Rowen said she was looking into a spell that kept you away. Maybe you weren't supposed to be here until you finally stepped foot on the town's grounds. Of course, I'm glad that you were on the road when you were since you saved me."

She smiled softly, and my bear groaned. I barely held it in. "I'm still not quite sure how I did that."

I shrugged. "I think your power somehow fluctuated so you could feel it, and it zapped me awake."

"Oh. Did it hurt?" She bit her lip, and I wanted to lean down and lick away the sting.

Down, bear.

I shook my head. "First, I'm a bear. Something like that wouldn't hurt me. And, second, you woke me up so I could move out of the way of the tree before anything else came at me or I drowned in mud or something. So, thank you."

"It was an odd way to meet. I'm glad you're okay." She let out a breath and looked around. "I'm in the middle of doing a few things, but I can show you around." She looked at me then, and I could see her tattoos peeking out from her collar as if waving at me.

"Do you feel them? Your anchor?"

Her eyes widened, and her hands moved to her neck. "Yes, it tickles. I'm trying to ignore them, but I don't think they want me to. The fact that they keep moving around my body is a bit jarring."

I grinned and pulled my shirt to the side slightly so she could see my bear peeking out. "It doesn't go well if you ignore them all the time."

Her eyes widened, and her hand reached out as if to touch. My bear preened, wanting her fingers, wanting her caress, but she froze as if finally aware of what she was doing.

"Oh, I didn't mean..."

"You can touch me anytime you want, Sage," I said and could have rightly kicked myself. "I mean. Well..." I was standing so close to her then, I could inhale that sweet rose scent of hers.

"Why do I feel like I know you?" she asked, her voice breathy.

I looked down at her, my bear pushing at me, but I knew I needed to pull back. "There are some things you don't know, Sage."

She let out a slight growl, and my bear perked up, my cock hardening at the sound. "I hate that. Everyone keeps telling me I don't know things. And it's true, but how am I supposed to learn them if you all won't tell me? I believe in magic now. It's only been a few days, but I'm going strong into opening this bakery and fighting revenants and working with magic and pretending that I know what I'm doing. Nobody is telling me everything, and I feel like I'm always a hundred steps behind. Just tell me, Rome. What are you hiding?"

I looked into her eyes and held back a curse. "We're mates," I blurted, knowing I would probably regret this. My bear pushed at me, even as it winced a bit at my brevity.

She blinked at me then. "What?"

I pinched the bridge of my nose. "Shit. I'm usually better at this."

"Better at what? How many women have you told that you're mated? What does that even mean?"

I ran my hand through my hair and then over my beard. "Many of those *other*—bear shifters, other shifters, even witches—have someone they're fated to be with. Through a series of choices, you can create a bond with your mate, and they will be forever yours—throughout eternity. The mating bond is different for each person or triad, and it changes over time to be what the people need it to be. It's personal, and it's everything. It's the future. It's a glimpse into who you could be. It's a connection of souls."

She looked at me then and shook her head. "No, you don't even know me."

I let out a breath. "My bear does. And the man wants to know you."

"This is all too much. I don't understand."

This was what I was afraid of—at least one of the many things these days. "I know. And most people find their mates either within their den, or it's someone who already knows all the histories that go into the concept of mating bonds. I didn't want to tell you. At least, not yet."

Sage narrowed her eyes. "I asked you to tell me all of your secrets, and now you're telling me I'm your mate? That we're fated?"

"We can say no. We can walk away." It was a complete lie. I reached out, unable to stop myself, and pushed a stray lock of her hair behind an ear. Her eyes widened, her pupils dilating as her mouth parted. "I don't want to walk away. At least, not until I know you."

"And if you find out who I am, will you walk away?" she asked, confusion etched on her face.

Never. "I don't know. But I'd like to find out. I want to see who you are. I want my bear to know you. The man wants it, as well."

"I don't understand what this means," she whispered.

"I know. I know you don't understand a lot of what's going on, and that you're trying to keep up. I didn't want to throw this at you on top of everything else, but you can feel it, can't you? The connection?"

She licked her lips, and I saw sadness there for a brief instant. I wanted to kick myself.

"It doesn't change how you loved him," I whispered, and she pulled away, her expression turning stony.

"Nothing can change that."

My heart ignored the punch. This wasn't about me. I'd never be a replacement. That wasn't what fate dealt. None of this was easy, and all I could do was lumber over and get in her space. "I know our hearts can do many things and not forget. So, I'm going to go now because I know you have a lot to think about. I feel the connection, and I know you do, too. Or at least I hope you do."

She looked at me, her eyes wide, a pleading look in her gaze. "I don't know what to think right now, Rome."

"I know. So, I'm going to go. I'll be back. Even if it's so you can push me away. I'm also here as the alpha of the bears to protect our town. So, I'll be back."

I wanted to reach out, to touch her, but I didn't. I turned on my heel and left, leaving her confused and in pain. I could feel it.

And I hated myself for it.

I closed the door behind me and frowned, sniffing the air. Had someone been here? Listening? I didn't know, but I pulled out my phone and called Jaxton to ask that his wing keep an eye on her.

My bear wanted Sage, and so did I. But something was watching us. Something was coming. And I knew that no matter what, regardless of the choice she made, I would always protect her, even if it took everything I had.

CHAPTER NINE

SAGE

In the blink of an eye, it was opening day, and Ravenwood Sweets was ready for the town. Only I didn't know if the town was prepared for me.

I had come to Ravenwood to start a new life, to open a bakery, to work for myself. To be near my aunt and try to settle in where I could be appreciated and not pushed away and painfully ignored by those who should have protected me.

I still couldn't quite believe that this was my life, that this was how I was living now.

Ravenwood wasn't a simple town. Far from it.

"The place looks amazing," Penelope said as she bustled around the bakery. People milled about, drinking coffee, talking to one another about what they were eating.

I nodded, smiling, exhaustion settling over me. "It's day one, and it's a soft open. I don't even have everything yet."

"You're getting the hang of it. You've worked at bakeries for years. You've got this."

I had. When I was married to Rupert. I'd worked for

other people, something his family hadn't appreciated, but that was neither here nor there. "This is still my first time opening my own business. It's going to be a little different."

"You've got this."

"You sure do," Sabrina, my new helper, said as she walked past, a carafe of coffee in her hands.

We wouldn't serve coffee like this on regular days since everyone would take theirs in the reusable cups they brought in themselves to protect the environment, but today was different. It was a soft opening, and we were having a little party. I had baked some of my favorite brownies, honey buns, cinnamon rolls, cookies, and pound cakes, and people were enjoying them with coffee. We were a bakery, not a proper coffee shop, so while we would have some espresso and coffee to sell, we were here for the baked goods and the bread. I had also made brioche, French bread, challah, ciabatta, round loaves, plaits, and so many others, and they were going out the door like crazy. People were buying them in droves, and I hoped they weren't doing it to feed the ducks outside. Not that the fowl didn't deserve my bread, but I didn't want the townsfolk to buy things simply to make me happy.

Jaxton had already come in, grinning as he looked at a large loaf of challah. He'd eventually taken four. I had raised my brow, and he'd only smiled. "I like challah, and I'm pretty sure you already have a lifelong customer in me." He had then leaned down to brush a kiss on my cheek in friendship and walked away.

I had been left there standing, blinking, as other people I only knew by sight around town laughed.

An older man smiled. "You're part of the town now.

Jaxton will know how to take care of you. In a fixer sense, of course."

"Jaxton is quiet, caring. A sweet boy. He will always be there to help you out. You have to remember that he needs help, too, even if he doesn't say it," Penelope said after the hawk shifter had left.

I tried to keep up with the orders, grateful that all the exhaustion I had put myself through for this opening day seemed to have been worth it. I didn't think people would continue buying at this rate once I was open officially, but they were already talking about special orders and asking what they could get once the place was open full time. I loved baking bread. That was my main focus at the bakery, but I would be making cakes, cupcakes, and other specialty items for order and some daily for the mornings. The town didn't have a bakery or a coffee shop, and I was filling that need.

Rowen walked in during a slight lull, even though there were still twenty people milling about, looking at bread and adding things to their small, handheld baskets.

She grinned and looked around. "You're doing well. I'm glad to see it."

I smiled, feeling as though I had known her for years, yet it had only been a few days. "I'm trying. Can I get you anything?"

"I love bread." She lowered her head as she studied a plaited loaf. "I've never been good at plaits. I always forget what goes over or under and end up with a nice little twist that I tuck underneath and pretend isn't messed up."

"I honestly can't believe you do anything that isn't perfect," I said, shaking my head.

She raised a brow. "Oh, I tend to do imperfect things

often. That's what makes me human." She winked. "Or, at least, marginally human."

"I love that there's a new witch in town," a smaller, older woman said as she bustled through the door. "And you can tell that every single thing made here is done with love, precision, and maybe a little extra something." The older woman winked as she said it and then went to the front counter where my new and only staff member, Sabrina, worked at the register.

"I'm not.... What was she saying?" I asked, swallowing hard.

Rowen reached out and gripped my hand. "It's okay. You're a witch. Of course, you're going to infuse some of who you are into your baked goods. Especially when you work with the liquid part of baking since you have an affinity for water."

I bit my lip and looked down at my hands. My tattoos pulsed, reminding me of who I was. "Am I hurting people?"

"No, I would let you know if I felt anything off. I only feel a part of who you are. You are a wonderful baker and a warm and loving person. And this place is a testament to that. They're here today to check you out because we're curious, and we want to know who you're going to be in Ravenwood."

I shook my head. "I don't even know who I'm going to be in the next moment. I can't keep up."

"I don't think you're supposed to right now," she said softly. "You're a baker. You infuse some of your magic into your goods. Not on purpose, but maybe simply what you're feeling at the moment."

"That's not good. It'll probably be all anxiety and me wanting to throw up."

Rowen grinned. "I don't think you can make anxiety rolls. More the welcoming feeling that you have when you think of your aunt." Her hands went to the French bread. "Here, it feels as if you were thinking about a certain someone." She winked and walked over to the honey buns. "And I know who you were thinking about when you baked these. Whoever eats these is going to be very happy later."

I blushed and shook my head. "I don't know what you're talking about."

"I think you do. But I won't pry. Yet. Though I know you probably have a few questions." She raised a brow. Thankfully, before I could say anything or she could continue, another townsperson came up and asked about a special-order cake for a birthday. I smiled and nodded and took some notes. I already had a pricing list in mind, but I'd never thought things would happen so quickly.

"You have to charge more than this," the older woman said. "We may be a small town, but we pay for what things are worth."

I smiled softly. "I'm only starting. And I am pricing decently high and for what I'm worth. I don't want to price out of the market, though."

"Thank you for that. But I expect you to raise your prices soon." She smiled. "You are a master at what you do, and you need to know your worth."

I shook my head. "I do know my worth."

The other woman left, and I looked over at Rowen. "I'm doing this, then? For real? Putting magic into my baked goods?"

Rowen threw her head back and laughed. "This is Ravenwood, Sage. You don't need to whisper about magic.

Everyone in this room right now knows who you are and what you and the rest of us can do."

The people milling about looking at bread and eating honey buns grinned and waved.

"I don't know how that's possible because I don't even know who I am or what I can do."

Rowen smiled. "Touché."

"Are you badgering her again?" Laurel asked as she walked up to a neat pile of brownies. "And I think I found my new lover," she said, cooing over the sweets. "These are all individually wrapped, but how much for the lot of them?" she asked, rubbing her hands together.

I snorted. "You do not need an entire plate of fudge brownies with a caramel center. You are going to end up sick."

"But I'll be sick in bliss. Look at these—hello, my darlings. Come to me. Love me."

"Are you crooning to brownies like you would a lover?" Rowen asked.

"I don't think I'm this sweet to my lovers," Laurel said, and Trace cleared his throat behind her. She blushed and then waved him off. "Oh, shush."

"I wasn't going to say anything, but those brownies do look good. However, are those honey buns?" the big bear asked as he walked forward, his gaze intense.

I laughed, and it felt like home. Why did it feel like I had always been here?

"I can't read your thoughts—I'm not that type of witch. But I can see them written on your face."

I looked at Rowen. "What?"

"You are home. Deep inside, you've always known who you are and who you could be. You might still be figuring it all out. So are we. But a part of you, some part of you will forever feel as if you've always been here. You fit in Ravenwood. And I know there are forces out there that make things difficult. Things we'll have to deal with. But you're also home. I hope you realize that."

"I was thinking that. Maybe you *do* read minds."

"No, but I feel that in the few weeks I've known you, I'm starting to understand what you're thinking."

"I've been suppressing everything all this time?"

"I don't know. You could have been. Or maybe it took walking into Ravenwood for you to understand. We may never know. However, you *are* home. And everyone seems to love your baked goods. You have a gift." She gripped both of my hands as Laurel grinned behind her.

"A true gift."

I smiled, looking at everything and everyone around me.

The hairs on the back of my neck stood on end suddenly, and I looked over to the doorway, wondering why I had been waiting all this time for someone else to walk through that door. Rowen gave me a knowing smile, but I didn't focus on that. Instead, I tuned into the man in the doorway. The one I shouldn't focus on.

"That's interesting," Laurel said as Trace tugged her away. Rowen merely grinned before walking towards a group of older women as they all spoke about my bread and sweets.

Rome moved forward, his gaze on mine as if he were afraid of what I might do. I didn't know what I would do, so I didn't blame him.

He came to stand in front of me and stuck his hands into his pockets. "Looks like the place is doing well." He studied the area, a small smile on his face.

"Maybe. I mean, yes, everyone's been so amazing. I'm almost out of bread."

"That would be horrible," he said. "I hear you have honey buns."

I smiled and gestured towards the stack. "I do. And I also have honey bread."

Trace's head shot up. "Honey bread?"

He let out an *oof* as Laurel elbowed him in the stomach. "Come on. You have enough honey."

"One can never have enough honey," he grumbled before he let Laurel pull him away.

I blushed and shook my head. "I made this honey white loaf, mostly because Rowen and Laurel said that I needed to make a lot of honey things for the bears in town." I still couldn't quite believe that I was saying these things aloud and that they made sense, but I was doing my best to roll with it.

"Yeah, we bears like honey. Not all bears, though. When the polars come in, they would most likely go for your salmon and lox."

"Seriously?" I asked, my gaze wide.

"Yes. And if you have any blubber, they'd like that more."

I shuddered. "I don't think I'm going to be serving that at a bakery."

"I thought not. But honey? Show me. Although I could probably follow my nose."

I smiled, not knowing what to say or do. I wasn't good at this. I didn't know what he had meant before about mates or what this pull between us meant. However, I planned to do my best to ignore most of it and simply focus on what I could do and what I did know.

"Can you follow your nose to the honey and the bread?" I asked, wanting to know more about this world around me, even if I was a little worried about what it would mean for me to get to know this man better.

"I can. My nose is best in bear form, but I have a better sense of smell than humans do while I'm in this form."

I shook my head, amazed that he could talk about this so openly. Rome seemed to know where my thoughts had gone because he smiled.

"That's the good thing about Ravenwood. We feel safe to speak freely because of the people around us. Everyone in this room is connected to magic or packs or some other form of the supernatural. And everyone feels safe. Well, as safe as we can be with revenants and darkness coming out of nowhere," he added dryly.

I winced. "We still don't know anything about that?"

Rome shook his head. "No, but we know that everyone who needs to be looking is working on it. It's the best we can do for now. But today's not about that. Today's about your new bakery."

I smiled and looked around at the place I was now beginning to call home. "It is, isn't it?" I asked. "This is mine. And the town's mine now, too."

"You're a major part of the town. Welcome home, Sage," he said softly, and my cheeks warmed.

"Thank you, Rome."

"You're welcome. Now, can I have an entire loaf of bread? Or would that be too much?"

"You're welcome to anything you'd like. Today, we're doing a sale."

"She's not offering her wares at the right prices," the older woman from earlier said. "She needs to raise them."

"We'll make sure of that," Rowen said, and I sighed. It seemed that everybody wanted to spend far too much money on me. And while the businessperson in me didn't mind, the woman who wanted this place to be her home didn't want to take advantage.

"Okay, folks, we've taken enough of Sage's time. We are past closing. The bakery isn't going anywhere. Sage is here to stay." I looked up at Rowen's words. Everybody began cleaning up their messes and then clapped, a little applause that made me blush from my head to my toes. I ducked my head.

"Thank you. All of you. I mean...thank you for welcoming me."

"You're a Prince. You're home," Sabrina said softly from the register. "Welcome."

"Welcome, my favorite niece," Aunt Penelope said as she kissed my temple. "Now, let's help you clean up."

I shook my head. "No, get back to what you were doing. I want a few minutes alone with my shop. Is that okay?" I asked, looking at Rome.

He nodded. "We'll all celebrate later. Promise."

I didn't know what he meant by that, nor did I know what I was supposed to say or do, so I simply nodded, smiled, and helped everybody with the last of their needs before going to help Sabrina clean up.

"The place looks great."

I looked at her. "It does, doesn't it?"

"Thanks for hiring me. I know this is your baby, but I'm glad to be a part of it. And I swear being near you while you're working...your magic infuses my latent powers."

I frowned, startled. "What?"

"I'm a latent earth witch. My whole family is. We can't

do much, except for some healing spells occasionally. But being with you while you bake makes me happier. So, thank you for that."

I shook my head. "I'm not doing it on purpose."

"Oh, I know. If you were, we'd have to charge extra." She winked, and I shook my head.

"I don't think that's how it works," I said, laughing.

"Maybe not, but Rowen and Laurel can show you the ropes. Even your aunt can."

"You're a witch, then?" I asked as we started putting things away to prep for the next day.

"Technically. I don't have any real power. But my family has a line of witches, so that's what we call ourselves. We're safe here in Ravenwood, although no one would come at us to burn us at the stake outside of it, I don't think."

I shuddered. "I don't know if I like that idea."

"Nobody does. The Salem witch trials happened for a reason, though. And it had nothing to do with true witchcraft."

I wanted to ask her more. I held off, knowing that if I started, I wouldn't stop.

"You've done enough here for the day," I said after we'd cleaned up a bit. "Why don't you head home?"

Sabrina frowned. "What do you mean? I'm here to help."

"And you did. We're nearly sold out of everything, and what didn't sell is what lasts longer than a day."

"Everybody loves your bakes."

I shook my head. "Maybe, but it was also day one. And a soft opening. We'll have to scale back."

"Not all of the bears showed up," Sabrina said dryly. "Once they do, things will change. You're going to be out of bread and anything related to honey very quickly."

My brows rose. "For real?"

"Only a few of the shifters came today since today was mostly about witches and the dryads and some of the fae."

I had so many questions I wanted to ask, but I didn't. Because I still didn't know who or what anybody was. It wasn't like anyone wore a name tag. Sometimes, I saw glowing eyes and figured they had to be shifters, but for all I knew, the fae's eyes glowed, too.

"When the shifters do show up, probably within the week, they'll eat you out of house and home. They put away far more than anyone I know."

"Oh," I said softly.

"Yes. Oh. It's pretty great. You have a hit on your hands. You filled a need. It's as if we were waiting for you forever."

She grinned and helped me clean up a bit more before she left.

I followed her out, locking the door behind her before I went to finish.

I felt as if I were still catching up, and yet, I felt at home. Finally. This was my place. A bakery I'd wanted since I was a little girl but couldn't afford on my own, both time and money-wise.

Now, it was all mine.

And I was a witch.

I shook my head and looked down at my hands. "What am I doing?"

"Isn't that the question?"

I looked up at the sound of an unfamiliar voice. The woman was blond, had bright blue eyes, and a cunning smile. She stood at the register, some type of manic glee in her eyes that worried me. I hadn't seen this woman before around town, but I didn't know what or who she was. Still, something inside told me she was dangerous. I needed to run, to do something—not let myself become prey.

"I'm sorry, I didn't know you were still here when I locked up."

"I came in through the back. You should be careful about the locks on your doors."

Alarm shot through me. "We're closed now. We'll be open tomorrow if you'd like something."

"Oh, I don't need anything from you. At least, not yet. I thought I'd introduce myself." She winked and came forward, her eyes glowing red for a moment. I blinked. Unsure what I had seen—if anything. "My name's Faith. We've met before, though you probably didn't know it was me."

My back was to the door. It was locked, and I realized there was no way out. "What do you mean?" I asked.

"You met some of my pets earlier. I'm kind of sad that you took care of them so quickly. It's okay. There's more where they came from."

"It's you," I breathed. Faith was the necromancer.

"It's me. It's amazing how long I've been here, and no one noticed. The town of Ravenwood is safe for all creatures, it seems. Even little old me. I wanted to introduce myself. And to give you a warning. Be careful when the darkness comes. Because light fades, and so will you." Before I could breathe, she held up her hand. Water sliced out, seemingly out of nowhere, and slapped me in the face. A trail of warmth slid down my cheek, and I reached up, only to see my hand come back red.

"You don't even know how to use your powers and you think to go against me? Oh, honey, you don't even know. Tell the others I'm here. This was a warning. If we're not careful, the game's going to end far too soon for my liking."

She held up her hands again, and I threw mine up in defense, not knowing what to do. Water pulled out of the small jars of water lilies around the room and flew at her. It soaked her to the bone, but the force of it pushed Faith enough that she slammed her back against the counter. Her eyes widened marginally, and it seemed as if I had surprised her as much as I had shocked myself. She winked, threw out another arm as water sliced into my flesh, and I ducked, holding back a pained groan. I wasn't trained. Could only do some magic. But she was a water witch, a necromancer. And, apparently, she could use water as a blade. I looked up and saw she was gone, but then the door behind me burst open. I looked over my shoulder as Rome appeared, his eyes gold and wild as he growled, huffing towards me.

"Where is she?" he asked, kneeling in front of me. Jaxton came in behind him, Laurel suddenly beside Jaxton with a sword in her hand.

"Her name was Faith," I whispered as Rome reached up to my face, carefully wiping away the blood. "She said this was a message."

I looked at the others and knew that the time of peace and to prepare was over.

CHAPTER TEN

ROME

My feet sloshed in the water on the floor, and my bear growled. My knee was soaked where I knelt in front of Sage. I reached out, grateful that my claws weren't extended. It was only by force of will that I kept them from poking out from my fingertips. I didn't want to scare Sage. She was still so new to everything as it was.

"Her name was Faith," she whispered, and I nodded tightly. I glanced over at Laurel and Jaxton as they moved to the back of the building, trying to catch whoever had been in here. Whoever this Faith was. Part of me needed to follow them, to discover who would dare touch my mate, who would dare to deface and harm my town. I had no time for that, though. Not when Sage was bleeding in front of me. The coppery scent of her blood burned my nostrils, and my fangs started to slide through my gums. I growled, low, deadly, and my fangs went back to where they should be. Sage's eyes widened, but she didn't cower away from me or say anything. Instead, she leaned forward and reached up as if to touch the cut on her cheek. I shook my head and wiped away some more of the blood, careful not to touch the open wound.

"Don't. I'll take care of it." My bear pushed at me, clawing. Needing to do something other than stand there. But I couldn't leave Sage alone. Not with blood on her face. All I wanted to do was slash at anyone who came near. The others seemed to understand that because they gave us a wide berth —for now.

"Is it bad?" Sage asked, her voice steady. She had to be in shock. That was the only likely reason she could be this calm and controlled.

"It's not," I said, knowing it was the truth, even though my bear thought it was the end of the world. I wanted to rip this Faith limb from limb for even daring to harm Sage. Whoever the hell thought they had the authority to touch my mate didn't deserve to breathe. "We'll get you cleaned up."

"Do you want help?" Rowen asked from the front door, her hair flowing around her, her eyes dark with magic.

I shook my head. "I've got this. You should go see who it is."

"I can scent her. It's the necromancer."

"Her name is Faith," Sage repeated. She was still in shock, but we also needed to ensure that she was unharmed in other ways.

"Other than the cuts, are you hurt anywhere else?" I asked, studying her face.

She shook her head and winced. "No, just a little rattled. I wasn't expecting her to come here when I was alone."

"And where are your helpers? Your aunt? You shouldn't have been here by yourself." My bear was in my voice, and I couldn't help it.

Sage's eyes narrowed, and I liked the fire I saw there, even if it *was* directed at me. "And you think I'd be okay with my aunt getting hurt? You don't know me, even though you seem to *think* you do."

Laurel's lips quirked, and I glared at her.

"Go help the others."

"You're not my alpha, bear. You would do well to remember that."

"I remember enough," I growled, my voice low and deadly.

"We will see."

She moved then, and I watched her walk away as Trace came in, gave me a tight nod, and followed her.

I let out a low snarl. "Seriously, let me get this cleaned up."

Sage shook her head again and then winced, looking around the room. "There's so much water damage."

"We'll be able to clean it up," Rowen said as she walked back in, her voice tight. "Faith is gone. Tell us what happened."

I helped Sage stand. She winced again, and I glared at Rowen for making her move so quickly.

"I was here closing up. I thought I locked all the doors, but apparently, I left the back door open because Faith walked in."

"She probably used magic or a spell," Rowen said. "I'll have to add another layer of protection that you'll need to learn to deal with quickly. The only reason I haven't yet is because you needed access to and from your place of business, and I thought I had enough wards on the town." She rubbed her temples, and I saw the exhaustion there.

"I'm sorry," Sage said. I growled again, and she sighed.

"Stop growling. I *am* sorry. If I knew more about magic or how to protect myself, Rowen wouldn't be working herself to exhaustion, trying to take care of me. And I thought a simple lock would work. I was wrong."

"It's okay," Rowen said before I could speak. "I'll teach you the simple spell, but I don't know if we're ready for a stronger one if we need it."

"How about I station one of my enforcers here?" I asked.

Rowen nodded, studying me as Sage frowned. "Why would you do that?"

"You know why," I growled, my voice low.

Her cheeks pinked, and she nodded. "I don't want anyone getting hurt because of me."

"You're going to learn how to use your powers. But you can't do it overnight. My people protect this town, and you are part of it now. I'll station someone here, you'll learn the simple spell, and eventually, you'll learn the harder ones. Give yourself some time. I'm sorry we didn't think of doing this ahead of time."

"If I'm not allowed to kick myself, you're not allowed to do it either," Sage added dryly.

"Fine," I grumbled.

"What did this Faith look like?" Rowen asked, and I brought myself back to the present rather than worrying about what I couldn't fix for the future.

"She was about your height, Rowen. Long, blond hair, straight. But I don't know if she straightened it or if she has natural waves. She had bright blue eyes and plump lips, but her eyes turned red at one point. I thought I was seeing things."

"I growled again, and Sage narrowed her eyes at me. "I'm

126

not growling at you, only at the situation. I'm a bear. You're going to have to deal with the growling."

"He's right. I would growl too if I could," Rowen put in. "The red eyes mean she's gone full dark magic. She's a low-power necromancer."

"She also has an affinity for water," Sage put in.

Rowen gave a tight nod. "She used a water blade to cut you. At least, from what I can tell."

"I didn't know that was possible," Sage said.

I cleared my throat. "I thought only powerful witches could do that."

Rowen sighed. "Yes, but the darkness she uses to feed her soul helps to boost whatever powers she has naturally. It's why those of us who don't feed the darkness need to train as hard as we do. Sage, the water on the floor, was that her or you?"

Sage blushed. "That was mostly me. I don't know how to control things yet, but I did push her back, at least. I fought. I need to learn more. I don't want to stand here and let everybody take care of me."

"We'll fix this," I said. Even as I said it, my bear preened at the thought of her strength. She'd tried to protect herself, doing what she could. She was strong and would make a good alpha's mate.

Sage shook her head. "I don't want anyone to get hurt trying to protect me."

"Everybody fights to protect each other and themselves. You need the tools, and we'll get them for you," Rowen said tightly. "I'm going to check on Laurel and the others. You should get cleaned up. Rome?" she asked, and I nodded.

I looked down at my mate. "Come on, Sage, let me clean

you up and call your aunt to make sure she doesn't hear this secondhand."

"I'm glad she and Sabrina weren't here," Sage said softly. "They have even less power than I do."

My bear prowled. "See? You're trying to take care of others even as you're annoyed that people want to help you."

Sage frowned. "I don't know if I like you throwing my words back in my face."

I smiled. "I can't help it. I'm a bear. Come on, I'll take care of you."

"You don't have to."

"Do you think my bear will allow anything else to happen right now? I'm on the edge, Sage. Hanging on by a thread. You might not understand what that means, but others in this room do. So, let my bear and me help you. Clean your wounds before I go find Faith for daring to touch you and rip her limb from limb with every ounce of power I have." My voice got lower, more of a growl with each word. Sage met my gaze. There didn't need to be any words in that moment.

"We're going to use magic to clean up your place," Rowen said. "Don't worry, everything that you put into this, your blood, sweat, and tears, won't have been for nothing."

"I just...thank you. I'm going to make sure Rome doesn't go full bear, and then I'll be back to help you clean up."

I growled again even as Rowen's lips twitched.

"We'll see that that happens," she said softly. Laurel, Jaxton, and Trace walked in at that moment, and they all looked around the place, at us, before they started cleaning up, too.

I tugged on Sage's arm. "Come on. Let's clean up that wound so it doesn't continue to bleed."

Or before my bear got any other ideas.

It was a short walk to my car, and I stuffed her inside before anybody could come out and ask what was going on. Rowen would deal with that. She was this town's leader. I was only the leader of the bears. I would explain to the pack what'd happened soon, but I needed to get Sage into my home and cared for before I lost it.

"You should call your aunt." Sage looked up at me and pulled out her phone. As she spoke, her voice was calm, *too* calm, as she explained to her aunt what'd happened. I was surprised at how well they were taking this, but Sage tried not to worry her aunt and vice versa. Soon, the reality of the situation would hit them both, and we'd all have to deal with the consequences.

"You're taking me to your place?" she asked softly.

"You're not settled into your home yet. You likely don't have your things unpacked, and some of your stuff is still with your aunt. I assumed you didn't want anybody in there until it was fully yours. Plus, I'm a bear. I want you in my place. Sue me." I winked as I said it, a small smile playing on my lips.

When her shoulders relaxed, and she smiled, I knew I had said the right thing. "It's so weird that I did everything online and over the phone without seeing it first. It didn't even occur to me that that wasn't normal until I was here."

"That's Ravenwood for you. The magic rubs off on people, even when we don't realize it."

"That doesn't seem nefarious at all." I ignored the sarcasm in her tone.

"It isn't," I said as I helped her out of the car.

I walked her into the kitchen and pulled out my large first-aid kit.

"That's a huge first-aid kit for the kitchen."

I shrugged at her words. "I have a larger one in my bedroom and another in my bathroom. And our pack healer has an entire infirmary for wounds like this."

"Wounds from a necromancer witch who used a water blade to slice into my skin?" Her tone was dry as if she still didn't quite believe what had happened. Sadly, it happened often enough that we knew how to heal things like this. She'd learn soon.

"You're already healing—witches heal faster than humans. But as to your question, yes, our pack healer has dealt with a lot of things. She's older than my parents."

Her eyes widened. "There's a lot to take in with that statement."

I grinned. "Sorry, sometimes I speak and forget that not everybody has been immersed in as much magic and shifter politics as I have."

I reached for gauze as well as a washcloth and began washing her face slowly. I gripped her chin softly, and her eyes widened as they met mine, her mouth parting. I wanted to lean down and brush my lips against hers, but I waited, at least for the moment.

I needed to breathe, to get myself under control, and then I'd figure out what to do. To say.

"Where do you want to begin?" I asked softly.

"That's a loaded question," she said with a laugh, and I grinned.

"Maybe."

"You said that witches heal faster than humans?"

I winced, knowing I'd probably sent her mind into another tailspin.

"Am I not human anymore?"

I sighed, put herbal ointment on a cotton pad, and began dabbing the cuts. She winced, and I blew cool air over the wound. "You have always been who you are. It's not an option anymore."

"I've never been human."

I sighed. "All of us are human. Though some with extra abilities. I can shift into a bear and there are pros and cons to that. You have inherent magic and face those, as well."

"I'm not...human."

"You are. It's sometimes easier to say human rather than use the other word: mundane."

"So those without magic or powers or shifting abilities, or who aren't fae, are mundane?"

"Everyone who's not fae is considered human. The fae are a whole other thing."

She shook her head. "This is all so confusing."

"I know," I said softly. "It's probably going to be very confusing for a long while. You'll get the hang of it, though."

"You say that, and yet I don't know if I believe you."

I rubbed her chin again, needing her touch. Her eyes darkened, and my bear smiled. "Give yourself time. It's the best you can hope for."

"I suppose so."

"Back to what I was saying. Fae are a whole other subset of those with magic and power. We don't know much about them because they're so insular. Some live within our borders, but usually, they are the ones outside of their caste system. Beyond their royal lines. Aspen, the fae leader here, is a friend of sorts. Shifters have their own governing laws and bodies and rules of magic. Witches are the most connected to humans, although depending on how the power is passed through generations, the magic is often so diluted that it feels as if they are mundane—at least to themselves. I tend to call them humans or mundanes, but not all non-magical creatures who know about the existence of magic like that word. It depends on the person."

She reached up to rub her temples, and I wanted to kiss the pain away. I resisted the urge. Barely.

"Either way, I'm a witch with a water affinity and far more power than I even imagined. And, I can heal quickly."

"You're going to be okay," I whispered.

"I don't know if any of us will be okay until we figure out exactly what's going on."

I looked at her then, my thumb rubbing across her unhurt cheek. "What *is* going on, Sage?"

"What is this?" she whispered.

"You know."

"I didn't expect this...this pull I feel. Is it magic?"

"In a sense. It's not bad. It's not pulling you against your will or going against your wants and needs. But it's there. A connection so instant, yet one you have to build on for it to remain true."

"I don't know what I want, Rome. I need time. I need to think."

I nodded but leaned forward, my mouth a breath from hers. "Well, before you think, I need to do this."

Meeting her gaze, waiting for her to say no in any way, I pressed my lips to hers. My bear growled, pushed at me, needing more. She tasted of honey and sweetness, and an intoxicating magic all her own. Her flavor burst on my tongue, and the man in me growled, needing more. I didn't lean in. I didn't grab her and pull her against me. I didn't throw her on the countertop and make her mine. I didn't sink into her. Instead, I let out another small growl, a breath, and kissed her again. She kissed me back, and I knew I was lost.

Because no matter what happened, no matter the darkness, or Faith, or magic, or whatever connections faltered, I knew this woman was mine.

No matter that my pack would reject everything and create more agony than was desired, this woman was my mate.

And I would die to protect her.

I would sacrifice anything to have her.

CHAPTER ELEVEN

SAGE

The following day, I swore I could still feel the burn of Rome's lips against mine. I had thought about dating again after losing Rupert. It had been more than enough time, according to some people in my past. And I would always love my husband. But before I even decided to move here, I had decided it was time for me to start a new life—including dating and possibly finding happiness again. I had no idea that it might include spending time with a man who could shift into a grizzly bear—one who called me his mate. But I had no clue about a lot of my life right now.

"Where is your head at?" Rowen asked as she paced in front of me, looking down at the book in her hands. We were behind her large home, one right off the main street near all the historical houses I'd loved that first day I walked through.

The night before, I had left Rome's place, my knees shaking and a goodbye sputtering off my lips as I tried to come to terms with the fact that I had enjoyed our kiss and wanted more. And then Rowen had texted me to tell me that we would be training today.

I was no longer of the belief that I imagined what I saw, what I felt. There was no way I could imagine all of this.

The world that I now resided in was far different from the one I had grown up believing in. And that meant I was finding my path, even if it was a little different.

I was meant to be here. Perhaps I had been all along.

Now, I needed to find my strength.

"Seriously, where is your head?" Laurel asked from beside me. She sat on a large boulder, the trees surrounding her framing her in a perfect, picturesque way. She had one ankle over her knee, her sword out as she polished it. It made a soft, metallic ringing sound every time she ran her supplies over the blade. Once again, I remembered that this was a new life for me. It would take a little bit of getting used to.

"Sorry, I was thinking about last night," I said quickly.

Rowen gave me a knowing smile. "You mean Faith? Or how a certain bear quickly hurried you off to take care of you."

"I don't think it has anything to do with Faith," Laurel said, her tone teasing.

I knew my cheeks blushed a deep red, and I shrugged. "He kissed me."

"That's all?" Laurel asked.

"Shush, let her finish." Rowen paused, leaned forward. "And?"

I shook my head, grateful I could speak about it at all. I hadn't had girlfriends in Virginia, and the lack of those relationships was only now dawning on me. "And that was it. We talked, he cleaned my wound after I told him exactly what had happened with Faith, what I explained to you, and then he kissed me. And I guess I kissed him back. I don't know."

Laurel blinked. "Huh, what don't you know?"

"I don't know anything. About any of this. Somehow, I can control water—but not well."

Rowen sighed. "And that's why we're here. There's a pond right in front of you. We're going to work through it. I'll make sure the spells we're about to go through are good for your skill level. It's been a while since I trained another witch."

I noticed that Rowen pointedly didn't look at Laurel. There was a history there, one I wouldn't get in the middle of.

"And? What else don't you know?" Laurel repeated.

I looked down at my hands. "As I said, everything. Rome says I'm his mate. As if I'm supposed to understand what that means. I just met him, and yet I can't stop thinking about him. There's like this...pull to him, and I don't understand it. When I fell in love with Rupert, it was nothing like that. We were gentle with one another and slowly fell into our relationship. It took a while, and it was sweet. When I lost him, I thought I lost everything. It's so different with Rome. And all we've done is kiss. Only I feel like he's claimed me somehow, and I don't understand it. I don't even know if I want it. Nobody is explaining anything in detail to me because they're all afraid of overwhelming me. Though what ends up happening is that I get even more overwhelmed."

The two women looked at me and blinked before Laurel put her sword back in its scabbard, set it down on the rock beside her, and stood. "Mates are for life."

"I assumed that," I grumbled and winced at Laurel. "I'm sorry. Please, continue."

Laurel smiled, her eyes distant. "We understand your

frustration, and I know you've read through the books, but they don't go over everything. Some things are so inherent with how we grow up and what family knowledge is passed down, that they're not always recorded."

"And my mom and my dad took me away from all this. And it wasn't like Aunt Penelope could tell me."

"Your aunt grew up in Ravenwood, but the rest of your family didn't. It makes sense that you wouldn't know," Rowen added, frowning. "Maybe you weren't supposed to be here until it was the right time."

"Beyond the prophecy," Laurel added.

"Aside from prophecies," Rowen continued, "mates are forever, as Laurel said. They're fated. It is said that within the world of the paranormals and fae—anything that isn't quite human, really—that there can be one or two people who are the perfect match for you, depending on whether you're a pair or a triad."

My eyes widened at that, and I nodded. "Fated. As in there's no choice?" I asked, not sure if I liked that idea.

Laurel shook her head. "There's always a choice. It starts with a pull. A connection. A literal metaphysical thread between two people—at least, in this case—that will forever tie you together. Unless you choose to walk away. You can choose not to be with your mate for whatever reason. And many are valid," she added quickly, and I wondered about the story there, but I didn't pry. "If you choose," she continued, "then you'll no longer feel the tug. You might feel as if something is missing forever and have an ache within you. But it will go away eventually. Or at least you'll learn to live with it."

"And what if I had come here with Rupert? What if I had felt the tug toward Rome but was still in love with my husband?" I asked, bile filling my throat. "I would never have cheated on my husband. You're saying that I could have this perfect romance and love with a man I don't even know, and not take anything from him?"

"No," Rowen said softly. "You wouldn't have come here if you were still with Rupert."

"You're telling me that fate decided that Rupert needed to die so I could come here and be part of the coven and mate with Rome?" I asked, anger pouring off me. "That can't be right."

"That's not what I meant," Rowen said quickly, stumbling over her words for the first time since I had met her. "I'm explaining it wrong. Rupert died, and it was a tragedy, and I'm so sorry I never met your husband—from what you've said about him, he sounds like a wonderful man."

"He was," I said, shaking my head. "And he's gone, and I can't change that. But I don't know what I'm supposed to do now."

"You don't have to make any choices right now," Laurel said. "Honestly, I'm surprised Rome is as stable and as nice as he is."

My eyes widened. "Rome isn't usually nice? He's lying about himself and pretending to what? Get in my pants?"

I knew I was rambling and probably acting like an idiot. I didn't understand any of this, and everything was coming at me so quickly I felt like I was behind. Always.

Laurel let out a breath. "I'm bungling this. Rome's being very good about not being overprotective and being...well, a bear. Of all of the magical creatures out there, shifters are the worst when it comes to protective instincts with their mates. Usually, once that tug begins, and they figure out that the person could be their mate or mates, the animal inside takes over and wants to mark them as theirs. Makes sure the choice is theirs, but helps it happen. It gets growly. And hot, if I'm honest."

I sputtered. "You have a mate?" I asked, confused.

Laurel's eyes widened, and she shook her head. "No, but I have friends with mates and have watched the guys get all dominant yet sweet and caring at the same time. And bears are the worst of them."

"I think the bears would say the wolves are the worst," Rowen muttered.

"Maybe, but there are a lot of bears in this town, and they do get growly. The fact that Rome is now kissing you? It's remarkable. It takes his alpha strength to hold himself back and not woo you, make you see who he is. I'm honestly surprised that he hasn't kidnapped you, simply taking you to his den to try and make you fall in love with him so he can mark you and make you his."

I ignored how heat lashed at me at that image. Rowen and Laurel gave each other knowing looks, and I cleared my throat. "What was that look for?" I asked.

"You got all blushy, and you bit your lip when I said that. Maybe you *do* want Rome to take you to his den and mark you."

"No. I mean, I don't even know him."

"You do. You know Rome. You might not know every-thing he's ever said or done, but you know the man he is. He's kind, alpha, and you'll learn more about him. Deep inside? You know. Maybe it'll take you some time to under-stand who he is and what he could be, but that attraction? That's not going away. It might not ever."

"What are you saying?" I asked Laurel.

"I'm saying that maybe you should let yourself believe."

"That's all I've been doing since I got here."

"Maybe. But have you believed in yourself?" Rowen asked, her voice soft.

"I don't know. I need time to think. And, honestly, I need to figure out what I want. Before I can do any of that, I need to catch up on everything else. Like magic."

Rowen nodded, set the book down. "Then let's begin. I am going to teach you a spell that will help create shapes with water. You won't need to recite the incantation each time, but the first few times, it'll help narrow the focus of your power."

"So, we're going to brush over the whole *she's going to mate to a bear thing*, right?" Laurel asked Rowen.

Rowen rolled her eyes. "Magic first. Mating will come. And we're here if she needs us."

My gaze bounced between them as they spoke to each other as if they'd done this a thousand times before. It felt comfortable. As if I'd always been meant to be here.

Laurel raised a brow. "We're not going to talk about Faith?"

Rowen threw her hands into the air. "What is there to say about Faith? She's a necromancer. We're going to find her. But we need to figure out what the hell she wants and who she is."

"I had never seen her before in my life," I added.

Laurel nodded. "We are going to find her. All of our trackers are on it, and I'm looking, too. I can't help you with magic, but I can help you find her." Laurel growled, and I knew why she was so uncomfortable. She couldn't do magic. At least, not directly. I didn't know the full story behind it or why she called herself cursed. I only hoped she would be okay.

"Why don't you go talk with Trace and Jaxton?" Rowen said softly. "Go over the hunt for Faith and check the wards." Once again, I saw the exhaustion on the witch's face. She was using her life-force to keep the town safe. What would happen if or when she used too much?

I needed to help. And that meant I needed to learn magic. So, that's what I would do.

"Are you sure you don't want me to stick around to make sarcastic comments, at least? I can't do much else."

Before I could say anything to try and calm the storm, Laurel moved away, grabbed her sword, and walked off.

After a moment, my heart finally stopped racing. "I wish I could help."

"Maybe you will, little sister," Rowen said. "For now, we need to train in what we can, so you can help her in other ways. I honestly think that it'll be Laurel who helps herself." And at that cryptic comment, Rowen began. "I need you to repeat after me. I will say the entire incantation, and you need to repeat it, word for word. You will feel the power of your element within you. All we're going to do here is make a sphere and hold it within your hands without touching it. Like this." She reached out her hands.

"*Guardians of the west, lend me your strength. Lord and Lady, lend me your ear. Shape this element into a sphere. Great Undine of water and sea, this is my will, so mote it be.*"

The hair on the back of my neck stood on end, and magic sparked across my arms as Rowen whispered the words, and a ball of water floated up from the pond in front of us. She created a sphere with it, her hands outstretched as she looked at me and winked before letting the water sprinkle back into the pond.

"Your turn. Now, I mostly use air, so that spell should

work even better for you."

"Will I be able to use other spells?"

"Yes. But first, let's do what you're good at."

"You mean what I *should* be good at," I said dryly.

I repeated the words, doing my best not to stumble over any, and magic sparked within me.

My body warmed, and I felt the water beneath me, slowly rising into the sky. I opened my eyes, not realizing I had closed them. A perfect sphere rose from the pond's surface, floating high into the air until it was almost at chest level. My hands shook, but not from strain, from the power. I could feel the water in the pond, the moisture in the air and earth, the liquid in the bottle behind me.

"Focus," Rowen murmured, and I did, looking at the perfect sphere in front of me as it twisted, slowly spinning as if it were a top.

"Now, let it fall into a trickle, not a mist. And not too quickly. Slow. Easy."

"How do I do that?" I asked as the water ball bobbed in front of me.

"Feel the particles and let the magic flow through you. Then, direct it."

I did as she said, warmth slicing through me as my magic ebbed and flowed. It did as I wanted it to, and the water sprinkled into the pond. At least for a few moments until the rest of the sphere popped like a balloon and splashed.

My face turned red, and I winced as I looked over at Rowen.

She raised a single brow at me and then spun her finger in the air. A wind tunnel appeared in front of us and air-dried her formerly wet skirt and shirt. "Next time we practice, you're going to stand a little farther away from me." She studied my face before she smiled widely. "Honestly, Sage, that was amazing. I'm not even sure I did my air equivalent of that spell so well the first time."

"I splashed you," I said, even though pride filled me. "Are you sure I did such a good job?"

"You're only beginning and already surprising me. I knew you had a wealth of power, but wow. Let's try it again."

I bounced on the balls on my feet and looked around, feeling the magic in the air. "I'm doing this."

"You've always had it in you. It's been in every loaf of bread you've ever made, and in every hope and dream you put your soul into. You have always been a witch, Sage. It's only now that you're truly able to realize who you could be."

"And who is that?"

"That's up to you. You are a witch. You could be a great power, but you are of our coven." She paused. "And you could also be a bear's mate. Or, you can stand alone but with strength." I opened my mouth to say something, and she pressed her lips into a thin line. "It's okay to be alone, Sage. Not everybody can stay with those they are fated for."

I didn't say anything and then understood that maybe it wasn't Laurel she had been talking about earlier. Perhaps it was Rowen, after all.

I might feel connected to these women, feel as if I could call them my friends even if our friendship was still a little new, but I didn't know everything. I always seemed to be two steps behind—maybe more. I had pulled a sphere of water out of the pond and hovered it in the air today, and I would do it again.

We would find Faith, and we would create our coven.

Because while I might be new to Ravenwood, I knew I belonged here.

CHAPTER TWELVE

ROME

"You haven't claimed her," Trace said, and I shook my head.

"No, I haven't." My bear grumbled at that, and I swallowed hard. "And please stop reminding my bear that I haven't. He's already in a fucked-up mood."

Trace snorted. "It's because you're a gentleman bear."

That made me laugh. "A gentleman bear? Like that's an actual thing?"

"You're making it so."

Alden came in from the kitchen, beer in his hand. "I'm glad you're not mated to her yet."

I raised a brow. "You're glad that my cock is so hard I can barely think, and I feel like crap? Thank you for that."

My brother shook his head. "That's not what I meant."

"Then why don't you tell me?" I growled the words, and Trace gave me a look, telling me to calm down. I loved my brothers, I did, but the fact that Sage was so close, and I couldn't do anything about it pissed me off to no end. It didn't help that I felt as if I were missing something in the grand scheme of things. Something was going on within my pack and in the town. It felt like we were all waiting for something disastrous to happen.

"You can walk away. You don't need to follow your base instincts," Alden said.

"You want him to be unhappy?" Trace asked, shaking his head. "That's not very kind."

"I'm not saying he should be unhappy," Alden growled. "I'm saying that mating a witch when our pack needs focus with the dark forces coming isn't a good idea."

My bear pushed at me, but I reined him in, knowing I needed to focus. "You're going to need to stop telling me I shouldn't mate with Sage. We've had witches and humans and fae and others in our pack. Sage wouldn't be the first witch."

"She would be the first witch as an alpha's mate; therefore, an alpha in her own right." Alden shook his head. "You know the elders won't like that."

I sighed. "Father doesn't mind. And since he is our Alpha, I don't give a shit what the old bastards think. They're so stuck in the past with their heads up their asses, they don't realize what's changed over time."

"Maybe some change isn't good," Alden said.

Trace cursed under his breath. "What change? The fact that our pack is strong and healthy?"

"How can it be healthy when the town wards are dying? The witches aren't doing their jobs. They don't have the same power they used to. Yet they're still the ones ruling the town? How is that fair?"

I froze, trying to understand what Alden was saying. "The witches have given their lives to protect our den and this town. Without their power, we wouldn't be as populated as we are. You know we're one of the largest dens in North America."

"There are larger ones," Alden said.

"Out in the forests and terrain that is nearly inhospitable to humans. Nothing near towns or in large cities. Everyone needs to hide who they are. Ravenwood is special."

"There are other places. Like that little town in Montana," Alden stated, speaking of a town that was different than any other city in America, including Ravenwood.

I shook my head. "There are witches there, too, protecting its secrets."

"There's only one witch here now. And I don't think she's strong enough to protect the town."

That worried me, also, but I didn't say that. I didn't voice my concerns about Rowen and prove Alden right. No, she wouldn't be enough to protect the town from Faith and whatever other dark magic came, but perhaps we could do something together. And though it scared me because it would put her in danger, I knew that Sage would lend her power, at least that's what we all hoped. She was training with the coven today, and that was good. She was learning to protect herself. And, honestly, that was all I cared about. Because even if she couldn't be mine, I needed her to be safe. There was something seriously wrong with me, but I couldn't focus beyond that.

"Come on, we have patrols to do," Trace said, standing up. "You, too, Alden."

"We never used to have this many patrols."

I growled, moving towards my brother. It didn't matter that he was my triplet. It didn't matter that I could see my face in his. I was done listening.

"We have always protected this town. Like the witches have. We might not always have the power to protect our secrets, but we can protect the people. There is a darkness out there, one even our elders acknowledge has been coming for years. Well, it is finally here, at least in some respects, and we need to protect those who cannot save themselves. Yes, we're going on patrol. We will do our best to protect who we can. And you are going to get over whatever the hell is blocking you and stand by our sides. You are third in the pack, Alden. So many people look up to you. You need to remember that."

"As you said, I'm third," he sneered. "I'm sure you and Trace can handle things."

And that was usually the case with Alden. He didn't like his place in the pack but wasn't strong enough to take Trace or me. Not that I wanted a dominance fight between us. We were blood, connected at the soul level because we were triplets. Yet there was nothing I could do to make him see reason. Something needed to change and soon. I hated the idea of how that might look, but I wasn't sure what else to do.

"Come on," Trace said after a moment. "We've got this. I know you have a call with Dad soon."

"Yes, I need to update him on the situation with Faith."

Alden's eyes tensed, but he didn't say anything, and I didn't ask. I honestly didn't want to know.

They left without another word, leaving me wondering what to do about my brother. Maybe it was time for Ariel to step in and challenge him in a dominance fight. She would win, and Alden would live, but things would be forced to change. Alden's bear wasn't in tight control anymore. The man not understanding what needed to happen to protect the den. And that meant our shelter wasn't as safe as it should be.

It was my job as alpha to protect my pack and my town, but now I wasn't sure how to do it. Not with my bear pulling at me like it was. I needed to talk to Sage. For many reasons, her being my mate only one of them.

I sighed and made my way out to the front lawn, sensing three little interlopers that should be with their mother.

"Baby triplets, what are you doing?" I asked the little bears as they crawled towards me, little bear smiles on their adorable bear faces.

They couldn't say anything in this form, but they rolled around and played with the leaves in the yard. I shook my head.

"Hi," Sage said. I turned, having scented her, thinking I was losing my mind.

Sage was here. On my land, in my home. Walking towards me. Without me forcing her here or tying her up in the house so she could be mine forever. Not that I would do that, but my bear had weird ideas.

I cleared my throat. "Sage."

The three devious little bears crawled right up to Sage, sat on their furry behinds, and waved their little paws at her.

Sage's eyes widened, and her hand came to her mouth. "You're shifters, then?" she said. Then flinched. "Not that I should ask that. That's probably a little uncouth."

I laughed and shook my head. "It's not."

"Don't laugh at me. I don't know anything." She knelt in front of the three cubs and smiled. "Hello, I'm Sage. I'm new in town."

The little bears approached her, the littlest one crawling into Sage's lap. Sage fell and laughed as all three bears sniffed at her then gave me knowing looks—far too knowing for little bear cubs—and continued pushing and tugging at Sage, wanting her to play.

"Hey, now, cubs. Be careful. She isn't a shifter. She doesn't play as rough as you."

"You are adorable." Sage laughed as she ran her hands over their little furry bodies. "It's very nice to meet you."

"Here, let me help." I knelt and pulled one cub into my arms as another crawled into my lap. The last cub stayed on Sage's lap and nuzzled into her side.

"They are seriously charming."

"Yes, they are," I said. "This is Honor, Jackson, and Henry. They should be with their mother. I can scent her somewhere near. She probably needed a break, and since I'm here..."

"Am I on den territory, then? Should I have asked?"

I met her gaze. "You never have to ask to be on my territory, Sage."

Her cheeks flamed, and the baby bears gave me curious looks. I cleared my throat since what I was thinking wasn't for baby ears.

"I wanted to see you. And to talk. And, wow, I'm not very good at this."

"As you can see, neither am I."

"Okay, darlings," the triplets' mother said as she came into the clearing, shaking her head. "You had your fun. Now it's time to leave your alpha alone. He has to speak with his lady."

And I knew with that, tales of Sage coming onto my land and playing with the cubs would be spread throughout the den in a matter of moments. Everybody likely had questions about my mate. Those who knew. And there was no hiding my reaction to her. Outside of that, they all wanted to know about the new witch in Ravenwood. The person that would help defend against the revenants, fight back the darkness, and potentially break through the prophecy. We all had questions, and for curious bears who always seemed to get into everything, they were actually being quite careful about it. They must have sensed Sage's fear or knew she was over-whelmed about her new world and were giving her space.

I didn't know how long that would last, but it was nice to see that they tried.

The baby bears went off with their mother, one stopping to wave again as they did. Sage waved back, her smile bright. She was stunning, breathtaking, but she wasn't mine yet. My bear wasn't in the mood to listen anymore. All it wanted was to claim her. I pushed that thought aside. I needed to. Sage wasn't a shifter and didn't understand mates. I didn't know if she would ever fully grasp it. So, I wouldn't push. But I would do my best to be my charming bear self. Hopefully, that would be enough.

I rocked back on my heels, forcing myself not to move forward or touch her.

Sage blinked up at me and studied my face. "You're holding so much of yourself back, aren't you?"

I swallowed hard. "What do you mean?"

She shook her head. "You have to be. You're a bear, and yet you don't act growly with me. I've only seen you that way when Faith attacked or when the revenants came. You protected all of us, but you were more bear than anything when you were protecting me. You're holding yourself back when it comes to everything else."

I couldn't lie to her. She was my mate. So, I shrugged. "You're not ready to see what being a bear shifter means."

Sage's eyes narrowed. "You say that. *Everyone* keeps saying that. That I'm not ready for the magic. I'm not ready to know the history of this town. But I've been through two attacks, have seen magic, and shifters, and everything else I didn't believe was real. And I haven't run away yet. Don't think so little of me."

I let out a breath, and my bear growled at me. "I would never think little of you, Sage. I'm an alpha bear. I could hurt you."

"Could you? Or are you worried that you don't know if it's fate or something real?"

I didn't know what I could say to that other than what I knew was our truth. "Fate is real. That's what makes us who we are. Determines how we push and pull against the force itself."

She swallowed hard and looked at me again. "Then talk to me. Who are you, Rome?"

How was I supposed to answer that? "I'm me. A bear shifter. An alpha. I grew up here."

"And you say that I could be yours forever. I don't know what that means."

"What do you want to know, Sage?"

She looked around us and bit her lip. "Can we go inside? I don't know who might be watching."

I tilted my head, inhaled. "No one's near enough to listen in, but yes, we can go inside."

She laughed, shook her head. "Extra-sharp senses could be handy."

"We should see if there's a spell to find out if someone or something's listening in. Witches are very handy."

She brightened slightly. "Maybe. I learned how to hold water today."

I grinned at the pride in her voice as I let her inside. "Seriously? That's great."

Sage practically bounced as she spoke. "It was a sphere, and I only got Rowen and me a little wet."

I looked at her dry clothes. "Did Rowen do her air thing to dry you off?"

She beamed. "Yes, something I will probably take another decade to learn."

"I've grown up knowing who I am and about the magic in our world. I don't know what I would do if I suddenly found myself finding out that everything was new and completely different."

"It feels like a veil has been lifted. Things were always different for me. The tattoos for one."

My bear anchor slid over my body and peaked out of my collar, wanting to see our mate.

Sage's eyes widened as she looked at it. "I'll never get used to them moving around."

"I find it funny that some of my ink doesn't move," I said with a laugh. "I have more tattoos than the bear."

Her gaze darkened a bit, and my cock hardened. Now I wanted to show her every drop of ink on my body, but I refrained. This was about getting to know each other, not stripping each other naked, and marking her as mine.

"I feel a pull towards you, Rome."

"Good," I said, relief pouring through me, even as undeniable hunger clawed at my insides. "We don't have to do anything about it, Sage."

She shook her head. "I don't know if that's what I want. You're a very handsome man, Rome. I love how you are around the cubs and how protective you are. I could see myself going out on a date with you. I really could. And this pull? I don't know. I'm not good at this. I wasn't even good about this with Rupert."

My bear sat up, intrigued, not jealous at all of the man she had once loved. There was no competition with a ghost, and there shouldn't be. There needed to be balance. Only I didn't know how to find that.

"You weren't like this with Rupert?" I paused. "You don't have to talk about him if you don't want to."

She shook her head. "I always talk about him. And I don't know if that's weird to anyone else, but he was a huge part of my life and will always be in my memories. So, I talk about him. I loved him. I love him differently now, a feeling that is more about a memory that feels difficult to hold onto. He'll always be there. I told myself when I was ready to start dating again, that I wouldn't compare anyone else to him. That I would try my best not to compare myself to who I was before with him. I'm not the same person who married Rupert. I'm not even the same woman I was when I first drove into this town."

"That person ran out in the middle of a storm to try and lift me out from under a tree. I like that person, just as I like the woman in front of me."

She smiled. "I still don't know what I was thinking. How did I think I was supposed to lift a man as big as you?"

I shrugged, my bear preening. "You tried. And I will be forever grateful for that."

Sage sighed and looked up at me. "I'd like to get to know you more. Discover everything. This pull? I can't stop it."

I moved forward then and slowly trailed my fingers across her chin. "This pull? It's magic. It's a bond that ties us together. We can walk away. Even if I kiss you right now, even if we find out who we could be together, that pull doesn't mean we will ever complete the bond."

She frowned. "What does that mean?"

"Once I mark you as mine, that completes the bond. Sex isn't part of it. It can be, and that's usually when someone marks another, but sex is more part of the pull, a bit of what completes us. If we slept together right now, I'd be claiming you as mine but not as my mate. Not forever. Does that make sense?"

She swallowed hard, and I wanted to reach out and bite her lip, have her taste.

"Why do I feel like everyone else understands this whole fated mate thing but I'm still falling behind?"

"You aren't. The fact that you're here right now? It's not you being behind."

"I used magic today," she said again, her eyes wide. "I used magic and power, and I have my store. I bake, I provide. Everything I'm doing...I'm changing. And yet, you're always there in the back of my mind. I want to know who you are, Rome. Can you show me?"

I nodded and leaned forward. "As long as you kiss me first."

She rose on her toes, and I leaned down.

When she brushed her lips against mine, I was lost.

CHAPTER THIRTEEN

SAGE

Rome slid his hands down my sides, bracketing my hips, and I moved closer to him, groaning. I couldn't breathe, couldn't think. All I wanted was to taste him, to feel him. I groaned again, needing more. And then, he pulled away.

I frowned, confused. "What?" I asked, my body shaking.

"I don't want to do too much, not when I want to strip you down and bend you over this table."

My eyes widened. "Oh." I shook my head. "That word seems to be the only thing I can say these days."

"I kind of like that I make you speechless."

"I'm not normally. Usually, I ramble. Especially when I'm nervous. And I'm nervous."

"You are?" he asked, his voice a deep rumble. His lips lifted into a smile as he studied my face as if he were trying to understand who I was. I did the same with him. I looked into those dark eyes of his, at that chiseled jaw beneath the big beard, at how he filled out the shirt he wore, and I swallowed hard. Magic and fate had brought us together at first, but I liked the man I saw. And I wanted to know more about him.

I swallowed hard and winced as I looked at the fish tank on the wall.

"I think I'm sloshing the fish around again," I said, frowning.

He sighed. "At least you're not knocking the water out. Don't worry. The fish are fine. If they weren't, I'd have moved them to a safer place. But Rowen helped with a spell."

"I need to get a better handle on my water affinity if I want to stand in this room again."

"You're already more controlled. I can see it."

"Are you telling the truth?" I asked as I walked towards him.

He nodded as he looked down at his fish. They happily swam and wiggled towards me, and I could have sworn that one little fish waved.

"The fish are fine, as is the tank. I've seen you as you bake and around town. You do have a stronger connection to your powers. As if you're finally waking up."

I bit my lip, hoping he was right. I needed him to be right. "That's still new to me, and I'm trying not to break everything."

"You're doing a fantastic job, Sage."

"Thank you," I said, giving him a shy smile. "Do you want to see some of it?"

His eyes widened. "See some of what?" he asked, and I blushed.

"My magic. Not, uh, anything else."

He laughed then, low and deep, and it did things to me that I didn't want to think about. Not that I didn't want what those feelings meant, more that I needed to focus on something else, or I would end up embarrassing myself.

"Show me some of the magic you've learned. If you can and feel safe enough."

"I can show you some. Rowen wants me to practice. Though I'm not sure I can do everything without her here."

He nodded, running his hands over his beard and looking far too attractive for his own good. "When we were first learning to shift as cubs, our parents were always around. And then when we snuck off to try to do it on our own, I swear our parents always knew. They didn't want us to hurt ourselves or lose energy because we did too much."

"Those baby bears are adorable." I smiled as we made our way to the back, remembering the little triplets. His yard was situated amidst a copse of large trees, creating a sanctuary.

"Those baby bears are trouble with a capital T, but considering I was pretty much the same way when I was younger, I can't say anything."

The thought of Rome as a baby bear made me smile, and I shook my head.

"You were in a gang of triplets like them, then?"

"Yes, for most of it. Alden was always a bit quieter than Trace and me, so we didn't get into as much mischief."

There was something he *wasn't* saying there, but I didn't want to steer the conversation to something that made him sad, so I moved on.

"You have a little pond here," I said, looking down at the waterscape.

"The stream is here, as well. Enough water for you to play with."

"Or severely mess up."

He shook his head. "Rowen wouldn't have you prac-
ticing on your own if that was the case."

"Sometimes, I feel like you have far more confidence in
my abilities than I do. But, sure, we can practice."

"What did you do before you were here?" he asked
suddenly, and I frowned.

"You mean, how did I handle the bakery before I came? I
did all of the baking and set up everything for Sabrina to
close. Or did you mean before I moved to Ravenwood?"

He tilted his head, studying my face, somehow
reminding me of his bear form, though I'd only seen his
brother as one. "The latter."

I blushed. "I baked. I worked at a bakery run by a
friend, actually, and did all of the baking for her. I pretty
much ran the place because she has six kids, and while she
was still the owner and made the tough decisions, I did the
rest."

"You have a lot of experience. Ravenwood is lucky to
have you."

I blushed again. "I hope so. It's scary but thrilling at the
same time. I love my shop. Ravenwood Sweets is everything I
thought it could be."

"I love the honey buns. And the honey bread. Pretty
much anything that you make that has honey in it."

I shook my head, my lips twitching. "Could you be more
of a bear stereotype?"

"I could, but you haven't seen me rub my back against a
tree yet."

I snorted, imagining it. "Wait, in bear form or human
form?"

"I'm not going to answer that for fear of humiliating
myself."

I laughed again and shook my head. "So, what is it that you do?" I asked.

He frowned. "What do you mean?"

"I mean, they said you're the cleaner and the fixer, but I don't know what that means."

He shrugged as he stuck his hands into his pockets. He was still so close to me that I could feel the heat of him, his need, but we were both excellent about not mentioning it. "I am all of that. I help build furniture and other things around the area, too. I've helped build houses, and I make other things. I'm good with my hands."

He winked as he said it, and I blushed. "Rome."

"Sorry. I am. And, one day, I hope you'll see."

"Maybe," I said primly.

He grinned, looking far more like a cat in cream than a bear. "This town takes a lot of upkeep, more than a normal one."

"I saw the damage the revenants did. And, sometimes, I see the small accidents around town from shifters or other witches who need help. Or maybe it's even the so-called fae since I don't know if they truly exist."

"First, you've seen the fae already. You've met them. You know them. You just don't know how to recognize them yet."

I frowned. "I know the fae?"

"You do. They look human."

I frowned. "Do they shift?"

"That's not my story to tell." He gave me a cautious look, and I nodded, understanding. He smiled softly again before changing the subject. "The town constantly gets damaged in some way. Windows are blown out and things. Random things happen when people have magic or turn into giant animals. Jaxton and I clean up after them. It's our job as alpha and wing leader, but more so as fixers to ensure that the town is safe. That means we're the ones cleaning up others' messes and making sure that things look as if it was a power outage or a gas leak. Covering up anything unsuspecting eyes see that they shouldn't. We—Jaxton and me—clean it up."

"And you do it because you're alpha?" I asked, trying to understand.

He shook his head. "No, other alphas would probably assign someone. Jaxton and I are just good at what we do, so we tend to gravitate towards that."

"You've been friends your whole lives, then?" I asked.

He nodded. "Jaxton and Ash were part of our group. It was the five of us, all through school and high school. Ravenwood holds our pack and wing and is our home, though my brothers and I go up to Canada often."

"Because your father is the Alpha of all bear shifters in both continents."

He nodded. "It's a heady responsibility, one I may have to assume one day," he said softly. My eyes widened.

"You'd have to move to Canada?"

He shook his head. "No, my father took over that pack because the alpha needed him to. If my father needs to step down someday and I become the next Alpha of all bears, I can do that from my stronghold here. Our mantle isn't forced to be in one area, but rather where the Alpha is the strongest."

"That's a lot of responsibility, Rome." I looked at him then, at the strength of him, and knew he could do it.

Except, if I were his mate, I would have to be by his side, right? "Shifters can only be born?" I asked quickly.

His mouth quirked into a smile. "Yes. If you're my mate,

you're not going to turn into a shifter. You would be alpha with me."

I ignored the squeezing in my chest. "As a witch. Is everyone okay with that?" I asked, speaking as if mating was a foregone conclusion. I wasn't there yet, but I could see it. Feel it.

"I'm not sure," he said after a moment, freezing me.

"What do you mean by that?" I asked.

"There's a lot going on with my pack, things I'm starting to see now that opinions are out in the open. Things that I need to work on, but I don't want to burden you with that. At least, not yet."

"Because we haven't made a decision one way or another," I said softly.

"And because the burden isn't one I know the details of yet to share." He shook his head, and I wanted to reach out and hold him, only I didn't know if I'd help. He cleared his throat. "Trace, Alden, Ash, Jaxton, and I pretty much roamed all over town and figured out where we fit. Being an EMT, Trace helps with healing, Alden is better with numbers and is an accountant, and Jaxton and I fix what we can around town. Ash, well, Ash was Ash."

I frowned. "Laurel's brother?"

"Yeah, he left town a few years ago and hasn't been back since. He grew up with us until things changed."

It sounded like every word he said was being pulled from him, so I didn't push. I didn't ask. I didn't want to hurt him. I hated that he sounded so pained while thinking about his friend.

"Now, are you going to show me some magic?" he asked, and I bit my lip.

"Maybe. Let's make sure I don't accidentally blow something up."

"You don't have an affinity for fire or earth. I think I'm good with water."

"Unless I drown you," I singsonged.

He snorted. "Bears can swim."

"Whatever you say." I let out a breath and held up my hands.

"Guardians of the west, lend me your strength. Lord and Lady, lend me your ear. Shape this element into a sphere. Great Undine of water and sea, this is my will, so mote it be."

Rome leaned closer towards me, and I could feel the heat of him. I felt his bear. I knew that no matter what happened, he would be there. I wasn't alone. A small sphere of water levitated over the pond, and I kept my eyes open, watching as it spun in a circle, flicking off little droplets as it did. I moved the ball from palm to palm, not letting it brush my skin but feeling as if I were struggling with a single ball.

Rome let out a rough chuckle, and I tossed the sphere towards him. He stumbled back, but I didn't get him wet. Instead, I pulled the water toward me and rose another sphere into the air. I juggled the two, but I could feel my energy drifting a bit, so I let them fall gently into the pond.

"You learned that today?" he asked, his eyes wide.

I rubbed my palms on my pants, magic itching through my body. I was full of energy, my body tight, my breasts full. I needed him, the energy pulsating through me reaching for him. His nostrils flared, and I knew that he could scent me. Sense the power, the *need* within me.

"I learned that today. But this? *This* is new. I didn't have this when I practiced with Rowen."

"Using that much magic? With that much skill? Oh,

yeah, it can pull you against something. And with me here? I can see why."

That made me laugh. "You're saying you're the reason I feel like I need to climb you like a tree right now?" I asked, surprising myself.

That seemed to surprise *him* because he threw his head back and laughed, a deep bellow that made me smile. "Now that's an image. And you're always welcome to climb me like a tree, Sage."

"Will using magic always do this to me?"

He shook his head. "No. But sometimes, with the right elements around? It can."

"Oh. Good." And then I jumped. I couldn't help it. Energy and need coursed through me. I could barely hold it back.

Rome caught me, though I seemed to have surprised him. He didn't move back. He was so strong, hard, and he held me, one hand cupping my ass as I wrapped my legs around him. I pressed my lips to him, and his mouth parted. I groaned, exploring him, needing him. He squeezed my ass, and his other hand moved to grasp the back of my neck. He tilted my head, deepening the kiss, and I groaned, needing more.

"Sage," he whispered.

"Need this. Need. This." I didn't care if it was magic or the shifter bonds I didn't understand. *It was real.* This feeling wasn't fake or contrived. Between us was desire I had been ignoring since I first saw him, and it had only built on itself as I learned more about myself and him.

I needed this. Needed him. Rome kept kissing me, my body shaking, his hands roaming.

I let my hands drift down to his shoulders and squeezed,

and then moved them around to his back, letting my finger-nails scrape him before grasping his hair. I kept exploring him, needing to touch him. He was so much taller, that if he hadn't been holding me like this, it likely would have been hard on me to kiss him.

He was so strong. He could touch me, do anything right now, and I probably would nearly fall over the edge. He kissed me again, and then he broke away, panting, his fore-head pressed to mine.

"Whoa," he whispered.

"Yes, whoa," I panted.

I kissed him softly again, and he smiled. "I'm enjoying getting to know you, Sage."

I looked at him then, and I was lost. I smiled. "I'm enjoying getting to know you, as well," I whispered. I kissed him again, this time slower, with more pressure. I somehow knew this was where I needed to be. If only for this moment. I raked my fingers down his chest, and he grinned down at me. "

Are you sure?" he asked as he bit my lip.

"Yes, I am." Magic sparked within me, and I let out a breath.

He ran his hand over my face, and I kissed him again. "I need you," he growled, and I swallowed hard. "We can stop. We can stop right here."

I shook my head. "The magic within me? It's like I'm so full of power, too full of everything. I need to release it. And I need you, Rome. Since the first moment I saw you, I've needed you." I couldn't imagine myself saying those words to anyone else or at any other time in my life, but it was the truth. I *did* need him. And I wanted him.

As he kissed me again, I groaned. He smiled and bit my

lip. "I need you, too, but I'm pretty sure you already knew that." He rocked into me, and my thighs trembled.

Slowly, he lowered himself to the ground, and I straddled him, running my hands over his body. "I don't know what's going on with me, but I know that I like you, Rome. I like you a lot."

He smiled, his eyes darkening. "I like you, too, Sage. Your power, your peace, how you feel on top of me right now."

I blushed and leaned down to kiss him again. "I'm not ready for a mark or anything that will bring us to full mating." I stilled, afraid I'd hurt him, then relaxed marginally as he nodded.

"We can take our time for that."

I looked up at him and then frowned. "Are you sure your bear will let you do that?"

His chest rumbled, and the sensation went straight to my warmth. I groaned. He seemed to smirk at that, knowing what he had done.

"My bear will listen to me because I have control of it. But you feel it, too, don't you? The pull? Of what we could be when together?"

"Of course, I do. And as I said, I like you, Rome. I like how you are with others, the way you are with me. I want you."

"Then have me," he whispered. I leaned down and kissed him again, and he rolled over on top of me.

He tugged at my clothes, and the magic within me pulsated, clouding my brain, pushing me towards something I knew I wanted. But the human part of me, the bit in my past, wouldn't have allowed me to think that. Before, I would've thought too hard, bit my lip over my indecisions, and then walked away out of fear.

I wasn't that person anymore. I had fought, I had used magic, I had faced down the darkness. And now, I was kissing the man I wanted, that I felt such a strong pull to that it was hard to sleep. Hard to breathe. And I wasn't backing down.

I tugged at his shirt, and he rose, pulling it over his head.

"Will anyone see us?" I asked, aware that we were outside.

He shook his head. "It's private, and I'll be able to scent or sense anyone who comes near. I promise."

I looked into his gaze and nodded. "I trust you." And I did. I trusted him with everything, even though it might be scary to do so.

He lowered his head and captured my lips.

I sighed, running my hands up and down his thickly muscled back. He was so strong, so full of energy. It was hard to keep up, hard to do anything but want him.

He lowered his head, nipped at my chin, and then slowly kissed his way down between my breasts and over my stomach. I groaned, and he undid the clasp on my bra.

"Oh," I said as I leaned up.

"Oh." He grinned and then moved to lick at my breasts, nipping at my nipples and slowly tugging on the turgid peaks. I leaned into him, sliding my hands through his hair as he kissed me gently and sucked at my nipples. My core tightened, and my legs pressed into his sides. He hummed against my nipples, and I frowned, watching how he gently played his lips along my skin. He twisted and tightened until I nearly came, my entire body shaking.

He kept kissing down my torso until he reached the

waistband of my pants. I looked down at him then, saw his dark hair between my legs, and knew I was damp—so damn wet. And when he pulled down my pants, tossing my shoes to the side, as well, I grinned.

"Rome," I whispered.

"Let me take care of you." And then he was kissing me, gently biting my inner thighs before paying attention to my clit, lapping at me, parting my folds.

"So pretty and pink," he whispered, blowing cool air along my heat. My body bowed, my toes digging into the earth, and I could feel the water in the air and in and around the pond, slowly rising to the surface. He looked around us, then raised a brow.

"Sleeping with a witch is going to be interesting."

I raised a brow right back. "Your eyes are gold. I'd have to say sleeping with a bear will be interesting, as well."

"I'll have to make sure I can keep up."

And then his mouth was on my pussy again, and I shook. He kissed me, sucked me until I came from his mouth and nothing else. I shuddered, my entire body quaking as my legs wrapped around his head. He hummed, flicking his tongue against my clit. And then he knelt again, tugging off his pants. I sat up, my body sated yet still strung as tight as a bow as I helped him with the button on his jeans.

"Condom," I said. "We need a condom."

He shook his head and frowned. "We're not fully mated. And I'm a bear. I'm not going to give you or get an STD."

"What?"

"We're fated mates, Sage. We can't get pregnant without the mating mark. And that's not what we're doing tonight. If and when we decide to go there, there are herbs you can take for that. Or birth control. STDs aren't spread among my kind. I can't get you sick, and you can't hurt me."

I blinked. "That's nice to know," I said and then nearly swallowed my tongue as he slowly pulled himself out of his pants. He was thick, his cock wide and long, and I had a feeling I wouldn't be able to even wrap my hand around him.

I reached out and slowly played with the droplet of moisture at the tip of his dick. "Um, Rome. I'm not sure that's going to fit," I said.

"I'm pretty sure we can make it work," he said as he slowly leaned over me and captured my lips again. The head of his cock played with my folds, and I groaned, letting my legs fall to the sides. "Don't worry. I'll be gentle."

I looked up at him then and only thought of Rome, nothing else. I wasn't the same person I had been before. Someone I would never be again. I was here, and this was now, and it was who I needed to be.

It might be magic, or it might be something I didn't understand fully just yet. Regardless, it didn't matter. Because this was the place I wanted to be right now, the person I wanted to be with. As he slowly entered me, I met his gaze and let my lips part, needing to say his name, wanting to say something. But I couldn't. All I could do was hold onto him and know that this was the beginning. The start of everything. He slowly slid deep inside me, my body stretching to accommodate him. He was thick and pulsating, nearly ready to come just like I was. Then his mouth was on mine, and he kissed me softly, his hands on my breasts before they tangled with mine as he slowly thrust in and out of me, treating me with such tender care that I almost cried. But I didn't. Not yet. I simply let myself fall. After so long of being scared to do more than just be, I let myself fall. I let myself be with him.

He kissed me, over and over again, his body filling mine. I looked up to see the bear in his eyes, the anchor on his body looking at me, all of us one. The water rose from the pond, my magic sustaining it as it twinkled under the lights from the forest. I knew this was now. This was who I needed to be. When I needed to be. This was forever. This was what I wanted, what I needed. And when Rome came, roaring my name, I saw his fangs elongate. My eyes widened, and he shook his head and lowered his brow. "Sage," he growled, and my fingernails dug into his back. I nearly tilted my head, almost let him bite me. Let him mark me. But this wasn't the time. Not yet. As we came together under the sky, surrounded by the forest that was his, and the water that was mine, I knew it was inevitable. We were inevitable. I would fall in love with Rome, and nothing would stop me—not my past, not my future, and not the magic running through my veins.

He fell to the side, bringing me with him, his hardness still deep within me. I sighed, needing more.

Needing everything.

Soon, we would figure out who Faith was and what the darkness wanted. But I was here now, a witch, part of something more than I had ever been before.

The veil of uncertainty that had been wrapped around me for my entire life was gone. I was here.

I was a witch. I had power. And soon, I would be Rome's.

All the choices I had made. Choices I would make. They were forever mine.

CHAPTER FOURTEEN

SAGE

"Sage, darling, will you work on this for me?" Aunt Penelope asked as she handed over an herb packet, as well as a vase of water.

I frowned and looked at it. "What do you need me to do?"

"It's a housewarming spell. I like to re-up it every month for this reading room. I'll add the flowers to it, new cuts whenever the blooms start to fade, and it'll be nice for whoever needs to sit in here and find comfort."

"Oh, I know this spell." I smiled as the magic within me rose.

She nodded and patted my hand. "It's a spell that I can do, so I'm sure you'll thrive with it. Maybe only add a pinch of the herbs rather than the whole sachet like I do since you have more power than I do."

It was so odd to hear her speak of that. My mother had no power, and yet I was told I had so much. I felt it, too. Yet if I could share some with my aunt, I would try.

I shook my head. "Are you sure? Maybe I should ask Rowen."

"Rowen wrote instructions right on that little scroll of paper attached to it. And knowing Rowen, she probably wrote instructions for you specifically." I laughed at that and unrolled the tiny scroll attached to the sachet.

Penelope, use the packet. A little pinch for Sage. She knows what she's doing. And good luck for hearth and home.

She had written out the spell, and I nodded, memorizing it.

"Okay, I can do this. I feel like I'm helping."

Aunt Penelope stopped what she was doing and looked at me before cupping my face. "You, my darling niece, always know what you're doing."

I sighed. "That doesn't seem to be the case all the time."

"You seem to know what you're doing with learning the magic, becoming part of the town, and learning to be a witch."

"True, but I don't know everything."

"Maybe we should talk about a certain bear you should invite over for dinner."

I blushed. "Aunt Penelope."

"What? Your mother isn't here. She can't get on your case about the very handsome man."

"I wouldn't be able to tell Mom about everything."

My aunt frowned. "No, my sister wouldn't be allowed to know everything. It's understandable."

"She must know some, right? I mean, she kept her maiden name even after she married Dad."

My aunt smiled. "Because she still believed in some things when she was younger and married your father. I think that memory faded away over time. Our family keeps our maiden names so the Prince line stays strong."

I frowned. "But I changed my name when I got married."

"You did, but you are strong. And the Prince family still lives in you."

"Did I harm us by not knowing? I should have known at least some of this."

"Your mother wanted to keep you safe. And then she didn't remember what Ravenwood was at all."

"Sometimes, I feel like it hindered me."

"There was a reason she kept you in the dark. There's a reason she doesn't remember much from Ravenwood. Once you leave the town, memories fade. And, honestly, I think that's on purpose."

"I don't know how I feel about that."

"We're all learning, darling. About who we are, and who we need to be."

"And yet I feel like I'm making a mistake. That I'm missing something."

"You are still figuring out who you are and who you need to be. And, yes, you may be taking things a little slow with a certain bear in our lives, but I trust Rome. And I like the idea of him for you."

I frowned as I looked at the sachet and the vase. "You do?"

"I trust Rome wholeheartedly. He's been alone for a long time. Never settling down with anyone. You don't have to marry your mate or even find your mate for true happiness, but for some reason, I always felt like he was waiting for a woman, the one who would step into his life and connect to him."

"And you think that person is me?" I asked softly. I

thought about his hands on me and how he took care of me.
The way I felt when I was with him. And I thought maybe
that could be true.

"I think it could be. I see how you two are with each
other."

My heart warmed, and the power within me flared,
wanting Rome, wanting to complete the bond. The other
part of me needed time to think. I was a thinker, even if I
sometimes jumped in too quickly.

"I like the man I know, and I can see myself being with
him. But a forever bond...that's something that could change
everything."

"It *will* change everything. And it should."

"I suppose I should focus on the magic at hand instead of
fated mates and bonds that are starting to stress me out."

"Say the spell, and let's work on that home and hearth."

I nodded, added the herbs to the water, and spoke the
incantation.

*"Herbs and words do magic bring, protect this space from
fall to spring. Invite those in who need this place, for comfort,
joy, and even grace. Powers rise of three times three; this is my
will, so mote it be."*

Heat and magic infused into my skin, and I looked down
at the now perfectly crystal-clear water in the vase and
smiled.

"Just a pinch of herbs, and wow," Aunt Penelope said
from my side.

"I already feel warmth, like I'm coming home."

"That's the point of the spell, and I love it. It doesn't
change how anyone feels. It doesn't alter their perception.
All it does is allow you to calm and to find your center.
Perfect for a bookstore when you are trying to relax for a

moment before you have to get on with the rest of your day."

"All of that with a single pinch of herbs." I shook my head.

"It takes me a whole sachet, and sometimes it still doesn't quite work out the way I want it to. You are so powerful, Sage. I'm sorry that I didn't understand that."

I frowned. "What do you mean?"

"I knew you were special before, but I thought it was because you were my niece. I didn't realize it stemmed from anything else. I think a veil of uncertainty shrouded us all. Sometimes, I wanted to talk to you and tell you everything. Bring you here. But at other times, I didn't understand that you were *needed* as you are. I missed so much of your life, Sage."

My throat tightened, and I nodded. "Rowen and I seem to believe that things were the way they were because of where we needed to be at the time. If any of us knew too much, maybe I wouldn't have had Rupert for as long as I did. Or we wouldn't have had what we had. I'm not sure. But if I keep thinking about the what-ifs, I'll never move forward."

Aunt Penelope touched my cheek. "You've grown so much, darling."

I smiled, my heart healing far more in the short time I'd been in Ravenwood than it ever had in Virginia. "I don't always feel that way."

We moved to the front of the bookstore, where Laurel was helping a patron. She smiled, although there was sadness in her eyes that I didn't understand. Aunt Penelope owned the bookstore and worked at it nearly every day. Laurel helped out where and when she could. I was there on my lunch breaks to be with my aunt, but this wasn't where I worked. I had the bakery next door, and Rowen had the magic shop on the other side. It was nice for all three of us to have places we called our homes away from home near one another. Laurel might not think she was coven, and I didn't know why she was cursed or what held her magic back. Since I was focusing on my power, I didn't want to hurt her by asking, but I still felt as though she was a part of us.

As if she were my sister.

As if Laurel could see into my thoughts, she smiled at me. "I couldn't sleep last night. I don't know why, that's just the mood. I felt your magic, though. You're coming along nicely."

I blushed. "It was the hearth and home spell."

"I remember that one. Rowen is probably the best at it, but she's of air, though my brother is of earth, so he can usually do more housekeeping spells than the rest of us. That always used to make his eyes roll, but he was good at it."

"Was?" I asked, speaking before I meant to.

Laurel's expression shuttered, and she swallowed hard. "He's a sorcerer, a male witch. He's of earth. When he was here, he was part of our coven. He's no longer here, no longer part of anything. He's still my brother, and I work with him every day, online and over the phone. I help him with his businesses, but he's no longer of our magic. No longer of Ravenwood. And maybe that's for the best."

I opened my mouth to say something, but I didn't know what to say. Everyone always treaded so carefully when it came to Ash, and it hurt to think of why.

Laurel's eyes widened, and she suddenly held her sword. I frowned, and then I whirled.

"Sage!" Aunt Penelope screamed, and I rushed towards my aunt.

It wasn't a spell gone awry. No, it was Faith.

And she wasn't alone.

"I tried to be reasonable last time, but you're not listening. Now, I need you to understand. Oriel will bring war, and then you will know the true power you've been missing. Join us, Sage. Stop working with Ravenwood and join us. Choose the winning side, not those who will perish fighting for what they cannot have."

She shoved out her hands, water pouring from her palms.

I threw my hands into the air, creating a wall of water to block Faith's. My aunt Penelope let out a sharp sound and moved behind the counter. Laurel shoved a dagger into Penelope's hands. "You know how to use it."

I blinked. "She does?"

Laurel gave me a tight nod. "She does. We may not be able to use magic, but we can still fight. Weapons training will be next for you."

"If there is a next," Faith said, grinning.

Faith slammed down her hands, and revenants poured through the windows. Glass shattered, the door fell off its hinges, and books began floating in the water Faith slowly made rise within the building.

My aunt's face blanched, and I wanted to kill this woman. I realized I would kill Faith if I could. At least hurt her if I couldn't take a life. Because she was hurting my aunt, the woman I always came to when I needed help. My family.

Damn this necromancer for daring to try and hurt her.

I stood in front of Faith as Aunt Penelope and Laurel used their blades against the revenants.

A screech sounded as a giant hawk flew through the broken window and began clawing out some of the revenants' eyes. Rowen was there an instant later, barreling through the line of revenants, using her air magic to push them out of the way.

"Faith is mine, Sage. Protect your aunt."

The hawk flew above us, clawing, protecting us, and fighting. I used my water magic to create a long sword. It was the only weapon I could make, as far as we had gotten during training, and thrust it towards the revenants. It pierced their flesh, and water began to gurgle out of their mouths.

I tried to propel the water out of the shop, attempting to protect the books, the shop itself, anything that my aunt loved. I needed to safeguard those I loved. Rowen and Faith began circling one another, and Faith just winked.

"This is only the beginning, dear Ravenwood. Oriel says hello."

Rowen frowned, her face fierce. "Who is Oriel?"

"You don't know? You should. And you will. Soon."

Rowen slashed out with a dagger, and a man came out of the darkness from the back door. I didn't recognize him. A stone flew through the air in front of him, propelled by his magic, and smashed into the dagger.

"Not today," he growled, and Rowen's eyes widened.

Laurel grinned for a minute, surprise on her face, and I wanted to know who this stranger was. He had dark hair, blue eyes, and a strong jaw. The hawk shrieked, and the man winked at him before going back to fighting at Rowen's side. My friend and fellow witch stiffened for a moment before she looked at the other man, nodded tightly, and they moved towards Faith as one.

Faith looked between them, a small smile playing on her lips. "Interesting. Very interesting."

And then she shoved out her hands, lightning crackling

on her fingertips. The revenants moved forward, and then...
she was gone.

Laurel cursed under her breath, and the rest of us went
to work destroying the remaining revenants. I hated what
Faith had done with these corpses, with the bodies that had
once contained the souls of those who had been loved. I
didn't see any of the bear shifters, but I knew they were out
on a hunt. Those who remained were here, protecting us.

I hugged my aunt tightly as everybody began cleaning
up. My chest heaved, and I looked over at the stranger.
Laurel smiled and threw her arms around him.

"I didn't know you were coming."

"I didn't know I needed to be here," he said, his voice
wooden.

Rowen rolled her shoulders back. "You weren't needed."

"What if I was?"

I now knew who this man was—this stranger who had
saved us. When I looked over, I saw Rome running towards
us, Trace at his side. They both had looks of surprise on their
features, and I knew who was here.

Ash was back.

As was Faith.

CHAPTER FIFTEEN

FAITH

F aith moved through the hallway and up the stairs to where her lover sat. He sprawled on a large chair, phone in his hand. He raised a single dark brow, a smirk on his face. "It's done, then?" he asked, his voice low, a deep, throaty purr.

Faith grinned. "Oh, it's done. He's back. Now, the key players are all here. Just like you said they would be."

Her lover grinned. "Of course, things are coming along, moving down the right path. It's our plan. I would never have even let us come here without everything in place. They don't even realize the chess game they're playing."

He held out his hand, lightning sparking off his fingertips and onto the dying wolf below. The shifter was in human form, naked, and covered in cuts. Faith grinned.

"A present for me?" she asked as she crawled onto her lover's lap. The man with dark eyes and a wicked grin kissed the top of her head as she snuggled against him.

"Of course." His voice was smooth as whiskey, low, deep, and tantalizing.

Faith leaned down and brushed her lips against his. He tugged on her hair, a punishing grip, then pulled her head back and crushed his mouth to hers. He bit her lip, causing her to bleed, and then lapped at the blood, laughing.

"They don't even realize what they have in that little girl, do they?" he asked, kissing down her throat.

Faith chuckled. "No, they never do. They think that fate decided to hide Sage from them all this time. They don't even realize that it was you."

Her lover grinned. "Of course, they don't. They didn't need to know that I was the one who forced them to never realize Sage was missing. They didn't know anything. Now, they will. They don't understand curses. If they did, they might've broken a few. Piece by piece, our plan is coming together. Soon, Ravenwood will be ours. He kissed Faith again, and she snuggled into him even as they tangled their fingers together. Lightning struck out from their twined fingertips, and the wolf beneath them screamed, agony pouring off him. Faith smiled again.

"What do you say we make things interesting?" Faith asked, a wider smile playing on her lips.

"How interesting?" he asked.

"A few players are a little too much for our board. I'm working on one of them. It will take some time, but it's been years in the making. There's another, one we don't need anymore. Their time is up, don't you think?" Faith asked, and her lover grinned.

"Oh, their time has been up for a long while. It will be good to hear them scream." He kissed her again, and she moaned. They stripped each other, both naked and writhing in the chair as they made love. Lightning pierced the air around them, blending with the screams of the dying man and sending them over the edge.

"Soon," he whispered as he slid his hands down her sweat-slick back, the jagged waves of her anchor tattoo wrapping around his hand.

"Soon," he repeated. Faith fell asleep, her lover wrapped around her, still deep inside her, and his magic soothing her soul—whatever she had left of it.

CHAPTER SIXTEEN

ROME

My hands clung to the steering wheel, my fingers turning white as I let out a slight growl. I nearly drove off the road when a gentle hand touched my forearm. I looked over at Sage as she gripped my arm, and she shook her head.

"Breathe, Rome. We're okay."

I let out a breath through my nose, inhaled again before I turned down the street towards her cottage.

"I'm not okay right now," I growled, my bear pushing at me. It wanted me to shift, to eviscerate anything in its path, but I couldn't do anything about it. The revenants were gone, as was Faith, at least for the time being. Someone had tried to hurt Sage again, and I hadn't been there. I didn't know if I could deal with the fact that I couldn't always be there to protect her.

"I'm going to need to run," I growled, hating myself for being so weak.

Sage patted my arm again as if she didn't know what to say. I didn't blame her. I wasn't acting like the bear she knew.

Hell, I wasn't acting like the bear I recognized in the mirror, for that matter.

I pulled into Sage's driveway. "Let me help you out."

"Rome, I can handle myself. You saw that."

"I know," I growled, my bear at the surface. I let out another breath and gripped the steering wheel tight enough that I knew I'd break it off if I weren't careful. Like when I'd been a teenage bear learning my first tendrils of control. "Let me do this. I need to."

Sage met my gaze. "Of course. Come on."

I turned off the car, got out, and went around to help her out. I opened her door, and she already had her seatbelt off, her purse clutched to her chest. I held out my hand. "Let me walk you inside."

Her gaze softened, and my bear wasn't sure how to take the look. "It's okay, Rome."

"I'm usually much better at controlling this."

"I know you are, and you are in control."

I shook my head. "I'm not. If I were, I wouldn't be growling and ready to rip off anyone's head who dared to come near you."

She squeezed my hand. "You're not. You're not hurting anybody. You're not hurting me. You're doing fine."

I still held her hand as I gave her an incredulous look before I went to the front door.

"How about I let myself in, and you walk around with me to make sure nobody's here?"

"How did you know I was about to take the keys from your hand?" I asked, swallowing hard.

"I was trying to think of what I would do if someone had attacked you, and I was the one who needed reassurance."

I nearly tripped over my feet. "Are you serious?" I asked, blinking.

"It's okay, Rome. We'll take care of each other. Now, your hands need to be free, or I guess they're claws. I will get the door open. Rowen has wards here, and since it's just me, it's easier than a place of business." Her lower lip trembled, and I cursed.

"We're going to clean up the bookshop."

"My aunt has put so much into it, and the revenants and Faith nearly destroyed it all."

I shook my head. "Between the fae, Jaxton, and Rowen, it'll look brand-new. The cosmetic things? We can clean that up. We can fix it."

"Not the insecurity that Aunt Penelope feels. Or what *you* feel."

"I'm not insecure," I growled as I stormed around the small cottage she rented. My bear was about to burst out of my skin and prove that, but I held it back.

"You might not be insecure, but you're still growling over the idea that we were attacked. We all took care of ourselves. I didn't know my Aunt Penelope was so good with a dagger."

That made my lips twitch. "Who do you think taught Laurel to use the sword?" I asked.

Her brows rose.

"We tend to fall back on what we're good at—witches do magic, same as the fae in their way. And shifters use whatever predatory skill they have. Those who possess small power but not enough to protect those they love? They need to learn other ways. And when Laurel lost her magic, your aunt stepped up and taught her how to protect herself. That way, neither of them was forced to rely on anyone."

"I hope Laurel explains it to me someday because maybe then I could help her find a way back."

I smiled softly and reached out, pushing her hair from her face. "One day, she'll tell you. But if anyone can find a way for Laurel to get what she's lost and break that curse, it'll be the coven. You'll figure it out."

"You say that. And yet, I sometimes feel that I'll never be able to catch up enough."

"Look how far you've come already."

"Possibly," she whispered.

I nodded as I looked around the rest of the cottage. "Everything looks good."

"Good." She looked down at her hands and sighed. "I'm going to have some tea and take a breath."

"I need to...I should go." I wanted to mark her right then, claim her so everyone knew who she belonged to. And that meant I needed to leave.

Her lips twitched. "Because you're afraid to be alone with me? Or you need to be with our newcomer? Was that Ash?" she asked, and my heart stuttered, even as I nodded.

"Yes, that was Ash. I didn't know he was coming back."

"From the look on everyone's faces, including his sister's, I don't think anybody knew."

"I should go see him. He was my friend."

She tilted her head, studying my face. "Was?"

My bear clawed at me, my heart racing even as my stomach rolled. "I can't...I can't talk about it."

"It seems many people can't talk about it."

I shook my head, my brain hurting. "They're not my secrets to tell. If I tell you what I feel about them, I'll break trust. I want to tell you everything, Sage. I promise, I do. But I can't."

She reached out and cupped my face. I froze, needing more, needing to push into her, hold her close, and never let her go. "Okay," she whispered. "I understand. I'm learning and figuring things out. I'm here if you need me."

"I don't want to leave you alone," I said as I leaned down and brushed my lips against hers. I couldn't help it. I needed to touch her. Needed to be with her.

She might not be my mate in truth, but I needed her because she was mine. And as she looked at me, I had to hope that maybe she felt the same way about me.

"Will you be safe here?" I asked, not wanting to leave.

Her lips quirked into a smile. "Yes. We have wards, and this is the best place I can be for now. I'm going to call my aunt because she wanted to be alone, but Rowen still set the wards at her house."

"I would feel better if all of you guys were together."

Sage shook her head. "Aunt Penelope needed time. Rowen is doing too much and won't let me help, and Laurel is off, either with her brother or dealing with other things. We're all working with what we have. I'll be safe in my small cottage with the wards set."

"And with some of my people on your place."

Her eyes widened. "What?"

"I'm going to make sure the bears watch your place."

"You've already had them doing it, haven't you?" She narrowed her eyes.

I shrugged and stuffed my hands into my pockets. If I didn't, I'd want to hold Sage close and never let her go. I was possessive. Sue me. "My bears protect this town. They protect the people I care about. And that's you, Sage."

She ducked her head then hugged me tightly. I wrapped

my big arms around her, not wanting to let her go. "As long as they're safe. Maybe I'll bake for them."

I grinned. "Just keep the honey buns for me."

She rolled her eyes. "No, I can't do that in this town. But I will find a special treat for you." My cock hardened at that, and she laughed. "I didn't mean it to sound so sexual." She paused. "You should go." She kissed me again, and I slid my hand around the back of her neck, tightening ever so slightly so I could hold her close.

"Be safe."

"I am safe."

"I'll always want to protect you."

"The same for me with you. Now, go see your friend. Rowen will be here soon. I think something's changing. "

"I felt it, too," I whispered and kissed her again, needing her taste, her touch. I wanted her, and with the magic swirling around me, I knew she wanted me, too. Tonight wasn't the night for that, though, not with what we needed to do separately.

As I walked out of her cottage, my bear growled to go back. I looked up to find Ariel.

"We'll protect her, boss. Go see what Ash wants."

There was a bit of a rumble in her voice. I knew she didn't trust him. I didn't know if I did either, not after everything that had happened.

"Thank you for doing this."

"She's going to be our alpha. Of course, I'll protect her. She'll be good for our pack."

I tilted my head and studied her face. "You believe that?"

"Of course, I do. Not everybody's as backwards as Alden." She winced. "Sorry. I try not to say bad things about him to your face."

I held back a curse. "No, you need to speak your mind. And I'm the alpha. I need to listen, no matter the topic. Keep Sage safe. I'll check in later."

"We'll keep her safe, but you do the same for yourself."

And with that, she walked around the back of the cottage where I could already sense Sage. It seemed she wanted to introduce herself to her protectors. I liked that. And I hoped to hell more people were on a page similar to Ariel.

I got into my car and made my way back to my home, aware that I had a thousand other things to do. But first, I needed to check in with the rest of my pack—although I had done a lot of that with Ariel. And then I needed to find Ash.

I pulled in front of my house and shook my head. Seemed I didn't need to look far for Ash. He'd found me.

The sorcerer stood on my front porch, coffee in hand as he spoke with Jaxton and Trace. If Alden were there, our group would be complete. I didn't think Alden would come tonight, though, not after everything that had happened. I didn't really understand what my brother wanted these days.

I turned off my car and got out, growling. "So... you're back."

Ash looked at me then, his dark hair falling over his eyes before he pushed it back. His blue eyes seemed unnaturally bright today, as if they held magic in them. Maybe they did. I didn't understand Laurel's brother, my former best friend, anymore. Then again, what had happened to Ash hadn't been his fault, and I didn't know how to fix it.

"I came because I was called," Ash said, his voice low, devoid of feeling.

"By who?" Jaxton asked, leaning forward.

"By the town. I'm still connected to Ravenwood, even if I don't live here or have any other connections."

"I'm glad you're back." Trace hugged the other man, his shoulders loosening. Ash slowly reached out and returned the hug before moving away.

"So, the town called you," I said, leaning forward. Jaxton silently handed me a cup of coffee, even though it was my mug, my cream, sugar, and beans, but every one of my friends acted like my place was theirs. I did the same with theirs, so I didn't mind.

"Yes, the darkness has finally come. And I have a feeling this is only the beginning."

"That wasn't cryptic at all," Trace said, and Jaxton snorted, sipping his drink. I shook my head. "Where are you staying?"

"I have a place. I always have a place."

Jaxton was a near-billionaire real estate developer and business owner. He had homes all over the world, and Laurel helped with most of them, though she did so within Ravenwood's wards. It was a family business, and Ash had made it even more remarkable. Ash did everything ruthlessly but still legally. Laurel was the one who kept them moral. Ash couldn't help himself, though. That was who he was, given what had happened to him. A curse that'd changed the very essence of someone made for profound consequences.

"So, what happened?" Ash asked.

Trace sighed and began marking off critical points with his fingers. "A woman named Faith brought revenants, she's a necromancer and is working with a man named Oriel, someone we've never heard of. He keeps attacking Rome's mate."

Ash's gaze went to mine, and a single dark brow rose. "I didn't sense a bond. I wasn't sure if that was because of me and who I am, or if it wasn't there."

My heart broke for him, even as I wanted to growl. "The mating bond isn't settled yet. I'm courting her."

"Interesting way to go about it," Jaxton said, not looking at me.

I wanted to push the bird off the porch railing, but I refrained.

Ash frowned, a subtle gesture that he quickly blinked away. "You should mark her quickly, just to keep her safe."

I nearly laughed at that. "You've been away from Ravenwood too long if you think that marking her without her permission's the way to go about mating consensually."

"I saw how she looked at you when you ran towards her. She wouldn't mind the mark."

"She's new to this whole magic thing. And Ravenwood." But, fuck, I wanted to mark her. To make her mine.

"Maybe, but she's learning. She'll be fine." Ash sounded as if he didn't care about the emotion and connection that came with bonding and claiming. Maybe he didn't. Not with what he'd lost.

"Is that your witchy intuition talking? Or do you not care?" Trace asked, his voice far more growly than it had been before.

Ash shrugged. "I don't know. I don't know much of anything anymore. I know I'm not welcome here by anyone other than my sister—and maybe you on a good day," he said, looking at us. "I need to be here, though. The coven needs me."

"You know she doesn't think you are a part of the coven anymore." I kept my voice low.

Ash met my gaze, the blankness in his eyes scaring me for a moment before whatever magic behind them shone brightly again. "I can't care what she thinks, Rome. You know that."

Jaxton sighed and set his coffee down. "You'd better. Because your sister needs you, the coven needs you. This town needs you. And you were gone way too fucking long."

"Jaxton's right," I added, surprised that Jaxton had exploded a bit just then. He was the quietest of us all, the hunter who stalked his prey as we bears growled and swiped.

"You can't fix a curse. You know why I left."

"Everyone is cursed in one way or another," Jaxton whispered, and I nodded.

"You're back. And you can't leave again when things get tough."

"So you think you can fix me, then?" Ash asked. "Because I've spent these years trying to fix myself, and it hasn't worked. I know Rowen doesn't want me here. But the town needs me. So, I'm here. Even if part of me still doesn't know why."

I leaned against the porch railing and sighed.

We were a broken bunch. All of us cursed in some way as Jaxton had said. Ash was back, and we were one step closer to a new coven, one step closer to keeping Ravenwood safe.

One step closer to keeping my mate safe.

CHAPTER SEVENTEEN

SAGE

"The amount of honey buns you make during the week is bordering on ridiculous," Aunt Penelope said from the other side of the counter.

My arms elbow-deep in dough, I looked over my shoulder and smiled. "What? I'm in a town full of bears. Of course, there are honey buns. And honey loaves, and honey-filled donuts, and everything else you can imagine with honey."

"Imagine what you'd bake if you didn't have grizzlies all around you," Rome joked from Penelope's side. "I wonder what all of the smaller bears would want."

My aunt shrugged. "Probably honey. If you had to deal with the polars from up north, then you'd make a lot of salmon."

"Ooh, honey-covered salmon sounds amazing." Rome rubbed his belly.

I rolled my eyes and looked between the two of them. I had a feeling Aunt Penelope had known the exact moment I slept with Rome. Not through magic or anything, but because I couldn't hide my feelings from my face. Rome and I weren't mated yet, but there *was* something there. Something between us—and not just sex, either.

One day, and I had a feeling that day would be soon, we would mark each other and fight together against the darkness, discovering what our lives could be. For now, I enjoyed taking it decently slow as we figured out who we were and what we needed to be.

"I get the first taste, though, right?" Rome asked, his voice low.

Aunt Penelope cleared her throat. "Wow, I feel like I'm interrupting," she said with a laugh, and I shook my head.

"Behave." I leaned down and began working on the next batch. "And, of course, you get the first honey bun. You're here early this morning. The dough is ready, and it needs to prove one more time before it goes in the oven."

"And to think, I used to buy store-bought everything."

I visibly shuddered. "We'll never have to deal with that again."

"Of course, you won't. You opened the bakery for the whole town," Aunt Penelope said, cutting through the tension I hadn't even realized had risen.

It made sense because we were all figuring out where we were, and my aunt gave me time to breathe—something I desperately needed.

"Here, let me help." Rome walked forward and took the heavy tray from me. I nodded in thanks and went to set the next items. Aunt Penelope was filling in for Sabrina today since she had a dentist appointment. My aunt would go over to the bookshop with Laurel later once Sabrina came back.

And Rome was here. I think just for me, but I didn't mind. It was good to get to know him better, to be with him, even as we worked on a thousand other things. He had to go in later to help Jaxton with a few ward issues and attend a meeting with the fae. And I would be here, working. On my breaks or when there was a lull, I'd practice spells with Rowen.

I had a routine and things to do, all while we waited for what would happen next.

"You're fortunate that you washed your hands before you stepped over here, or I wouldn't have let you behind that counter," I said, teasing.

Rome shrugged. "I want some honey buns. I have to follow the health code." He leaned down to almost kiss me but looked over at my aunt first. She rolled her eyes.

"Pretend I'm not here," she singsonged and went over to work on the display. Since Rome's and my hands were empty, he leaned down and kissed me softly.

"I'm pretty sure that's against the health code," I whispered.

He shrugged. "They can give me a citation. I don't mind."

I warmed, my magic tingling at his closeness. "You need to head out soon, don't you?"

"I have a couple of hours."

His phone buzzed, and he frowned. He pulled it out of his pocket and shook his head. "Apparently, I don't. Alden wants to meet with me now so we can go over what we're going to say to the fae."

I frowned, wondering why my magic felt off at that. "Alden will be there?"

"*I* will be there with Alden. Ariel and Trace are securing the pack. We try to never have all of us in one place—except for when we're in the den itself."

"That makes sense," I said. "What do you have to talk about with the fae, anyway?"

"Our normal peace treaty. There's never been a war with them. At least, not us personally. But there was one a century ago. So, we meet once a quarter to lay out our rules." He sighed and kissed me again. "It hasn't changed in a century, and it won't now. I don't know what Alden wants, other than to tweak something as usual, but nothing ever changes. The fae are long-lived and don't tend to like change.

"Witches and shifters do?" I asked, teasing.

He shook his head. "Not even a little. I think the fae are even worse than us, though. Anyway, I'll be back soon. Be safe."

I sighed. "Rowen and Laurel are watching out, and I'm doing okay on my own. You be safe, as well. After all, you're going to treaty negotiations."

He snorted. "Yes, by *negotiations*, you mean I'm going to have coffee with a couple of people I've known for my entire life, and we're going to sign a document that already has our signatures on it. It makes total sense."

"Oh, bureaucracy. Who knew it would touch the supernatural, as well?"

I laughed then sighed, looking at the door, daydreaming about what could happen.

Aunt Penelope cleared her throat, and I nearly dropped the spoon I forgot I was holding. "You are a goner, darling," Aunt Penelope said.

I looked over at her, my heart racing. "What?" I practically squeaked out the word.

"It's so nice to see you falling again."

I swallowed hard. "You think so? That I'm falling?"

"I see how you two look at each other, the way you're so careful with one another as if you're learning each other's needs and wants. So, yes, I think you're falling. And not because of a bond that could happen."

"It feels like I just arrived, but it's been a couple of months now."

"It has," my aunt said. "You were always meant to be here. I still think something was pushing you away."

She frowned as she said it, and I leaned forward. "You're thinking of Faith."

"Yes, I've been thinking about it for a while now. Why didn't I ask you to come up earlier? When Rupert first passed. Why didn't I ask you to come when Rupert was still alive? He would have loved it here. He may not have understood it right away, but he would have felt at home."

I frowned. "What about Rome?"

"Nothing would have happened with Rome because you were already married. Mating isn't as harsh and cruel as that. It doesn't make sense that I wouldn't want my niece, my blood, a future member of the coven to be here, though. And not because it's fate and it wouldn't make sense for you to be here until the time was right. Why wouldn't I want my family here?"

"You think Faith kept me away. Kept me from thinking about my ink or how magic seemed to be all around me, even when I didn't realize it."

"Her or this Oriel, whoever he is."

I swallowed hard. "I think you're right. I've been thinking about it for a while now. Yes, I was meant to be here now, but I think fate is also a choice, and something kept me away."

"And that scares me, Sage. Because why didn't it want

you here until just this moment? And not so that you could meet Rome. Because mating can take years to develop. You can know someone for your entire life until, finally, the magic within you clicks, and you understand who you should be with. So, even if you had been here for years, you and Rome might not have realized who you were to each other until this moment. It was as if something was holding you back, and now it's pushing you like a rubber band snapping. You pull too hard or for too long, and when it comes together, it snaps or breaks in half."

"All mating isn't this intense, is it?" I asked, rubbing my heart.

"It doesn't have to be. But I don't know. It feels like something kept you away on purpose. And I don't like it."

I opened my mouth to say something more, but I stopped, looking up as water began dripping from the ceiling.

"Is that a leak?" Aunt Penelope asked, and I swallowed hard.

"I think you should get your dagger," I said, the hairs on my arms rising.

She met my gaze and pulled the blade out of the sheath on her hip. I spread my fingers, allowing my magic to come to me. We had wards on the town, the bakery, and each of our homes. We had done our best to protect ourselves. And yet, it seemed we were missing something.

Water poured from the ceiling in earnest, but none of it reached the floor. Instead, it hovered above it, over the wood and every piece of furniture. My aunt gave me a worried look.

"Is that you, Sage?"

"No, it's not me."

"She only wishes she was this strong," Faith said as she walked into the building.

My aunt whirled, looking at the necromancer. "How did you get in here?"

"You think your wards can stop me? All it takes is a bit more magic, a few more drops of blood. That's why you and your precious little coven will never win. You're not strong enough. You never will be. You are wasting much of your power so you can save your moral code, and you'll end up losing much because of it. You aren't as strong as I am. You never will be. And it's your fault that this is even happening."

I rolled my shoulders back, prepared to fight and protect my aunt. "You should go now. The others will know you're here."

"The others are already taken care of. Why do you think you're all alone here with only this little human to help you out?"

Fear coated my stomach, my tongue, and I tensed. "What did you do?"

"Do you think I'm alone? The others will be along shortly, I suppose, but we needed to keep them busy first. Now, about you." Faith sneered. "You think you know everything? You don't know anything. All you know is that you came here thinking you would find a new life. You didn't realize that the life you had, wasn't yours to begin with."

"What do you mean?" My pulse raced, and I tried to keep up, my mouth going dry.

"What I mean is that I took everything you thought you wanted. Your perfect little husband. That perfect little family. I took that, too. Did you ever wonder why Rupert's family never loved you?"

Pain sliced through me. This wasn't true. It couldn't be. What she said didn't make any sense.

The witch sneered. "I didn't let them love you. A spell here. A whisper there, and they never *would* love you. They would never trust you. As for Rupert... Do you think he died of a brain tumor, just out of the blue, with no symptoms until he suddenly had a slight headache and had to go to the doctor? No, that's not how things work."

I felt as if I couldn't breathe, as if someone were screaming in my ear, yet I couldn't keep up. This couldn't be right. What Faith was saying couldn't be true. It had to be a mistake.

"You...you killed him. How? How could you do that?"

She grinned, her eyes going dark. "Look at you. You're so lost. I took Rupert. I took your precious little husband because I could. And Oriel was right there with me, waiting. All I had to do was sit back and watch your pain grow and grow, and you got nothing. I'm the one who got everything."

"No, that's not right." My hand shook, and water sluiced into the air as if it were trying to catch up with me.

"What? You thought somebody could love you like that? No, Rupert was a part of the plan to push you back here. We're the ones who kept you where you needed to be. Now, you're lost. And alone. You think this little human in front of you will protect you. You've got nothing. You wanted to find goodness. You wanted to find a home. Still, you've got nothing. And I'll make sure you understand that."

She had killed Rupert. Somehow, she had orchestrated all of this, along with this Oriel. I couldn't bring myself to think more on it. I needed to protect my aunt, but Faith would pay.

"Who do you think you are?" Aunt Penelope asked,

standing in front of me. I wanted to reach out and pull her back, but I couldn't. Any sudden movement, and I knew Faith would lash out and do something to hurt my aunt. I couldn't let that happen.

"I'm your future." Faith flicked her hair over her shoulder. "I'm the future of this town. All you are is a little human who never got enough magic. It's so sad that you'll never be enough. It would have been nice if you'd ended up being the future of this town. Of Ravenwood. But you're nothing. You've never had enough magic. And you never will."

"Don't you dare come any closer," Aunt Penelope said, her hand outstretched. I moved closer then to stand by my aunt's side, Faith's attention on Penelope.

"Don't you dare hurt her," I growled.

"You're so cute to think you can stop me." She lashed out, ice sliding from her fingertips, forming into blades. I sent up a wall of water, protecting us and likely destroying part of my bakery. I didn't care. I had to defend my aunt. However, I needed the others to help me with Faith because she was still stronger than me.

And there was nothing I could do except fight with everything that I had.

"Oh, I see you've learned a few new tricks. They're not going to help you." She sent out wave after wave of ice blades. I blocked them. My aunt picked up a tray, stopping them as well, though some started to pierce the plastic.

"We need to get out of here," my aunt said.

"I feel the water all around this place. She set up wards. We're trapped."

"I'm not going to let her hurt you," my aunt said.

I looked at her then and shook my head. "I'm not going to let her hurt *you*," I said.

"Touching, but I'm bored." Faith raised her arms again. This time, the daggers flew into the air, larger and sharper than before. I threw up my hands again, but I couldn't stop them all. The water wouldn't be enough, not with the power she pushed at us.

My aunt met my gaze for a moment, and I screamed. Because the blades weren't coming for her, they were headed directly for my heart. It didn't matter. I wasn't quick enough.

Aunt Penelope looked at me and then push me out of the way, her grip hard on my arm as she knocked me down. And then she screamed, echoing my shout.

I yelled and reached for her, but the ice pierced her skin, near her shoulder, through her heart, her stomach—another through her neck. Blood pooled, gushed, sprayed, and I reached for her, catching her as she fell.

The other ice shattered all around us, and a blade struck my arm. I screamed as Faith grinned, and held my aunt as she shook, bleeding out in my arms.

"No!"

Faith laughed. "You can try all you want, but you'll never be as strong as me." This time, she took my aunt's dagger and smiled. "Never." Lightning wrapped itself around the blade as I held my aunt's dying body in my arms and reached up, trying to summon my magic. I couldn't. I was so scared. I couldn't do anything.

Instead, Faith winked and threw the dagger at me. I put up another wave of water, partly deflecting it, but it still slid into my stomach instead of my chest. My aunt gasped, and I looked down at her, trying to hold her, trying to do anything. My tears fell, turning to ice as they slid down my face. Pain erupted from my side as the dagger dug deep, lightning sparking and slicing into my skin. I felt my magic leaching from my body and tried to do something, anything.

Blood pooled, its dark and sticky residue coating my hands, my knees, everything. My blood mixed with my aunt's, and I felt helpless.

All I could do was lean down and hear the screams of others as they came in. As magic pulled from me, I felt my soul leaving, right along with my aunt's.

Then, there was nothing.

Only screams.

And death.

CHAPTER EIGHTEEN

ROME

My bear roared within me, and I twisted, looking over my shoulder at the town.

Alden's eyes went wide at the sound of my growl, and the two fae in front of me frowned.

"What's wrong, Rome?" the leader asked.

"Sage. Something's wrong with Sage."

Aspen, the fae leader's eyes widened. "I didn't realize you were bonded. I would say congratulations, but I do not believe it's a good time for that."

"We're not, not yet, but something's wrong."

"Go, we'll be right behind you," Aspen shouted, and I ran, my feet pounding the ground. I didn't know if Alden had joined me, but he would. He was my brother. I trusted him to be at my back, no matter what. The fae would likely be there, too, and so I ran, keeping my gaze on the town in front of me as I made my way towards the bakery. I ran as quickly as I could, my bear pushing me, scraping at my skin as I saw the water main break at the end of the street.

Jaxton flew over me, his hawk form shrieking as he

passed by before landing in front of me as I stood and looked at the bakery. I felt him shift and saw Trace running towards me, garments in hand. He tossed clothes to Jaxton, and I tried to push my way through the wall of water.

"What the hell is this?" I growled, my hands burning as I touched the scorching water.

"Faith is in there," Jaxton said. I shot him a look.

"How do you know that?"

"She's the only one I know who could do this."

"She's there." Ash came to my side, tilting his head as he studied the water. "We can make our way through."

"How?" I asked, my bear growling.

Others joined us then: the fae, Alden, Rowen, and Laurel. We were all there, looking at the wall of boiling water blocking us from getting into the bakery. None of the rest of the town had been touched, only this. I frowned.

"We'll need to push through it with magic," Ash said. "It will take everything we have to go against water since Sage is in there."

My bear could only hear the name Sage. I growled again, pushing at the water.

"You'll hurt yourself," Trace scolded.

"Maybe, but I need to see her. She needs to be okay. She's hurt," I growled again.

"Fine, we'll help," Rowen said.

"I won't be much help," Laurel added.

"You'll be enough." Ash took Laurel's hand, not Rowen's I noticed, and Laurel took Rowen's. The three of them pressed their hands to the water and began chanting a spell I ignored. Instead, I pushed my hands towards the water, trying to get through, attempting to break it down so we could get into the bakery and I could get to Sage. So I could save her.

Jaxton and Trace were at my sides, pushing at the water, as well, scalding themselves to help me get to her. The fae muttered something under their breaths, and I knew they were trying to help, as well, trying to break through the new ward. The others did what they could, each using their type of magic or power to get through. Jaxton stripped again, turned into a hawk, and then he and some of his winged brethren began flying over, hopefully to find another way in.

The town was working their hardest as one to get through. Finally, *finally*, Laurel screamed, blood pouring from her ears as Trace ran to her and caught her.

"Go," Rowen said, falling to her knees. One of the fae was there to catch her, and Ash looked down at her. I saw something flash in his eyes for just a minute, but then he was at my side as I pushed bodily through the water. The wall scorched my skin, leaving blisters, but I ignored it. I could make my way through. Ash was behind me in the hole I had made. One of the fae came, as well, and then Jaxton was there, but I couldn't see any others. I couldn't pay attention to them. Instead, I looked down at the blood on the ground and roared.

Claws burst through my fingertips, and I fell to Sage's side as I looked down at the blood covering her stomach, her arms, and chest. Then at Penelope's wide, vacant eyes.

I threw my head back and roared, the windows shattering, the wall shaking.

"Control yourself," Jaxton said, pulling me back. Sage was still in my arms, gasping for breath. I put my hand over her wound.

"Rome," she muttered, blood trickling out of her mouth.

Lightning and electricity shocked my system as I touched the dagger. I growled again. "What is this?"

"Damn it, Faith is siphoning her power," Ash said.

Jaxton was there, putting his fingers to Penelope's neck. He met my gaze and shook his head. Pain shocked me, the loss staggering. Penelope was dead. I could sense the other woman here. I knew that Faith had been the one to do it. She had killed Penelope.

A latent witch, a kind woman, someone who had been at our sides for as long as I could remember. Now, she was dead, and given their positions, I had a feeling she had died to save Sage.

"How do I stop it?" I growled, my voice so bear, I knew I was one second away from shifting.

"Mark her," Ash said, and I looked up at him.

"What?" I snapped.

"Mark her. The bond will help her push out the dagger by giving her that boost of your strength and will help her keep her magic. It'll drain you slightly, but you'll be able to keep steady and recuperate. You're strong enough for this. You're alpha."

"You can take power from me, too," Trace said.

"All of your pack will help," Jaxton said, though I didn't know if that was quite the truth. Most of the pack would, but not everybody.

"I can't take her choice from her," I growled, my bear so close to the surface, I would shift and prove that I wasn't strong enough to be alpha.

Ash snarled. "If you mark her, you'll save her."

"It's her choice," I growled.

"She can't choose if she's dead," Ash said, a hint of anger

in his tone. For a man who rarely showed emotion, that was something.

"Do it. Sage will understand," Rowen whispered as she supported Laurel. Laurel was still bleeding, probably from the pain it had caused her to use magic, and then Trace was there, keeping her steady.

Rowen looked around, her entire body shaking. "Faith is gone. But she'll pay for this. She'll pay for all of it. But we can't do anything unless we have Sage. Save her, Rome. She's our only hope."

I looked down at the woman in my arms, her eyes closed, her breaths coming in shallow pants as her magic and life seeped out of her.

"I'm sorry," I whispered.

I let my fangs elongate and pulled her neck closer to me.

Marking was how our kind mated one another. It was passionate, private. Emotional. It was an intense and personal moment. And now, everyone would watch. They would see that I would take this choice from her by force. I would take away her will. I didn't deserve to be alpha; I didn't deserve to be her mate.

But I couldn't let her die.

And so, without looking at anyone else, I slowly slid my fangs into her neck and winced as she let out a shocked gasp. Electricity shocked through my fangs, and I knew it was the magic of the dagger. Penelope's blade was coated in Faith's dark, necromancy magic.

It was killing my mate, and I couldn't let that happen. I needed to save her, even if it took part of my soul to do it.

I bit down harder, and my bear roared. A bond between Sage and me finally snapped into place. It was pure life, energy. Magic. It wrapped around my soul, and I could feel it do the same to Sage's as we became one in every way.

She was my future, my past, my present. She was everything in my life that mattered, that would prove who I could be and the man I would become.

And at that moment, nothing else mattered but her.

She was my power, my salvation.

She was everything.

I could feel her. I could feel everything.

Her eyes shot open, the gold around them echoing mine for just an instant as my bear pushed into her, saving her.

Magic shook around us, lashed at my skin, pulled at my hair as it dug into me. Ash let out a few words, a soft spell, and I witnessed him pulling the dagger slowly out of Sage's body. She began to convulse, and I pushed more energy through the bond to her.

She had to be okay. She had to stay alive. We were bonded. She was my mate. She was my future.

And she would hate me.

The others began to murmur, putting their hands on the wound to stop the bleeding. I held her and threw my head back, roaring again. Whatever glass was left in the place shattered, but Rowen used her wind magic to stop it from hurting anyone. They all gave me pitying looks, but I ignored it.

"I need to help save her," Rowen said as she knelt in front of me. "There are spells, Rome... I need to hold her."

I looked down at Penelope, the one we couldn't save, and my bear knew I needed to let go. Because my bear and I weren't in control, and I didn't want to hurt her. I couldn't hurt anyone. I handed Sage over to Rowen and staggered back, coming to my feet as my hands shook, my body now covered in blood.

I didn't say anything. I simply left. I left my mate, my family, everyone.

I needed to leave.

My bear had taken her pain, but I had to go before I saw the regret on her face. The others could stay. They could save her. I needed to go. Because I had done the one thing I'd promised I would never do, the one thing a shifter should never do.

I had taken her as my mate without her permission.

It might've been to save her, but I had crossed a line. And I deserved whatever consequences came because of it. I staggered out of the bakery, knowing the others were there, ready to hear something from me, but I couldn't say anything.

Instead, I threw back my head and roared again. The town shook, and I knew that whatever wards Rowen had in place, had to be working double-time to keep the secrets of our town.

I rolled my shoulders back and then shifted, my bones snapping into place, fur sprouting all over my body. I dropped to all fours, roared again, and then ran into the forest. I needed to breathe. I needed to push out the pain and the energy the bonding had brought.

Sage would be safe for now. I needed her to be. Because there was nothing else I could do. I had a mate.

She would hate me.

But I deserved it.

CHAPTER NINETEEN

SAGE

I could hear others around me mumbling words over and over. I couldn't tell what they were saying, and it hurt too much to focus hard enough to figure it out. There were hands on my body, soft, healing touches, but I wasn't tuned in to the outside.

I was focusing on what was inside. What clawed at me. Was it claws? Or was it something else? I wasn't sure. I had never felt this before. It was as if a thread connected me to another. What was this?

I reached out almost internally, trying to understand what was going on, and dug my fingers into its spindly yet sure grip.

It was a thread.

A bond. Something I didn't understand. What was it? What could it be?

Then I heard a soft growl. And fur slid along my skin.

It was a bear

Rome's bear.

I knew this bear. He was *mine*, creeping along the bond,

reaching for me. And then it reached out to the power within me. My magic. It pushed towards the bear, and he butted his head against my side. I smiled.

"You're here," I murmured. "Or am I here?" It didn't make sense.

Where was I? I didn't think I was awake. This had to be all in my head. If this was in my head… Where was Rome?

His bear butted my hand. Again, I smiled. This was definitely his bear. His anchor. He was here. And if there was a bond… That meant we were mated.

It had to be. This was the bond the others and he had spoken of. I could feel it wrapped around my soul as surely as I saw the bear who stared at me now.

Rome and I were mated. When did that happen? When had he marked me? I didn't know. I should be worried, but I wasn't because this was Rome.

Was this all a dream? Rome's bear headbutted me again. I looked towards the bond and blinked.

Who was that? What was happening?

"Sage, I need you to wake up. Sage, wake up."

I pushed out those thoughts—that voice that wouldn't go away. I wanted to follow Rome's bear. I wanted Rome. He would tell me what was going on. He was the one I trusted above all others. He would help me find Aunt Penelope. Pain seared me, and emotion choked me.

Aunt Penelope.

She was dead. No, she couldn't be dead. Not Aunt Penelope.

It didn't make any sense to me. How could she be gone? Did I imagine it? I had to be dreaming.

I blinked open my eyes and tried to breathe. Pain seared

my side and my chest. My heart. Everything tried to overtake me. Wanted to kill me. It felt like death.

"Sage, keep your eyes open."

I looked at Rowen and tried to breathe, attempted to call out, anything. But I couldn't.

"Sage. Keep your eyes open. Focus on me. You're in pain. I know it hurts, but we will get through this. We need to move you, though. Do you understand? We need to move you."

I tried to blink, attempted to say *something*, but no words came out. My throat was dry. Everything hurt. Why couldn't I do anything? Where was Rome?

"Rome."

"He's coming. He'll be back."

I must have said the word aloud, though I hadn't realized it. If Rome wasn't here, then where had he gone? Because I could still feel his bear. I could feel him. Therefore, he had to be near. He wouldn't leave me. Rome would never leave me.

"Where. Am. I?" Each word came out in staccato as I tried to breathe. And then I let out a sharp cry, as someone pulled me to their chest.

"Be careful with her. Don't let the stitches tear." What was Laurel growling about? It didn't make any sense.

"Stitch-es?"

"They were a quick fix to keep you steady, but we need to take you to the bookshop or maybe the magic shop. I don't know where we should go." I'd never heard Laurel sound so panicked before, and it worried me more than the pain in my side and the agony flaring through my heart.

Rowen cursed. "To the magic shop. We may need herbs that Penelope doesn't have."

Hearing Penelope's name sent pain through me. I

wanted to cry out, but I couldn't. I couldn't do anything. I hated feeling helpless. That was *not* who I was—not the woman I'd been before, and sure as hell not the woman I'd become. And yet, I couldn't do *anything*.

"What do we do with Penelope?" Trace asked. I could hear him close to me and knew he was the one holding me. I could scent his bear, detect the barest hint of forest, but it wasn't *my* bear. It wasn't my Rome. It was his brother.

This wasn't Rome. Where was my mate?

My thoughts moved in circles, and I knew I was panicking, trying not to think of my aunt or the pain making me want to throw up.

"Come on. We're going to go to the magic shop. It's the best place," Rowen ordered everyone. Rowen would help. She had to. She was so bright. She knew everything. She was my friend.

Someone set me on a bench inside Rowen's magic shop, and I realized that I must have passed out again because I didn't remember anyone moving me or taking me outside. I didn't remember anything. I did remember Penelope. I remembered her blood. I remembered death. And I remembered Faith.

"She killed Rupert," I whispered. My lips were chapped. Someone gave me water, and I could finally breathe a bit better.

"What about Rupert?" Laurel asked, her voice sharp.

"Faith. She killed Rupert and cursed his family. She did everything. I don't know, but she killed my husband, and I think she wants to kill Rome and the rest of you." I didn't know where my sudden strength came from. Still, I didn't know how much I could do just then. The others needed to know, though. I had to speak. I had to tell them what had happened and what I had learned.

"Where's my aunt?" I asked, my voice shaky. She couldn't be gone. She was, wasn't she?

"Come on. We need to get you asleep," Rowen soothed.

"No, I can't. I need something. Someone help me. Please. Where's Rome?"

"He'll be back," a familiar voice said, and I looked up as Jaxton appeared above me. "I need to go on patrol, but he will be back. You're safe, Sage. We will take care of Penelope. Trust me. We will take care of her with dignity and respect."

And then Jaxton was gone. I looked around at the others —Laurel, Trace, Rowen, and Ash. I didn't really know Ash, but he stood there, anger on his face, his eyes dark as if waiting to protect all those in his charge. But who was in his charge? Who was this man, really?

"We need to fix the rest of you," Rowen said after a moment and then hovered over me before whispering words I could barely understand.

"*Lord and Lady working for me and through me, heal this witch in her time of need. Bolster her strength, plant the seed. By air and water, earth and fire, banish the dark in these times most dire. Bring her peace, bathe her in light, make her whole this very night. With the power of the coven and blessings times three, this is my will, so mote it be.*"

I woke as if I had been asleep for centuries. And yet, my head ached as if I hadn't gotten even a moment's rest. My chest hurt, but not from an injury, from the loss of something that screamed at me. And my side burned. Yet, I was alive.

At least, I thought so.

"Sage, you're awake." Laurel walked into the room, a frown on her face as she studied a piece of parchment. "Rowen gave me a list of what I'm supposed to give you. I hope it's right."

"What do you mean?" I asked, my voice dry.

The other woman looked up at me and raised the brow with the scar as she smirked. "It seems the first thing I'm going to give you is water. Because you need it." Her voice was light as if she were afraid to hurt me, scared to say anything that might set me off.

I didn't understand. I didn't understand anything.

"It wasn't a dream. Aunt Penelope is gone, isn't she?" I asked, my voice a breath.

Laurel raised her chin, her eyes filling. I'd never seen her look like this, as if she were in pain, as if she had lost someone close to her. But she had worked with Penelope for a long time; she had been with her day in and day out. I might be Penelope's blood, but Laurel was just as much her daughter as I was her niece.

"She's gone. Faith killed her. She bled out. I'm so sorry. I'm so sorry I wasn't there to help. I'm so sorry I wasn't there to kill Faith for you."

Tears fell, and I sucked in a sharp breath, my soul bleeding. The bond I knew was there yet couldn't hold pushed at me, a very bear move where it seemed to butt its large head against me almost if to reassure me that I would be okay. "She threw her body in front of me. Why did she do that? Why did she think that it was okay for her to do that? It wasn't, Laurel. She shouldn't have done that. She shouldn't have risked everything and sacrificed herself for me. Who am I? Who am I to deserve her death?" Tears fell freely now, and suddenly Laurel was there, pressing water to my mouth, her lips pressed into a tight line as she fought for control.

I chugged it quickly, letting the comfort seep into me. My body pulsed, my magic quickening at the first taste of the healing liquid. I was dehydrated. My body needed water. But my magic needed it more.

"Faith is a strong witch with a water affinity, even though she's a necromancer. She can make weapons that I can only dream of. I tried to do so much, but I couldn't do enough."

Laurel nodded and pushed her hair back. "She put a ward around the entire building so we couldn't even get to you."

"How did you get in?" I asked, frowning.

Laurel sighed. "My brother helped Rowen and me with a spell. One I had forgotten long ago. We chanted and weakened the barrier. Then Rome barreled his way through, practically bleeding and burning himself in the boiling water to reach you."

I nearly shot out of bed, and Laurel grabbed the water before it fell to the floor. "What? Is he okay? Where is he? I haven't seen him since...since I think I was dying."

Because I *had* been dying, I knew that much.

Laurel didn't look at me, and I knew something was wrong. "He should be fine. Everybody healed soon after we cleaned up your shop. It's as good as new. You know what I mean. But they burned themselves in the boiling water that surrounded the building. That was something I have never seen before, by the way."

I tried to keep up as she told me everything that had

happened, going over the details. I sat back again, thinking. "What does this all mean now?"

"It means that we're at war. Faith and her master want us dead for some reason. They orchestrated this all, and I still don't understand it. But, hopefully, we will figure it out soon because they killed someone we love. And we will have vengeance."

I looked at her, then over at Rowen, who had walked in as Laurel spoke.

"What am I missing?" I asked, my voice soft. The water had helped more than it would have if I'd been human. "Where is Rome?"

Rome will be here soon. At least, I hope," Rowen answered. She gave me a look, then continued. "It hurt him to save your life. Do you understand that you were near death? That blade Faith shoved into you was coated in magic and was siphoning not only your powers as a witch, but also your life-force. You were dying. You *would have* died without Rome saving your life."

My hand moved to my neck. I touched the slight indentations there that I knew had fully healed and remembered the bond and the bear that had butted me in my dreams.

It was the mate bond with Rome.

One that was only between him and me and no other.

"I'm mated..." I whispered.

Laurel and Rowen nodded before giving each other a look before looking away.

"He's upset about it," Laurel whispered.

I felt like my heart broke. As if I had been shoved off a cliff. He didn't want the mating. After all this, he didn't want the mating.

"He...he didn't want this?" I asked, my voice shaking.

"No, that's not what I meant," Laurel added quickly before looking at Rowen, her gaze pleading.

Rowen shook her head. "Rome wanted this more than anything. But you see, Sage... Mating is supposed to be a consensual agreement between parties. It's a cherished bond. When mates take that risk and leap towards another, it's beautiful. But because of how things were, because you were dying, you weren't able to mark him back. Not in a way that mattered. The mark on him is one of his own making. The pain that he took into himself because he marked you without your agreement. You were unconscious and dying, and he marked you to give you part of himself."

Tears fell again, and I clutched at my chest as if trying to feel the bond. "Is Rome dying because he saved me?" I didn't know what I would do if they answered yes.

Laurel shook her head. "But he likely feels like it inside. He blames himself."

"What do I do?" I asked. "What *should* I do?"

Rowen raised her chin. "Soon, you'll need to go to him. To reassure him in ways only you can. Because I know you. You are kind, and you are strong, and you will ensure that our alpha is whole, just as he did for you. But, first, we need to make sure that you are fully healed so you can protect yourself and others."

I nodded. "I want to go to him. Help me get up." I tried to move off the bed, but Laurel kept me in place. And then we weren't alone anymore.

Trace, Jaxton, and Ash walked into the room, and I pulled the sheet up over my chest. Rowen or Laurel had dressed me in my sleep since I was fully clothed, and I assumed it was because blood covered my outfit from before. But I felt far too vulnerable at the moment for so many

CARRIE ANN RYAN

people to see me in bed. I did my best not to think about the
blood that had been on me. Everything hurt, and I felt like I
was in a fog, probably because of the drugs they'd given me.

I could face my near death because I had to. I would
think about my mortality when the time came, but the fact
that the person I loved most here was gone...nearly crushed
me. She was gone. Aunt Penelope was dead. And it was my
fault.

"She's blaming herself," Ash said into the void. His voice
was low and devoid of emotion.

Rowen sighed. "I knew she would feel like this." She
turned towards me. "You can't blame yourself. This was
Faith and Oriel. Do you understand? You didn't kill her. It is
not your fault that you weren't strong enough to protect her.
Because honestly? That wasn't the case. Strength had
nothing to do with it. Not when you were fighting pure evil.
Do not make Penelope's sacrifice be in vain by self-sacrificing
yourself or blaming yourself for what happened. You will
fight and train harder to take vengeance. Get stronger. But
you will not take the blame. Do you understand me?" Rowen
asked, her voice a whip. Laurel smirked, and I wondered
what it meant.

I shook my head. "I need time. Do you understand that I
need some time to process everything?"

"We might not *have* time," Ash warned. "Death magic
and necromancy take sacrifice. And that's what Faith has
been doing for who knows how many years. You said before
that Rupert died because of her. That was all set up. I have a
feeling they were trying to curse this town long before you
showed up, Sage. Why weren't you here before? You should
have been here." Ash frowned, and I realized that was the
most emotion I'd ever seen on his face.

"And why did *you* leave?" Jaxton asked softly, and Laurel and Rowen both flinched.

"This isn't the time," Ash growled. "What I do know is that Faith has been circling this town for long enough that she knows all our secrets—or at least most of them. And that means we need to be prepared. She has something up her sleeve. And so does this other necromancer we need to figure out and identify. I don't know how they know about this town or what they want from it—other than our destruction."

Rowen narrowed her eyes, her magic wild as it blew her hair back from her face. "Well, then, we're just going to have to stop her. We're stronger together." She wasn't looking at Ash when she said the words, but I saw his face tighten as she spoke.

"I'll help however I can. I promise. I need to get to Rome. I can feel him inside me, and I don't understand it. I really need to get to him first. Okay?" I hoped I was making sense.

Trace nodded. "I'll help you find him. He needs to get his head out of his ass. And not just because of you, also with the pack."

"What do you mean?" I asked.

Trace shook his head. "You're going to be thrown into a lot, Sage. There's a reason matings don't happen this way, why it sometimes takes a little bit of planning to make sure a person's ready. But you're strong, you'll be a good alpha."

I started and nearly fell off the bed. "Did you say alpha?" I couldn't have heard him right. Because there was no way I was going to be alpha.

Trace raked his hands through his hair, looking so much like Rome just then that it was a little startling. "You are mated to an alpha now. That means, you're also alpha. And not everybody will be happy about that."

Laurel cursed under her breath. "Do you think this is a good time for you to mention all this?"

Trace smirked, but I didn't see humor in his gaze. "No, but I figured it's as good a time as any. And, frankly, she needs to be prepared. So, let's get you to Rome. Let's fix whatever the hell is wrong with him right now, and then we're going to save this town because I'll be damned if one of the sweetest ladies I've ever known died for nothing."

I nodded, my heart breaking. But I pushed those thoughts away and tried to get out of bed quickly.

Rowen just shook her head. "Give us some privacy, boys. Let's get the final herbs into her so she's healthy, and then we will send her on her way to meet her mate. And then, we fight. Because our town needs to be protected, and I will not let another person die because of that necromancer and her senseless hatred."

I nodded and leaned into the girls as they helped me get ready. I knew I needed to get to Rome. I needed to find out how to protect my mate and make sure he understood that while some things were taken out of our hands, we still had to face them.

I could barely breathe as grief overwhelmed me. I tried to push it away because I needed to focus on other things. I couldn't focus on Penelope right now. I couldn't concentrate on Rupert. I couldn't focus on why I was here. I could only take one step at a time.

Anger radiated through me. I would grieve later. I would cry, rage, and I would likely break. But I would be Rome's mate. And I'd do everything in my power to make sure he understood what that meant and how I felt about it.

CHAPTER TWENTY

ROME

I sat by the pond and looked at the water, trying to understand how I had ended up here. It didn't make any sense to me that this was how my bond had been created.

I shouldn't have crossed that boundary, but I couldn't lose her. Ravenwood needed her. The coven needed her. I needed her. And yet, there was nothing I could do now. I had bitten her. I had marked her. I had taken her as mine without her permission.

She would likely be awake now. She would know what I had done. She would now understand that I had taken everything from her: her choices, her future, her ability to be herself without the pack surrounding her. She was only just learning how to be in the coven and Ravenwood. And now, she would have to do more with the pack.

I didn't know how to fix this. I didn't know what I was supposed to do. All I knew was that Sage would never forgive me.

And, frankly, I was never going to forgive myself.

Her scent hit me first. I froze, wondering if it was a

dream. But that rose scent was here. One that wasn't cloying but slowly softening as it wrapped itself around me. Pulsated and seeped into my pores. I couldn't breathe. Because if I did, I would inhale more of it.

And I would realize there was no going back.

My bear pushed at me, crawling over my body as my anchor tried to lift off and move towards the woman that it loved. The woman *I* loved. The bond flared. I closed my eyes, willing it to stop. Willing myself not to feel. I knew it was there, waiting. Waiting for me to do something about it. My bear played with that thread and knew that our mate was on the other end, but I couldn't. I couldn't do anything about it because I would only end up wanting the bond more than I already did.

Our mating should have been a joyous occasion. But it couldn't be now. I couldn't let it become that for me. If I did, I would break. Though I deserved any pain that came because of the choices I had made.

I inhaled again and knew that she was in the house, not in the yard or the forest near me. I shook my head. I didn't want to go in there. Every part of me knew I needed to. My bear pushed at me and I let out a breath.

"Okay, I'll go."

I stood up, wiped the dirt from my pants, and looked over the area. No one was around. However, I did see a tip of a wing out of the corner of my eye. I knew Jaxton had brought Sage here. Had brought her to me.

She was awake. She was healed. And she was mine. Now, I needed to face the consequences of my actions. I could scent Trace, as well, but I knew he was on the other side of the house. Watching, protecting.

I let out a chuff, a deep growl that only other bear

shifters would hear, and Trace did the same in answer. There was no need for words, not now.

I needed to speak with Sage. I needed to make sure she knew that I wouldn't force her into anything more. That I wouldn't make her be my mate beyond the bond we now shared forever. She would bear my mark, just as my soul bore hers. The one I had placed above my heart because she couldn't.

I walked into the house and inhaled again, her scent wrapping around me.

"Rome," she said as she looked up at me, her eyes wide. She looked beautiful with her hair flowing in soft waves around her face. Her lips parted. Her eyes were wide—the hazel hue alluring.

I tried to catch my breath. I couldn't. My bear pushed at me. Suddenly, I was moving forward. And then I had my hands around Sage's face, cupping her cheeks, the tips of my fingers in her hair.

I leaned down and brushed my lips against hers. "You're okay," I whispered.

She looked at me. "Yes, because of you. You saved me."

I shook my head and wrenched away. I shouldn't have touched her. I shouldn't have done anything without permission. And yet, here I was, doing it all over again.

"It's not because of me. I took away your choice."

She shook her head and took a step forward. I held up my hand, afraid that if she touched me, I would never let her go. The bond flared between us, pulling me towards her, but I forced myself to stay put. I made myself not touch her.

"You didn't take away my choice. You and I slept together, Rome. I gave myself to you that night. You know you were the first person I was with since Rupert. I gave myself to you. That was my choice. One I would make readily again. We were waiting for the mating mark; until we got to know each other better. But you know it was inevitable. I would have chosen you, Rome. You didn't take that choice away. It was Faith. She's the one who took everything. She's the one who hurt me. Who killed Penelope. It wasn't anything you did. You aren't the one who hurt me. You aren't the one who took away my will. That was her. She's a dark witch. A necromancer. What else were you supposed to do? Were you supposed to let me die in your arms, bleeding out? Was I supposed to let my blood mix with Penelope's as I died near her? What were we supposed to do, Rome? You need to stop blaming yourself. I can feel it in the bond. I can feel your pain, and it's killing me. Please, don't walk away. Don't stop touching me. Just hold me."

She was crying then. And I tried...tried so hard to hold myself back. I couldn't. Instead, I took the three steps between us and crushed her to me. "I'm sorry."

She let out a breath. "No, don't be sorry. You saved me, Rome. And I can feel you. You are my mate. You're *mine*. Do you understand that? I hope you do. I hope you realize that I would have chosen you if given the time. We were already making our path. We would have ended up here. Maybe not in the same way, but we would have. And now, we have a future. We will fight Faith. We will protect this town and the pack. Though to do so, we need to be together. You can't walk away. You can't look at me and only see the choice that someone ripped away from us. I need you to look at me and see who we are and who we could be. I'm falling in love with you, Rome. Don't you understand that? I'm falling in love with you. And it has nothing to do with the bond but because of the man you are. So, please don't walk away. Look at me. Be with me. Kiss me. Can you do that? Can you kiss me right now?"

The floor nearly fell out from under me, and I staggered. "Of course, I want you, Sage. I've always wanted you. From the moment I saw you in that forest. When you were saving my life, when you used your magic without knowing to protect me, I wanted you. I will forever hate Faith for what she did. Because when I close my eyes, I can still see your lifeless form in my arms. I marked you, Sage. I engaged in the biggest taboo I could."

She studied my face. "Now, what do we do? Do we go back to who we were? Or do we find a way to make this mark ours?"

I was holding her, and in answer, I leaned down and brushed my lips against hers. "You're mine."

"Good, because you're mine, too."

I kissed her. She tasted of sweetness, tea, and of the herbs that had made her healthy. I could feel her within my soul. My bear grappled as I held her. Tasted her. I picked her up, unable to stop touching her. She wrapped her legs around my waist. Thanks to the bond and the magic within the coven, I was able to keep her safe. For this moment, she was whole. We both were.

I would take every step I could to make sure she knew that I was the right choice—if she'd been given one.

"Kiss me, Rome. Be with me. Always."

I retook her lips and carried her to my bedroom. She had never been in here. We had made love outside under the stars before. I had fed her in my kitchen. But she had never been in my bed. Now, she would be. In *our* bed if I had anything to say about it. Of course, she would be the one to make that ultimate choice. I would never again take away her will.

"Be with me, Rome," she repeated.

"Always, Sage. I'm never letting you go." I hadn't meant to say that last part, but as the bond flared between us at my words, I knew she felt the same.

"I can feel you. Deep inside." She blushed. "I mean the bond."

"Since we're both still clothed, I knew what you meant." I paused. "Is that okay? I know it will take some getting used to. Bears come by it naturally, but I know as a witch, you'll have to figure out what works for you."

I gently placed her on the bed, and she reached up, resting her palm on my chest, over my heart. "I like the feel of you around my heart, Rome. I like the idea of you knowing where I am, and that you'll be able to find me. That I'll always know how to find *you* if you're hurt. That I'll always know you're *there*. That might be too much for others, but not for me. Be with me, Rome," she repeated. "Let's make this *our* choice. No one else's."

"I don't want to scare you." I swallowed hard. "I'm a bear, Sage. I could hurt you."

Her eyes darkened. "Be yourself, Rome. And I'll try not to hurt you, either." She winked as she said it, and my bear roared, craving her more than I ever thought possible. I lowered my head and kissed her again before gently nipping at her collarbone and neck.

She moaned, tugging on the bottom of my shirt. I leaned up and pulled the shirt over the back of my head. She groaned and looked at me, licking her lips. No words were needed, not between us. We could feel each other along the bond.

I lowered myself again and took her mouth, this time greedily. Far harder than before. She moaned again, scraping her fingernails down my back. I grinned; my bear happy yet needy.

I tugged at the bottom of her shirt. She sat up, and I pulled it over her head before I did the same with her bra.

Her eyes widened, and I kissed her softly as I pulled away to look down at her beautiful breasts. They were heavy, full, her nipples a dark red. They were more than a handful and perfect for the size of my hands. I groaned then leaned down, taking one supple nipple into my mouth.

"You taste fantastic," I ground out before I latched on to her other nipple, using my free hand to palm her breast and play with her. She slid her fingers into my hair, moaning. I looked up as her head fell back, her long hair cascading around her.

She looked like a goddess. *My* goddess. My mate.

I was so fucking excited to have her, to have her body and soul as part of me.

This was where we should have marked one another. This was where we should have become true mates. I needed to push the thought of how it had happened out of my mind and focus only on the woman in my arms. I looked up at the slight scar on her shoulder, the one that would be there until the end of time. The one that told the world that she was mine. I licked the slight ridges. Sage shivered and pressed her thighs around my hips. "Rome. That feels..." Her voice trailed off.

"Yes. I could probably make you come by sucking on it. Do you want me to try?" I asked.

She let out a shaky breath, even as her thighs clenched around me. "Not yet. I need you inside me."

I groaned. "That I can do." I kissed her again. And then I licked and nipped down her body until I reached the top of her leggings. I slowly pulled them off her legs, taking her underwear with them. I tossed them over my shoulder, and then I knelt in front of her, pressing her silky thighs down as I spread her. She was pink and wet and perfect. I could barely hold back a growl. My bear pushed at me, wanting to taste her sweet honey.

I latched on to her clit, sucking and licking and letting the sweetness coat my tongue. She tasted of perfection. I wanted to continue tasting and eating her until she came on my face, over and over and over again. She let out a breath, her back arching as she kept her hands on her breasts. I held her thighs spread, knowing her taste would be all for me.

I rubbed my beard along her thigh, and she shivered before I latched on to her clit again and sucked, twisting my lips and darting my tongue. She moaned, her whole body freezing for an instant before she came, her pussy tightening around my tongue.

I groaned, lapping up her orgasm. She continued coming on my face, writhing as she whispered my name. I lapped at her again, spreading her folds more as I continued exploring her sweet pussy.

Then she tugged on my hair. "Please, I need you."

I gave her one long, sensual lick, stood up, and slowly undid my pants. She held one hand over her breast, the other over her pussy as she stared at me.

"Rome."

I grinned and patted her hip before I undid the button of my jeans. "Roll onto your stomach, Sage. I want to see how deep I can go."

She licked her lips and then slowly slid onto all fours.

She put that pert little ass in the air as I pulled off my pants. I nearly came right there, gripping the base of my cock.

Sage looked over her shoulder at me, her eyes dark with need. "Rowen gave me herbs. I can't get pregnant unless we want to."

I groaned, remembering that we were mated now. I could get her pregnant with my seed. I hovered over her, my dick playing between her soft folds. As I slowly licked her mate mark, her whole body shook.

"Good. We will make our choices about that later. Together."

"Please come inside me. I can't wait any longer. Make me yours just like you are mine."

I nodded, the need the same inside me, I latched on to that mate mark and bit down gently so it was ours. I slid home, and her pussy clamped around me like a vise. She pushed that soft ass of hers back into my hips.

She was so tight, so warm that I nearly came right then. I put one hand on her hip, the other looped around her body, keeping her steady. And then I started to move. She slid back to me, meeting me thrust for thrust as I pumped into her, needing more. Needing everything.

She panted, called out my name, and I continue moving, knowing I was close as my balls tightened. I was afraid I would come before she did again, and I couldn't let that happen. I reached around and flicked her clit with my finger, and she came, clamping around my dick.

I shook, the need far too great. I pumped deep inside, hard, once, twice. And again. And then I roared, shouting her name and shaking the windows with my bellow. As I filled her with my seed, with everything I was, I realized I was alpha. I was bear. And I was Sage's mate. She was mine.

"I love you," I whispered. I wasn't falling. I had fallen.

As we moved so I was on my side with her facing me, she curled into my body, her eyes closed but a small, beautiful smile on her face.

And we slept.

CHAPTER TWENTY-ONE

SAGE

My heart ached, and it felt like somebody was stabbing me from the inside. It didn't make any sense. I had left one sense of loss and darkness, and once again, I stood staring at that abyss. At what I couldn't change. My Aunt Penelope was gone, and there was no coming back from that. And I wasn't even sure how I'd gotten here in the first place. Rome slid his hand over mine and squeezed it as we stood near my aunt's grave. Rowen stood at the head of the casket, her hair blowing in the wind, though it was just of her making—her magic. Laurel stood on the other side of me, still as a stone. She had been closer to my aunt than even I was.

I reached out and gripped her hand. She was icy-cold, which was odd for a woman full of fire. I squeezed, and she clamped down on my hand so painfully, I knew I might have bruises later. But I didn't care. She needed me, just as I needed her. Trace, Jaxton, and Ash stood on the other side, three stone pillars of strength and confusion. There were others from the town there. Customers who came in to help at the bakery and wanted to meet me. People who had known my aunt for years and wanted to be part of this final goodbye. They all knew who had taken her. They knew who had killed her. They all understood that we would have vengeance. However, it was difficult for me to realize that I couldn't fix anything.

"Our Penelope was one of our founders," Rowen began. I looked up at the woman who was my coven sister, my teacher. Someone breaking inside just like me. "She fought for her family, for this town. She was a founder of more than the hope that drives us. She was of the blood that brought us together, that has protected us for so long. She might not have had the magic to work the spells, but it was her hope and tenacity that protected us all. She will be missed. She was a light in the darkness. A beacon of steadfast loyalty and hope. She is gone, but she will never be forgotten." Rowen looked at all of us, and then at the town, before staring back at me, her eyes fierce, that wind in her hair picking up. "She might be gone, but we will find who took her from us. She was of hope, but we will be vengeance. We will not let her die in vain. We will not let her go to ash, to the soil, without knowing that we *will* fight for her. We will continue fighting for her and for ourselves. Our Penelope is gone, but not the hope she brought. Not the protection she sought."

"In this time of darkness, bring us back to light. Ease the sorrow and burden on these next harrowing nights. Penelope's time here is done, for with life is given death. Keep with us the memories; Goddess, please alleviate the rest. For only She is eternal, even the sun must disappear. Gone from body but never from heart, our sister is always near."

Magic churned within me, and I let out a breath as Rome, Trace, Jaxton, and Ash slowly began lowering Penelope into the ground. Rowen had her hands up, and I knew she was using air to buffer the casket.

We would bury my aunt whole so she would be of earth, and she would be ours. I had come to Ravenwood from loss, and yet here I was, surrounded by loss again. I wasn't sure what I was supposed to do with that.

Others from the town came to me to express their sorrow. They held my hand, and they hugged me. I could see the sincerity in each of them. I could also see the fear. One of theirs had been taken, and who would be next? If we didn't stop Faith, my aunt would only be the first we lost. The townsfolk were scared. I would do my best to be strong for them. Somehow.

Rowen stood after the others had left, and only our small group remained. "Come with me to the magic shop. We can eat, speak, and then we will meet with the rest of the town for the wake."

"Are you sure you don't want to go take a nap or something?" Rome asked, and I frowned up at him.

"Do you think me so weak that I need to sleep right now?" I asked before I shook my head. "Sorry, I'm tired, but I need to do something. We need to do something."

I met Rowen's gaze, and she gave me a tight nod. "That's what we will discuss. Before we meet the others and grieve with our town, with our people, we will decide what we must do."

"Sounds like a plan to me." Trace held out his hand for Laurel. "Come on. I'll walk you."

"I can walk myself," she said, but she still took his hand. She squeezed it slightly, and I saw the grin play on her lips. He was trying to make her smile, trying to make her laugh or feel at least some joy, and I was grateful for that. Jaxton followed them, whispering something to Laurel that made her smile, as well. Ash followed his sister after giving Rowen a long look. Rowen didn't walk with him, instead falling into step with Rome and me. The three of us followed the group towards the magic shop.

As soon as we stepped into the building, I inhaled the sweet scents of herbs and magic. It warmed me, settled into my skin as it soothed me. I wasn't sure how we would protect our town and those we loved, especially after losing my aunt. But I knew we needed to try.

"I know we're here to protect the town, but first, there's something else we must do," Rowen said as she cleared her throat.

I looked up at her. "What do you mean?"

"There's someone we need to say goodbye to."

I froze, the hairs on the back of my neck standing on end. I turned, and I knew that shape, that soft smile. She was but a shade, but not the same that Faith could raise. I knew this woman. I knew this spirit.

"Aunt Penelope," I whispered.

Laurel sucked in a shocked breath and held out her hand. "No, you can't be here. They will use her." She rolled on Rowen. "What have you done?"

Rowen shook her head. "It wasn't me." A single tear fell. "It wasn't me."

"It was none of you, my children," Aunt Penelope said, her voice sounding faraway, distant. "I lingered just for a moment because I wanted to make sure you knew what must be done. I love you all. You were all strong, together. Remember that. Know you must be together. I love you. Stand strong and fight. Remember who you are. Where you come from. And know that you always have one another."

She faced me as tears fell freely down my cheeks now. "I love you, daughter of my heart. I love you so much."

Pain shattered me, and if it weren't for my bond with Rome, I'd likely be on the floor without strength. "I love you so much. How are you here?"

"As I said, I lingered. Now, I must go." She looked at Rowen. "I need to go before they find me."

Chills spread over me. "Could Faith use her? Her spirit?"

"Maybe not Faith, but the one she calls Oriel," Rowen answered, wrath in her tone. "We need to be careful. There's something I could say to send her away." She turned to my aunt. "This means you can't come back. Ever. The necromancer cannot get you."

Penelope nodded. "I understand. I only lingered because of the magic here. I do not want to stay. It's not my place any longer. It's yours. I love you all. Fight. Remember who you are."

"Come with me, Laurel," Rowen said. "We need to gather the rest of the herbs. I did some before the funeral, but now it's time to do the rest."

Laurel looked frozen for a moment before she shook herself and went to help. "I can't use magic."

"You can do this spell. It won't hurt."

"You say that, and yet I feel like it will."

I looked between them, nodded at Rowen, then followed. "Here, let me help," I said, standing between them so they would stop bickering and looking as if they wanted to hurt one another because of their pain.

Rowen gave me a tight nod. "Come now, the three of us will work as one."

"I'll help," Laurel asserted. "For Penelope."

Rowen gripped the other woman's hand. "I know. If I could take all of your pain, I would."

The two women shared a look.

"I know that, too," Laurel said, and I lowered my head and gathered what Rowen told me to.

We gathered the herbs, mixed them in the cauldron in the middle of the store as the men watched. I knew Ash wanted to say something, I saw his mouth open to speak every once in a while, but he held back as if he knew it wasn't his place. Wasn't his time.

Rome, Jaxton, and Trace stood there as protectors. And I was glad. I wasn't sure I could do this without Rome here.

Tears freely fell down Rowen's cheeks now. "Repeat after me." She took a breath.

"Beloved spirit, sister ours, your time has come to grace the stars. Go with light to live again, for we all know this is not the end. Your time here is ended, but not your memory. Merry part and blessed be."

I looked at my aunt. She smiled, and then she was gone. Tears slid down my cheeks again, and I let out a choked sob. Magic washed through me, and I looked over to see Laurel bent over at the waist, pushing everybody away.

"I'm fine. I'm fine," she bit out.

"Damn it, you shouldn't be in pain," Rowen said, her hands shaking. "I'm so sorry. That shouldn't have hurt you, not with the intention and the protections I put in place."

"It's the curse. It doesn't care what you think or what protections you use. It grows stronger," Ash whispered, and Rowen froze.

"Let me help." Jaxton moved forward.

Laurel pushed him away. "I said, I'm fine. Now help me

get this bitch. Because Faith deserves to die for what she did."

Laurel stood, wiped the blood from her nose, and I leaned into Rome, the tension in his chest stiff yet comforting.

"Laurel..." I whispered.

"It's none of your concern. I did it for Penelope."

Rowen had her chin up, but I saw the pain there. She hadn't wanted to hurt Laurel, hadn't wanted to cause any pain but she knew what must be done. I wished I knew what I was supposed to do or how I could help. I had the power within me. I knew that much. Hopefully, I would be able to use it against Faith.

"So, we are the seven," Rowen began.

"The seven who are doing work together to take down Faith. Because she's going to hurt this town, and I don't want anyone else to die like my aunt did," I added.

Rowen nodded. "Exactly."

"What do we know?" Rome asked, his voice a growl behind me.

"We know she's a necromancer. And we know she must be close," Ash said. "We also know she's working with someone named Oriel."

"Do we know anything about him?" Rowen asked.

"No," Ash said. "At least, not yet. I'll find out more."

"How? Rowen asked.

"I have my ways," Ash insisted.

I stepped between them, delaying the inevitable fight. "You'll both figure it out. Right now, it's Faith. She's the enemy we know. She's the one we can try to beat before all is lost. We have to find her." I had to believe we would, or I didn't have much hope for anything else.

"We will. We're going to scry for her. But the potion I was thinking about using takes until the full moon. It will take time," Rowen said.

"You can't just use the regular scrying method?" Jaxton asked, frowning.

Rowen shook her head. "I tried, but Faith is too strong. Whatever dark magic they're using is blocking me."

I frowned. "You did that on your own? Are you searching for her without us? What if it hurts you?" I asked.

Laurel scowled. "You don't do any magic on your own that has to do with that woman, got it?"

"I am a coven of one and have been for a long time. You can't use magic without it killing you. Sage doesn't know enough to help yet. I've always done things on my own."

"Not anymore," I snapped. "I don't care if you're used to being a coven of one. There are seven of us here now, and it looks like we're at least a coven of three. We may not be the best coven or the strongest, but we will be who we can. So, anything that's Faith-related, you do not attempt on your own."

Rowen tilted her head, a sad smile on her face. "Look at you, little witch. So strong."

"I don't much care for the mocking," I snarled, and Rome growled behind me.

Rowen winced. "I'm sorry. I was only teasing because I need to do *something* or I'm going to break right here. And that's not something I'll allow myself to do. You're right. With Faith, I can't do things myself. I promise. I'll change."

"We'll scry," Rome said from behind me. "And then our witches, the pack, the fae, and whoever else has power will go after her. To protect the town. We have to be together for this to work."

I nodded along with the others.

"We will. We're stronger together than we ever were apart." Rowen rolled back her shoulders, but I noticed she didn't look at Ash as she said it.

I let out a breath, leaned into Rome, and listened as Rowen went through her plans and what spell would need to be used for the scrying. We were just about ready to move on to the wake when the door slammed open, and Ariel ran through. "I'm sorry, but you need to come," she said, looking at Rome.

"What is it?" he asked, his bear in his voice.

"Alden is at the den, calling for a pack circle. He's challenging you. You need to come. Now."

I froze as everybody looked at one another, their eyes wide.

"What?" Trace asked as Rome stood beside me, his whole body shaking.

"Alden is trying to take the pack. And he has people on his side. If we're not careful, he's going to take it. And I don't know what that means for the town. We need to go," Ariel said.

"You're right, we do," Rome said after a moment. "It's time to take care of my brother."

I gripped my mate's hands and looked up at him, feeling the ice and the anchor along the bond. I knew that no matter what happened next, I would be by his side.

Even if this was the worst possible time for a challenge.

In the back of my mind, I wondered if that was indeed the case, or if the timing was just perfect for what was to come.

CHAPTER TWENTY-TWO

ROME

My bear clawed at me as I walked into the pack circle area. I couldn't believe Alden would do this, and yet, why shouldn't I? Why shouldn't I think that the brother who had been slowly pulling away from us all this time would do this? He wanted power, not the change that came with an ever-evolving world. He only wanted the title. He hadn't wanted Sage as my mate. I shouldn't be surprised Alden would stoop to this.

A pack challenge? One for alpha?

I couldn't walk away from the path before me, but given the way Alden had set things in motion, only one of us would walk away from the circle tonight.

My bear chuffed, anger radiating through both of us.

Sage gripped my hand before I stepped into the circle, and I looked back at her. "What's going to happen?" she asked.

I squeezed her hand. "I'm going to introduce you to the pack, and then we're going to see what Alden wants."

Her eyes widened, but she lifted her chin. "Anything

you need. I'm here for you. But, Rome? Will you have to fight him?"

I knew any other bear near us would be able to hear, but I didn't lower my voice. "If Alden forces my hand, I will. Let's see what we can do first." I leaned down, gripped the back of her neck, and kissed her hard on the mouth. Sage rose to her tiptoes, meeting my kiss. I deepened it, claiming her as mine in front of the entire pack.

"Be safe."

"Be safe and be with me," she whispered back.

I nodded and met Trace's gaze. My brother lifted his chin and moved to stand on one side of her, Jaxton on her other. Rowen, Ash, and Laurel were with us, as well, the six of them by my side. Ariel had gone on ahead to meet with the others and the elders, and I hoped to hell she didn't get into trouble for warning me. Alden should have waited to call the pack circle until I was here. Since he hadn't, he was trying to forego some of the formalities, and Ariel leaving her post as she had could be seen as treason.

All because Alden wanted power. And if he won, he would kill Ariel—if not others, as well. I would not let that happen. I would not let any of this happen.

"You finally arrived." Alden smirked as if he had been the one to invite me.

"I see you've called a pack circle without me. Care to explain?" I asked, my voice a growl.

"It is time the pack comes back to where it was best. We must make our pack what it once was, make it good and righteous again."

I narrowed my eyes at him. My anchor slid over my skin, wanting blood. I didn't blame the bear. "Our pack is strong. We are compassionate. We have strength in numbers, in our bonds, and in our purpose against a common enemy. Why are you calling a pack challenge now of all times? On this day that we buried a friend. On a day we are formulating plans to protect our town. Why are you doing this?"

Alden narrowed his eyes, just for an instant, then went back to looking like his perfect businessman self. He played with the cuffs on his long-sleeve shirt and shook his head. "Don't you see? *This* is why we are here. You have spent so much time with your witch and this coven, you have forgotten what our pack needs."

"I am alpha, dear brother. I know precisely what this pack needs. And that is strength and protection. Of all sorts."

Alden tilted his head as he stared at me. "Strength of all sorts? And yet you spend all your time protecting the coven and not yourself. Where were you when I called this challenge? You were with the witches and the hawks. You were with others. Not your own."

"I was with him, brother. The town and most of our den was with him when we buried Penelope. Where were you?" Trace asked.

I nearly bit back a growl. Trace was allowed to speak since we weren't in a full alpha challenge yet, but I didn't want Alden's attention on him. I didn't trust the man I called brother.

"You were there for a witch, yet you haven't been here for your pack. You were alpha. You were supposed to put your pack first above all else."

"No, he's supposed to put his mate first. Together, they rule as an alpha pair to keep our pack safe," Ariel called out.

"No one asked you, *fourth*," Alden growled.

"We are not a full pack circle yet, as I have not called it.

251

Therefore, Ariel can speak however and whenever she likes," I ordered.

"I have called the pack circle about you, dear brother. Therefore, I am the one in charge here."

There were murmurs from all around, and I shook my head. I was grateful that those who had come to this hadn't brought the cubs. The triplets weren't here, nor were the other cubs of the den. They didn't need to see what could happen next. What *would* happen next.

"You are mistaken. I am here, I am alpha. And as such, since we are having a pack circle, and I have arrived and allowed it to be, let me introduce you to my mate. Your *alpha*." I held out my hand. As if we had rehearsed it, Sage stepped forward and slipped hers into mine. "Sage is my mate. She is a witch. And she is of the coven. She is part of this town, Ravenwood. *We* are Ravenwood. She will protect us, as I will protect both you and her."

"I will protect you, as well," Sage said, looking at me. I winked at her, even though my bear was on alert because I knew this couldn't be the end of Alden's plans. Something would happen; I just had to figure out what.

"You see?" Alden gestured with his hands towards the center of the circle. "He brings her here to our pack circle. We don't need the coven," Alden said, staring at me.

I tilted my head, studying him, alert. "Oh? The coven formed this town. If it weren't for them and their magic keeping our wards, we wouldn't be able to congregate en masse like we are. We are the largest pack in the nation because of Ravenwood. Sure, there are other towns like Ravenwood, but they aren't as large as ours, and their packs aren't as considerable. We are symbiotic with the coven and those of magical nature. We work with them. And yet, you say we should cut ties?"

"The coven has done nothing but hurt this town. Look at what the witches are doing now. Look at their necromancers. They are witches, too, don't forget. And they are bringing death and destruction. They are scaring our cubs and hurting our future."

There were murmurs, agreements about the necromancers, and I could hear Rowen and the others whispering to one another. They couldn't get involved, and I knew they would understand. Sage was the only one who might be confused, but she stayed silent, standing by my side. I could feel her magic pulsating within her. She'd be ready to defend me if I needed it, but she also understood that this was my time to speak.

There was so much strength in her, and she surprised me at every turn.

I had fallen in love with her the moment she showed her true colors, how she fought for herself and others.

She was my mate now. My alpha, as well.

The rest of the pack would have to get on board with that.

"The necromancers are a problem, yes. Just like there are rogue shifters, there are rogue witches. And when we had to fight our last rogue, Rowen and Laurel were at our side to help. The fae and the hawks were with us and did not judge the whole for its parts. Penelope was at our side to help heal our wounded. She is gone now, and we need to avenge her. We need to protect this town. We don't have time for your dominance games, Alden."

"If you do not unbind yourself from the coven and this witch, then you'll force my hand, brother," Alden growled.

I didn't understand any of this. My triplet had always wanted power yet there was something else here that I wasn't seeing, and it worried me. Something was behind and beneath this. I just didn't know what it was.

"I'm not leaving my mate. You know you have no right to tell me to defy fate. We are bonded now."

"And I will protect this pack with my life." Sage's voice was calm, collected, and firm. "I might be new to all of this, but I want to get to know you. An outside force shielded me from the world of magic. Faith and the other necromancers and whoever's working with her wanted me kept away from Ravenwood. But I'm here now. I'm going to catch up. I promise I will protect you. I'm learning my magic, and I will use it to safeguard you and this town. You don't need to push Rome away. I promise I won't do anything to take him away from you. I will use all of my power to keep you safe."

My bear preened at her words, and I could see some others nodding as if they saw her strength and felt the passion in her words—her magic. They could likely sense her power, but she couldn't do anything more right now.

All she could do was wait. But, hopefully, they would see the strength she had and feel the truth of her words.

"This means nothing," Alden growled. "I call for an alpha challenge. To the death."

I blinked as someone gasped, and Sage gripped my arm. There were other murmurs, shouts, words. I wasn't listening to it. Instead, I just looked at my triplet, at my brother, my blood. And I knew I would have to kill him.

Because there was no going back. Magic snapped within me, and the challenge called me forth.

Once you were in a pack circle and someone called for an alpha challenge to the death, there was no going back.

One of us would leave the circle alive, the other would be gone forever.

Even in my wildest nightmares, I hadn't thought Alden would do something like this. I had been wrong. Terribly wrong.

"So be it," I growled, my bear in my voice.

"Rome," Sage whispered.

"There's no choice. You can feel the magic, right? Through the bond?"

"It feels like a vise. It's so tight."

"It's the ways of our people. I'm sorry this is how you're being introduced to the pack." I leaned down and kissed her, and she gripped my shoulders, pulling me closer. "Be safe. There's nothing we can do?" she asked.

"Nothing."

And I could feel through the bond that she understood. If I didn't die here today, if these weren't my last words, I would have to kill my brother.

And I didn't know who I would become afterward.

Alden stripped off his shirt and slowly crept into the center of the circle. Four men stood beside him, all in his corner. Those were the traitors I would have to deal with. I looked at Trace and Ariel, who nodded, Trace staying beside the witches, and Jaxton, who could do nothing since he wasn't bear but a shifter of another group. Ariel moved closer to my other trackers and the elders, and I knew they would protect those weaker.

Because if I beat Alden here, it wouldn't strip out all of the rot. It was only the beginning.

"What do I do?" Sage asked.

"Go stand by Trace. Get the others out if this goes poorly."

She shook her head, her eyes narrowed. "You mean if you die?"

"Yes. If Alden becomes alpha, he will kill you and anyone else he can. Protect the weak, the cubs. Get Faith. Do all that you can. I need to take care of my brother."

I kissed her again, even as rage filled her face. I could feel it dancing across the bond, but she simply gave me a tight nod before walking to Trace. Ash and Rowen stared, ready. Jaxton and Laurel had gone to the other side of the circle, and I knew that they would protect those on their side, as well.

We didn't have to speak. We knew each other so well that it was understood we would do what we could to help those who couldn't help themselves. I had to push that from my mind, though, and focus on what was in front of me.

Alden, my brother. My challenger. "Are you ready?"

"You didn't have to do this," I said. "I don't understand why you're doing this."

"You had everything handed to you. You were alpha, and Trace was beta. What did that leave me? Nothing. You never gave me a chance. You never listened to me. Instead, you went to the witches, the hawks. You listened to everyone else and ignored me. And, in the end, you hurt your pack. We needed you, and you did nothing. Now, you have to reap what you sowed."

I shook my head and stripped off my shirt. "No, dear brother. It is you who will have to do that."

"To the death," Alden growled, his bear in his eyes.

"To the death."

We shifted. It was bear against bear, and I could hear Sage's small gasp from behind me. My bones cracked, my magic flared, and I dropped to all fours, roaring. The ground shook beneath me, the trees reaching out in their effervescence.

I did not want to do this, but I would. I would kill Alden to protect my people. Protect my mate. Some part of me would die in the process.

Alden was the one who swiped first. I ducked. He was slightly smaller than me in bear form, the only difference between our nearly identical human halves. Alden bit and clawed, and I rose, slicing out. I gouged out part of his side, but he came back at me. Claws and fangs. Alden roared again, and this time, he pushed out with something that wasn't his.

It tasted of magic. Of witch.

I knew whose it was. That's when I noticed that while Alden might be in bear form, there was still an amulet around his neck.

Faith.

Coldness swept over me, and I understood. The circle was a distraction, one part of many. Alden was the one helping Faith get into the town. While I worked with witches through the coven, Alden had been using magic far more sinister.

He had betrayed us all.

I exploded, my heart ripping and rending as magic sliced into me, tearing holes in my body. I heard Sage yell, and Rowen curse under her breath.

"Alden has used magic," Rowen called out. "He's cheating."

"Liar," one of Alden's people spat.

"No, your so-called bear is a traitor," Ariel screamed.

People were shouting, yelling, as blood poured from my

side from the magical wound Faith's amulet had allowed Alden to give me.

I ignored the pain, the burn, and leaped. Alden's eyes widened for just a moment, and in that, I saw the young boy he had once been. The one who had smiled and laughed and rolled around on the ground with Trace and me. The one who was part of us with Ash and Jaxton. Who had been sweet, if a little quiet. Who had always stood off to the side because he hadn't known how to play well with others. But he still tried. When had I missed the change? Why had I forgotten that he was no longer that boy but a man who couldn't fit in or fight for what he wanted in the ways of our people?

When had I lost my brother?

My fangs dug into Alden's neck, and I bit down. It was quick, a bare moment, and then Alden shifted back to human, blood pouring from his throat, his breath coming in pants. I shifted back as well and caught my brother before he fell.

I didn't cry, but my bear roared inside, and I clenched my fists as I held my triplet close.

"Why?" I asked, my voice a rasp.

"It was worth it," Alden said, blood on his lips.

I frowned and then looked to where Alden's gaze went, but I was too late. I couldn't say anything.

Borrowed power that was not of the witch I had seen before filled the circle, and then Faith stood there, a dark dagger in her hand. She gripped Trace by the shoulder, and he slashed, trying to get her with his claws as he pushed Sage down to protect her.

But it was too late.

Faith took the dagger and stabbed Trace in the heart,

twisting her wrist. The trees shuddered, and the pack howled and growled and yipped, and every other shifter around us made a noise that would forever echo in my dreams and haunt me.

Trace fell to his knees, blood pouring out of the wound and his mouth as others came through the woods, their stumbling grace not human. Revenants.

Trace stared at me, his mouth open, but the light in his eyes dimmed.

Alden lay dead at my feet as I screamed, and Trace lay dead at Sage's as she did the same.

Faith smiled.

I threw back my head and roared, and the town answered my call.

CHAPTER TWENTY-THREE

SAGE

Rome was on the other side of the circle from me, and I screamed, blood pooling at my feet and splattered across my face. I had fallen to my hands and knees after Trace pushed me out of the way. I called out, the bond within me nearly breaking but still holding firm. Trace was dead. Alden was dead.

Rome was still in the circle, howling. He might be in his human form, but he was still roaring. Faith had done all of this. Somehow, she orchestrated all of it.

I yelled and scrambled to my feet as Ash pulled me away from Faith. He muttered a spell under his breath and shot out his hands. A wall of rock slid between the necromancer and us, and then I was beside Rowen, trying to catch my breath.

Rome moved forward, pulling on sweatpants that Ariel had tossed to him before moving to my side, tugging at my arm.

"Protect the young."

"No, we need her here," Rowen said. "We need the strength of the coven."

"I don't want her hurt. The cubs will follow her," Rome growled. I pulled on his arm, and I knew he was breaking inside. There were bonds between triplets, and now they were all broken, torn apart through pain and terror. Through revenge and betrayal.

There would be time to go over it all soon and grieve, but first, I needed him to understand. "The coven needs me, and so do you. Your people are protecting the young. They aren't here at the circle." We only had a few moments, and I needed to make sure I made the right decisions.

He narrowed his eyes. "No. They're safe somewhere else."

"Good. Now, protect those here. The coven needs me. And your pack needs you."

"Our pack." His voice was all bear, no longer human.

I nodded, my hands shaking. "Okay. Let me do what I can. And that's with the coven. You do what you can. With your bears." I wanted to say that I was sorry. I wanted to hold him and say *something*, but there wasn't time for that. We only had moments. Ash could only hold off Faith and the others for so long. And the necromancer wasn't alone. She had brought her revenants. There were more than I had ever dreamed there could be. She must have pulled the dead from around the country, perhaps even the world over time. Maybe she kept them stabled. There were so many, and we needed to protect our people.

I swallowed hard, and my feet dug into the earth beneath me as I tried to find my strength.

"Protect yourself. If you get hurt, I'll never forgive you."

I looked at him then and waved my hands over his

wound in his side that was still seeping blood. "Same to you. Now, fight."

Then, there was no more time for words. Faith was using borrowed power. I didn't know exactly how I could tell, but it felt different. Not like hers. It didn't feel as it had when she fought us before. Was this Oriel's work? Or some other dark magic I didn't yet know or understand?

I wasn't sure, but no matter what, I had to fight Faith.

Jaxton and Laurel were there in the next instant. Laurel was shaking, her eyes dark, and I swore I saw flames in them for a moment. She blinked, and suddenly, her sword appeared in her hands. "Let's do this."

"I'll be better in my hawk form," Jaxton said before shrugging out of his clothes. With his talons and that beak of his, I agreed. He shifted and soared into the air before he began dive-bombing the revenants that came at us.

Ash and Rowen moved as one, as if they had been doing it all their lives. And perhaps they had in a way and had only forgotten that fact in the past few months. The two of them used air and earth to push at Faith, shaking her foundation. Faith was strong, far too powerful, and she kept shoving at us all.

Rome used his claws in his human form, lashing out at the revenants, ending their pain and protecting us. Ariel was there, too, fighting, using her claws, as did the rest of Rome's trackers. The fae and other town members I knew could fight, came forward through the trees as if they had heard Rome's roar. They jumped into the fray, as well. It was claw against magic, sword against sword, but we were all fighting. I was at Laurel's side, and she used her blade against them as I dug into myself and pulled out my magic. I pulled water from the pond beside us and dug in. I threw the revenants into the pond, ending their sorrow and their screams. And then I did my best to create water daggers and lob them towards Faith. She knocked them away, one by one, but I was distracting her—which was the point. Because Rowen and Ash were getting closer, their hands clasped together as their magic whirled.

"I need to take care of something," Rome growled and moved towards the four bears who had stood with Alden. I looked over at him, and Laurel nodded. "I'm right beside you. That way, he's not alone."

I nodded and followed Rome, using my water magic to make more daggers, arrowing them at the four bears who had hurt Rome and betrayed their pack.

"You'll never be our alpha," one snarled.

"That's fine. Because if you don't give up now, I'll kill you."

"Then kill us. We don't care. You're never going to have everything you want."

"So be it."

"Alden was always better than you."

"That's enough of that," I said and shot an ice dagger towards the one who had spoken last. He clutched at his neck where the blade met flesh, his eyes wide. He fell to his knees, and the other three turned towards me. Rome gave me a look, one filled with heart and pride, and then he lashed out. Laurel used her sword on the final one, and then the four traitors were gone. We were shaking, but this still wasn't over. Dozens upon dozens of revenants still came, and we kept fighting, but we had to get back to Ash and Rowen. They needed us. We needed to take down Faith.

As soon as we got to them, though, my heart stuttered,

and I cried out. I hadn't meant to, hadn't meant to get Rome's attention, but he saw them anyway.

Faith stood at the other end of the clearing, having moved back to get out of the way of a blow. Behind her, two dark shapes formed, their bodies solid. Two revenants with familiar faces stared toward the center of the circle. My heart shattered. Trace looked at us, his eyes vacant, blood still covering his chest. Alden stared, his neck covered in dripping blood, his eyes dark, also vacant.

She had made revenants of Rome's brothers. I couldn't breathe. I screamed, and Rome roared. Everything felt as if it were fragmenting around us. I couldn't believe this was actually happening.

"She will not get away with this, not this kind of evil. She dies. Tonight."

I hoped Rome's words were true.

We moved then, Jaxton initially overhead until he shifted back to his human form. He stood there naked and picked up a fallen dagger, and we all went at Faith. The necromancer held up her hands, and the revenants moved forward, some with swords, some with shorter blades. She pulled the water from the ground and the pond, creating at least a hundred daggers, maybe more.

"You're so weak. If only you had my power, understood what I do, you would win. You are nothing. And now, you will understand that." She shoved many of the daggers forward. Not all, but enough. People screamed as the blades met their marks. I ducked out of the way of one and shouted as Rome pulled a second out of his arm, tossed it to the ground, and kept going.

Another dozen ice daggers came out of the air, and we moved, Laurel using her sword to deflect them.

"We need to stop Faith. We stop her; we stop all of this," Rowen said.

"Tell me what to do," I replied.

Ash lifted his chin. "Clasp hands and use the magic. Repeat after me."

Before I could, another dagger came forward, and Rome let out a shout as he tossed himself in front of me. The blade sliced into his collarbone, another embedded itself in his chest. I cried out, using my water magic to melt the ice and pull it from his flesh. He groaned, blood seeping, but he shook it off. "I'm fine."

"No, you aren't," I said.

Then the Trace and Alden revenants were there, and nothing made sense anymore.

"Let me do this," Laurel said.

Rome shook his head. "No, this is mine."

I moved forward, and I knew it was my responsibility, as well. I would not let my mate do this alone. No matter the cost, no matter the pain. When Alden moved forward, I used my ice and my water, sliding a dagger home through his neck. He fell to his knees, gone once more.

Rome growled and looked at me, reaching out. I thought he would hold me or do something, but instead, he pushed me out of the way as Trace lunged. One of Trace's claws sliced my arm, and I cried out at the pain. I looked down, saw the blood pouring, but then I saw my mate. I wanted to do something, wanted to call out, but there was nothing I *could* do. Instead, I watched as my mate, the man I loved, placed his hands around his brother's neck and twisted. Trace fell to his knees, his mouth open, and I swore I saw something there for a second. Hope? A thank you?

I didn't know, but I was bleeding, and so was Rome, and Trace and Alden were gone once again.

I could barely keep up.

Laurel tugged at me, and we moved towards the others. Faith was there, lobbing more ice daggers, as well as directing her revenants.

She was so powerful. She was sacrificing something, but none of us could get close.

"The spell. We need the spell."

Rome threw himself in front of me again, taking another hit, and I growled. "Stop it. I can take care of myself."

"Use the spell. Let me protect you."

I knew he was right. I had to. I had to let him. Because I would protect him. I was going to save everyone. I gripped Laurel's and Rowen's hands. Rowen gripped Ash's. And we chanted.

"*Earth, air, water, fire, seek the one that we desire. Stop this evil, purge this blight, banish this witch to darkest night. Lord and Lady, ancestors, too, lend us your strength for what we must do. Take this witch so we may be free. This is our will, so mote it be!*"

I screamed, water and fire and earth and air searing through me as I threw back my head, and magic poured out of my mouth. Blood began trickling from my nose, but I didn't reach up to wipe it away. There was so much power, so much more than I'd ever felt or used before. It was almost too much. I didn't know what I was supposed to do. Instinctively, I pushed it towards Faith, and I knew the others did the same. I had to trust in my coven.

Because there was nothing else I *could* do.

Ash shouted, a guttural scream that echoed in my mind. Laurel stood firm, despite the blood trickling out of her ear.

She scared me the most. My hand burned, but I didn't let go. She was burning from the inside out, her entire body shaking. I knew this was too much for her. We had asked too much of her. But I couldn't end the spell early. We had to stop Faith.

I looked up at the necromancer, her blond hair floating in the wind, blood pouring out of her eyes, nose, and mouth. Still, she kept moving, kept chanting. Another dagger came forward and sliced me across the stomach, another embedded in my shoulder, but I stood steady.

I could not fall. I would not falter. Rome and Ariel, and the other shifters were taking care of the rest of the revenants because Faith was still alive, and her necromancer power was still too strong.

And then I heard a shout and pushed forward with my magic. Something broke inside me. I fell to my knees, my hands dropping in front of me as I let go of both Laurel and Rowen. Rowen fell beside me, cupping her head as she screamed. Ash stood there, staggering back as his whole body shook. Blood soaked my clothes, and my wounds felt as if I'd been stabbed over and over again.

Faith burned, her body turning to ash, smoking as she stared at us and screamed. She shouted, she screeched, and then the revenants fell where they stood, the magic around us popping like a balloon.

Faith's screams suddenly cut off, and then there was nothing.

I looked to my left and called Laurel's name. She stood, her sword suddenly falling from her hand as her whole body burned. Not just fire magic but fire itself. She stood in embers, a living flame as her magic consumed her. I knew this had been too much. Rowen rose and staggered beside me, reaching out, tears falling from her eyes. Ash was beside her, his gaze dark as he looked at his sister. I knew he was likely trying to think of a spell to stop what was happening to her, but I didn't think there was anything we could do.

She was burning, dying, and we couldn't do anything. I coughed, blood spurting from my mouth, and knew that whatever had snapped inside of me had cut something deep. I could feel my life draining from my body. And then Rome was there, holding me close as I watched Laurel.

I couldn't breathe. I couldn't stop the bleeding. We had stopped Faith. But had it been enough?

Jaxton jumped and threw himself on top of Laurel, the only one of us able to move. I heard the hiss of his skin as flames burned flesh, and they both fell to the ground. Laurel curled up in his arms, and their magic together doused the flames.

I looked up at Rome and tried to speak, but blood poured from my mouth.

Rome held me close and roared.

I looked down at the jagged dagger still in my flesh and knew that I had been impaled not by magic but by metal. The final throw Faith had leveled wasn't ice but steel.

I didn't know if this was goodbye. I attempted to speak in case it was, tried to do something.

Somehow, we had won. Somehow, we had defeated Faith. And yet, as I tried to speak, I knew death was coming. And I didn't know if we had lost everything else, as well.

CHAPTER TWENTY-FOUR

ROME

The wolves howled, and the hawks screeched overhead as I lowered my head and mourned. We had lost seventeen pack members as a result of Alden's betrayal. However, we had lost more than numbers. I had lost two of my triplets. I had lost my family. And I had lost something inside myself that I wasn't sure I would ever get back.

Sage put her hand on my back, and I looked down at her, aware that I'd almost lost her, as well. She had nearly bled out in my arms. It had only been Rowen's quick thinking and our pack's healer that saved her. Laurel was still healing as far as I knew, but she was stiff, and I could smell the burnt flesh on her body. Nobody spoke of it. There was nothing to say. Nothing we could do.

We had all lost enough at the betrayal of our pack and our town. Now, we needed to face what came next.

Faith was gone, but someone had given her the power she wielded.

This Oriel, whoever he was, needed to be stopped.

"I think your parents are coming," Sage said after a

moment once the song of our people had ended, and the pyres burned.

There would be nothing left for a necromancer to take. We would never allow that. Rowen and Sage and Ash and possibly Laurel would do a spell to keep the spirits of those we had lost away from the necromancers. We had to hope it would be enough. Penelope had been buried, as was done for witches of her family line. Her bones would be safe, and her spirit had been sent to wherever witch souls went in the afterlife.

It was odd to think that our lives included keeping our afterlives safe, but there it was. We were mourning everything we had lost, and I still wasn't sure we had considered what would never come.

"Rome," Sage whispered again.

I shook my head. "I'm sorry, I see them."

My parents walked towards me and stood on the opposite side of the circle from me. This was traditionally how two alphas met. He was my father, my Alpha, and I felt like I had failed him. I lowered my head as he came closer, something I had not done in years. I didn't need to lower my gaze when it came to him. The other alphas of the country understood that I had the power to challenge him, but I wouldn't. This was my father. And I trusted him.

"Rome," he said softly as he rested his hand on the back of my neck. "Don't bow to me. Look at me, son. You are an alpha, too. You are strong. And your people need you."

"As does your mate," my mother added, her voice steady. She was tall, her shoulders broad. She was a bear sow, one who had raised triplets who would become three of the country's most powerful bears. She ruled at my father's side and kept our people safe. My mother was not weak. And right then, I wanted her to hold me and tell me that everything would be okay. However, I was not a young child anymore. I couldn't think that way.

"I'm glad to meet you," Sage said after a moment. "I'm just sorry it's under these circumstances."

My mother reached out and pulled Sage close, hugging her. "It is an honor to meet our son's mate, the alpha of the Ravenwood pack. "I am glad we found you. That we are here. And I am glad that you are with Rome during this time. He will need you more than ever."

"I will always be here," Sage said softly. "For him and our people. Always."

Nothing she could have said would have been better. My father smiled softly and tugged her close, giving her a big hug. Sage let out a little oompf, and a small smile played on my lips. She was so tiny compared to the giant bears around her, but she didn't falter. Instead, she hugged him back, and my father kissed the top of her head.

"We will mourn our sons and the choices they made. In the end, Trace protected. He did so much. My heart feels as though there can be no hope, but I have to hold onto the fact that my son died protecting those he loved." My mother's voice broke, and my bear mourned.

We did not speak of Alden. There was nothing more to say. He had gone down the wrong path, and we couldn't change that.

I slid my hand into Sage's and nodded as Ash, Jaxton, and Aspen came over. Aspen, as the fae leader, looked calm and remote as he nodded at my father. "We are sorry you're here for this occasion but know we still stand with your son and the shifters. We will stand against the necromancers."

"All of us," Ash whispered.

"We will fight, and we will avenge your sons," Jaxton added, and it wasn't lost on any of us that he had mentioned both Trace and Alden.

My heart would forever have a jagged crevice at losing my triplets, but Sage was here and could fully help me heal it. I could feel her within our bond, wrapping herself around my bear, my anchor, and my heart.

She was healing me, and I wasn't even sure she was aware that she was doing it.

We spoke to my parents and the others as Ariel came up, her expression solemn. She was my beta now. Perhaps not as strong in power as Trace, but she would be strong enough. She would protect our pack. Honestly, she should have been our third, to begin with. However, there was no time for those regrets now.

"It's my shift now on the perimeter. I just wanted to stop by and give my condolences." Ariel nodded at my parents. "We'll meet soon?" I lifted my chin in affirmation. It had only been two days since the attack in the pack circle that had changed everything. It had taken those two days to make arrangements, to get my parents here, and for our wounds to heal. And even then, they weren't fully healed, not physically, and definitely not emotionally.

"We'll speak soon." Ariel met my gaze for a brief moment before her bear forced her to lower her chin. "Alpha." She turned to Sage. "Alpha." My beta walked away just as the three triplet cubs ran over. They had shifted to bear form, far more comfortable that way with so many strangers. Sage immediately dropped to her knees, and the three hugged her tightly, crawling all over her. She let out a soft laugh, and my bear hummed, relaxing slightly at the sound of her voice.

My father cleared his throat. "She will be a good mate. And despite what Alden thought, it will be good to have a connection to the coven."

"He's always had a connection to the coven," Ash corrected my father.

My father gave Ash a look. And there it was again, those unspoken words. We did not speak of why Ash had left, nor why he had come back. At least, not yet.

I knew we would have to do so soon. "There's always a connection to the coven, but my mate is part of its heart and soul, so the connection is even greater now."

"Take your mate home and hold her. Tomorrow, you will make plans, and you will tell us of those plans," my mother ordered, and I smiled softly.

"We'll tell you what we know, but you should also protect your den. We don't know where this necromancer might reach out to next."

"Understood," my father said, "We'll protect ours, but you are ours, as well. Remember that."

We spoke a bit longer, and then I watched as Laurel walked away, limping. I knew we would have a conversation later. She would kill herself if we weren't careful, and I knew none of us could handle that. She had lost Trace, just as I had. We needed to speak, but first, I needed my mate. We met with the elders and the other bears who needed us but were soon in my home, *our home*, as I held Sage close.

"We haven't even had time to talk, beyond a few mentions about the fact that we're mated."

She looked up at me as I spoke, and she smiled softly. "I know there are logistics and discussions about what will happen next and who we will be. But this is our home. It's closest to the den, and I was only renting that cottage. It'll be good to be with you, in the den, for when they need you. They're broken. I can feel it through the bonds. I hope I can help."

I kissed her. My mate was so strong, and my bear approved. "I know we need to speak with the others, but can I have you? Are you healed enough? My bear needs you. And so do I."

In answer, she tugged off my shirt. I kissed her again. We slowly stripped each other, and I led her to the bedroom, laying her on the bed. I kissed her, and she kissed me back, her lips soft, her touch gentle. She would have a scar on her side, just like I would. We'd both nearly died of perverted magic not our own. It would take time to heal, but these scars would never fade. I kissed the ridges on one and then moved back to the mating mark before I hovered over her and slowly slid deep inside.

She wrapped her arms around me, and we moved as one, riding each other, needing one another.

I wasn't sure where I ended, and she began, but my bear groaned. When I rolled over onto my back, she rode me. My hands moved to her breasts, her nipples hard against my palms. She looked down at me, her hair flowing around her in honey-brown waves. She was gorgeous, and she was mine.

The water in the vase beside the bed started to spiral out, and I smiled, knowing it was her magic, her magic of warmth and home, and when she came, the water sprinkled down like rain, back into the vase with a mist sliding over our faces.

She grinned, and I followed her into bliss, holding her close.

The pack would need time to heal, our friends would need even longer, and I didn't know what our future might bring.

No matter what, though, I had my mate.

We had defeated Faith but had lost something in the process. However, I had found Sage, the one person I hadn't known I was searching for.

And, in the end, I had to count that. Maybe as everything.

My witch, my Sage, my future.

My mate.

CHAPTER TWENTY-FIVE

ORIEL

Oriel looked around at the large home he'd built for himself in the mountains, long before the others thought they knew who he was. No one knew precisely who Oriel was or where he had come from. And that was the point. They had forgotten him. Ignored him.

Others called dear Rowen the perfect witch, the last of her kind. They didn't know anything. He was here. And that was all that mattered.

He would finally take what he was owed, what should have been his to begin with by all rights. The others would understand what they had taken from him and what he deserved.

He looked down at the photo in his hands and growled before tossing it into the flames, the glass shattering against the hearth. He lowered his head, letting out a breath. He would mourn Faith. He would regret losing what they had and what they had built. He knew her death was needed, however. She might not have seen what her purpose was, but he had known.

He had needed somebody to scout Ravenwood and let them know that somebody was watching, ready to take their place. Oriel's journey was only beginning, while Faith's had come to an end.

Yes, he would mourn her. He had loved her in his way. After all, someone like Oriel couldn't love like that earth witch, who called himself a founder and a power. He *was* a side of a coin that others didn't realize yet. Soon, they would know his true purpose.

It was time to fight for what came next.

And what was his.

Because Ravenwood would finally be his. Rowen Ravenwood was not the last of her kind, and soon, the town with all its secrets would understand that. Soon, it would all be his, and the power that Rowen neglected and ignored would come to him, as well.

If only she knew what lay beneath her feet. If only she understood what she was about to lose.

CHAPTER TWENTY-SIX

SAGE

Rowen, Laurel, and I stood in the clearing behind Rowen's home, the three of us holding hands around a small fire, our heads tipped back.

"*Guardians, Watchtowers, ancestors, friends, we gather in the presence of our Lord and Lady to ask for peace. Bring this town and its residents into the light and hold them in your embrace. Shelter them from the evil that lurks and let us find our way. From this day to the next, let us manifest plenty and more of everything we need, and bring happiness even in our darkest hours. With thanks and blessings to the great divine three, this is our will, so mote it be.*"

Magic flowed through me, wrapping its arms around me, and I could feel the water in the air, in the pond, the earth, the stream, everywhere.

Rowen let out a breath as air slid through her hair and around mine, as well. Laurel's hand heated up, and I squeezed it before daring to look at her. She gave me a tight smile and nodded, and I knew she was trying.

She was trying so hard. All of us were.

"That's enough for now," Rowen said as she took a step back and wiped her hands. "Now, we must close the circle. And, Laurel, let's work on those burns."

"I'm fine," Laurel said, pulling her sleeves down. "This was nothing, just settling in."

"Let me help," I said, picking up the pouch from beside my bag. "I've been looking through my aunt's things, and there was a whole book on healing."

"The Princes always were good with healing," Rowen said, a small smile playing on her lips.

My heart hurt thinking about it, but I swallowed hard to clear the lump in my throat. "Really, let me help," I whispered.

Laurel pressed her lips into a thin line. "Maybe. But I need a minute."

Rowen shook her head at our friend's words. "The guys are watching. I guess we should let them join us."

I could feel Rome through our bond, and I looked over my shoulder and smiled at him. He came through the trees, the darkness sliding away from him. Jaxton was by his side, and then Ash brought up the rear.

Ash nodded at all of us, his gaze lingering on Rowen. "You know that blessing spell works better with all four."

Rowen's eyes narrowed. "We're of the three, and we're the ones that needed to do this one. Another time, we might need earth, but for now, you know why you cannot be part of that spell."

Ash nodded. "You're looking for the darkness, and darkness can't be part of it."

I knew now why Ash had left. Rome had told me one night in the dark when it had been the two of us. There would be no hiding the past and no changing it. Not yet.

However, there would have to be soon. A lot of changes needed to happen. As Rome slid his arm around my waist and spoke of our search for Oriel, I had to wonder what the next chink in our armor would become; what the next piece on the board would be and how it would move. We had already lost so much. But not all.

We were the Ravenwood coven, and while I was still learning my craft, I could feel the magic pouring through me. I no longer had the veil of secrecy put on me by Oriel or whoever he worked with or for. Nothing pulled me back anymore. Yes, I missed Rupert and the life we had, but that hadn't been my truth. That hadn't been the life I was meant to have. And while I would be forever grateful for the moments I'd shared with him, I knew I was where I was supposed to be now. Where I was always meant to be.

In Rome's arms, with my coven, and my town.

We would fight, protect Ravenwood, and as changes beget more, we would roll with the punches and learn.

We would search for Oriel, and I would find my powers.

I would protect everyone I could.

I was not the same Sage I had been when I first came to Ravenwood. And I had found so much more than I had ever been looking for.

I was alpha of the Ravenwood pack. Member of the Ravenwood coven. Rome's mate. Rowen and Laurel's sister.

I was a witch.

I was part of Ravenwood.

And I would protect my home at all costs.

CHAPTER TWENTY-SEVEN

LAUREL

I stared into the mirror and winced. My body ached, and it felt as if I were burning from the inside out. Then again, maybe I was.

I was dying.

I knew this. I knew that another spell like the one we had done on the battlefield would probably be my last. Of course, if I wasn't careful, *any* charm or use of my magic could be my last.

This damn curse had taken everything from me and those I loved. Now, it would take my life. I could say I didn't want that to be the case, and I didn't, but I knew what was happening next, and there would be no stopping it. I gripped the edge of the sink and forced myself not to let the tears fall.

Trace was gone. He was supposed to be the one for me. Somehow, he should have been mine. We had danced around each other for so long, taking our time to find who we were, but now, he was gone before we even had a chance to be with one another and overcome our mistakes. Soon, I would join him. I would join him on the other side because there was no coming back from this.

I wore only a bra and jeans, riding low on my hips as I stared into the mirror. Once again, I fought back a cry of rage and pain. If I kept doing this, I would die. I let out a breath and slowly picked up the satchel to rub my burns with the ointment and herbs Rowen and Sage had given me.

Rowen had tried her best to help me unbind myself from the curse, but she'd failed. As had I. Maybe it was because of the curse itself, or perhaps it was because Rowen hated that I couldn't help her. She'd always helped me soothe my burns. Only I didn't think she realized how bad it was. Nobody was allowed to realize that.

Not even my brother.

Especially not Ash.

I slowly cleaned the burns, and let the tears fall. Every ounce of pressure on the wound felt like I was dying. It wasn't fair that this was happening, but at least it was me and not Sage. Sage was far too new to this world to deal with pain like this. She had been dealt blow after blow in her life already, and I did not want her to ever face this kind of pain. Everything hurt, and it literally felt as if I were dying.

I looked into the mirror and swallowed hard. Every time I used my magic, every time I pulled on the fire within me, it scarred me from the inside out. I *burned* from the inside out. This time, I had been too close to flaming out completely in a gulf of fire and ash.

My eyes were aflame. Pure fire—blue and red and orange and purple. Everything that fire could be, even in its most dangerous and beautiful form.

I looked over my shoulder and pressed my lips together.

Jaxton stood there. He didn't lean against the doorway. Didn't look relaxed as he always seemed to be.

He stared at me, his jaw set. "It's time."

I shook my head, even as the tears fell faster because the pain was too much. I really was burning from the inside out, and I couldn't stop it. There would be no dousing this flame. Whatever was coming needed all of us at full strength, but I couldn't be. I was nothing. Sure, I had a sword, but I couldn't use magic because I nearly died every time I tried. The next time would mean my death. I was sure of it.

"It can't be." My voice sounded as if I'd swallowed smoke. Then again, I had, in a way.

He shook his head. "You can't keep doing this."

I looked at him in the mirror, then down at the scars that would never fade from my body, and then stared at him once more.

"I have to."

Even if it killed me.

Want more of the Ravenwood Coven?
Laurel and Jaxton's romance is next in Dusk Unveiled.

A NOTE FROM CARRIE ANN RYAN

Thank you so much for reading **DAWN UNEARTHED!**

I love writing paranormal romance and a few friends of mine have been betting the universe for witches, covens, and girl power books and that is what sparked the idea of the town of Ravenwood. I cannot wait to show you more of this world!

Next in the series is Dusk Unveiled. I cannot wait to break open Laurel and Jaxton's secrets.

If you want to make sure you know what's coming next from me, you can sign up for my newsletter at www. CarrieAnnRyan.com; follow me on twitter at @CarrieAnn-Ryan, or like my Facebook page. I also have a Facebook Fan Club where we have trivia, chats, and other goodies. You guys are the reason I get to do what I do and I thank you.

Make sure you're signed up for my MAILING LIST so you can know when the next releases are available as well as find giveaways and FREE READS.

Happy Reading!

The Ravenwood Coven Series:
   Book 1: Dawn Unearthed
   Book 2: Dusk Unveiled
   Book 3: Evernight Unleashed

Want to keep up to date with the next Carrie Ann Ryan
Release? Receive Text Alerts easily!
Text CARRIE to 210-741-8720

ABOUT THE AUTHOR

Carrie Ann Ryan is the New York Times and USA Today bestselling author of contemporary, paranormal, and young adult romance. Her works include the Montgomery Ink, Redwood Pack, Fractured Connections, and Elements of Five series, which have sold over 3.0 million books worldwide. She started writing while in graduate school for her advanced degree in chemistry and hasn't stopped since. Carrie Ann has written over seventy-five novels and novellas with more in the works. When she's not losing herself in her emotional and action-packed worlds, she's reading as much as she can while wrangling her clowder of cats who have more followers than she does.

www.CarrieAnnRyan.com

ALSO FROM CARRIE ANN RYAN

The Montgomery Ink: Fort Collins Series:
Book 1: Inked Persuasion
Book 2: Inked Obsession
Book 3: Inked Devotion
Book 4: Inked Craving
Book 5: Inked Temptation

The On My Own Series:
Book 1: My One Night
Book 2: My Rebound
Book 3: My Next Play
Book 4: My Bad Decisions

The Ravenwood Coven Series:
Book 1: Dawn Unearthed
Book 2: Dusk Unveiled
Book 3: Evernight Unleashed

ALSO FROM CARRIE ANN RYAN

Montgomery Ink:
Book 0.5: Ink Inspired
Book 0.6: Ink Reunited
Book 1: Delicate Ink
Book 1.5: Forever Ink
Book 2: Tempting Boundaries
Book 3: Harder than Words
Book 3.5: Finally Found You
Book 4: Written in Ink
Book 4.5: Hidden Ink
Book 5: Ink Enduring
Book 6: Ink Exposed
Book 6.5: Adoring Ink
Book 6.6: Love, Honor, & Ink
Book 7: Inked Expressions
Book 7.3: Dropout
Book 7.5: Executive Ink
Book 8: Inked Memories
Book 8.5: Inked Nights
Book 8.7: Second Chance Ink

Montgomery Ink: Colorado Springs
Book 1: Fallen Ink
Book 2: Restless Ink
Book 2.5: Ashes to Ink
Book 3: Jagged Ink
Book 3.5: Ink by Numbers

The Montgomery Ink: Boulder Series:
Book 1: Wrapped in Ink

Book 2: Sated in Ink
Book 3: Embraced in Ink
Book 4: Seduced in Ink
Book 4.5: Captured in Ink

The Gallagher Brothers Series:
Book 1: Love Restored
Book 2: Passion Restored
Book 3: Hope Restored

The Whiskey and Lies Series:
Book 1: Whiskey Secrets
Book 2: Whiskey Reveals
Book 3: Whiskey Undone

The Fractured Connections Series:
Book 1: Breaking Without You
Book 2: Shouldn't Have You
Book 3: Falling With You
Book 4: Taken With You

The Less Than Series:
Book 1: Breathless With Her
Book 2: Reckless With You
Book 3: Shameless With Him

The Promise Me Series:
Book 1: Forever Only Once
Book 2: From That Moment
Book 3: Far From Destined

Book 4: From Our First

Redwood Pack Series:
Book 1: An Alpha's Path
Book 2: A Taste for a Mate
Book 3: Trinity Bound
Book 3.5: A Night Away
Book 4: Enforcer's Redemption
Book 4.5: Blurred Expectations
Book 4.7: Forgiveness
Book 5: Shattered Emotions
Book 6: Hidden Destiny
Book 6.5: A Beta's Haven
Book 7: Fighting Fate
Book 7.5: Loving the Omega
Book 7.7: The Hunted Heart
Book 8: Wicked Wolf

The Talon Pack:
Book 1: Tattered Loyalties
Book 2: An Alpha's Choice
Book 3: Mated in Mist
Book 4: Wolf Betrayed
Book 5: Fractured Silence
Book 6: Destiny Disgraced
Book 7: Eternal Mourning
Book 8: Strength Enduring
Book 9: Forever Broken

The Elements of Five Series:

Book 1: From Breath and Ruin
Book 2: From Flame and Ash
Book 3: From Spirit and Binding
Book 4: From Shadow and Silence

The Branded Pack Series:
(Written with Alexandra Ivy)
Book 1: Stolen and Forgiven
Book 2: Abandoned and Unseen
Book 3: Buried and Shadowed

Dante's Circle Series:
Book 1: Dust of My Wings
Book 2: Her Warriors' Three Wishes
Book 3: An Unlucky Moon
Book 3.5: His Choice
Book 4: Tangled Innocence
Book 5: Fierce Enchantment
Book 6: An Immortal's Song
Book 7: Prowled Darkness
Book 8: Dante's Circle Reborn

Holiday, Montana Series:
Book 1: Charmed Spirits
Book 2: Santa's Executive
Book 3: Finding Abigail
Book 4: Her Lucky Love
Book 5: Dreams of Ivory

The Tattered Royals Series:

ALSO FROM CARRIE ANN RYAN

Book 1: Royal Line
Book 2: Enemy Heir

The Happy Ever After Series:

Flame and Ink
Ink Ever After